ALSO BY E.

THE WORLD OF THE GATEWAY

The Gateway Trilogy (Series 1)
Spirit Legacy
Spirit Prophecy
Spirit Ascendancy
The Gateway Trackers (Series 2)
Whispers of the Walker
Plague of the Shattered
Awakening of the Seer
Portraits of the Forsaken
Heart of the Rebellion
Soul of the Sentinel
Gift of the Darkness
Tales from the Gateway

THE RIFTMAGIC SAGA
What the Lady's Maid Knew
The Rebel Beneath the Stairs

TALES FROM THE GATEWAY

TALES FROM THE GATEWAY

A Companion Novel to the World of the Gateway

E.E. HOLMES

Lily Faire Publishing

Lily Faire Publishing
Townsend, MA

Copyright © 2020 by E.E. Holmes
All rights reserved

www.lilyfairepublishing.com
www.eeholmes.com

ISBN 978-1-7339352-7-2 (Print edition)
ISBN 978-1-7339352-6-5 (Digital edition)

Publisher's note: This is a work of fiction. Names, characters, places and incidents are either the product of the author's imagination or are used fictitiously.

Cover design by James T. Egan of Bookfly Design LLC
Author photography by Cydney Scott Photography

If these characters have become like friends to you, and these pages like home, then this one, dear reader, is for you.

CONTENTS

1. Savannah's Story — *1*
2. Annabelle's Story — *23*
3. Carrick's Story — *49*
4. Karen's Story — *81*
5. Milo's Story — *115*
6. Finn's Story — *143*
7. Hannah's Story — *177*

About the Author — *207*

I

SAVANNAH'S STORY

I'VE GOT NO BLOODY IDEA why anyone would give a tinker's fart about what I've got to say, if I'm honest, but here it goes just the same, and good luck to you.

I saw my first ghost when I was four. Well, I reckon I'd been seeing them for a while before that, but I just thought they were people like everyone else, right? That first one certainly looked normal—just your regular, wrinkled old pensioner with spectacles like magnifying glasses and a face like a piece of fruit that someone left on a windowsill too long. She was sitting in my dad's favorite chair by the telly, which was what made me stop and stare at her, seeing as how no one was allowed to sit in that chair but my dad unless they wanted to get knocked around good and proper.

"Hello, you dear wee thing," the woman said, looking at me with a friendly smile.

I kept my trap shut because I was still so surprised to see her sitting there.

"You're a very pretty little girl, aren't you?" the woman asked.

I figured there was no harm in nodding, seeing as I agreed with her on that score.

"Would you like to come sit on your Nanny's lap, my love?" she asked, patting her knee with one of her shriveled old mitts.

I shook my head because I wasn't a bloody fool. No way was I about to climb up into some old stranger's lap, no matter how pretty she told me I was. I may have only been four, but I had sense enough to know that much.

"Ah, well, no matter. You'll warm up to me yet," the woman said, shrugging her shoulders.

I opened my mouth to tell her that it wasn't bloody likely when my dad walked into the room with a beer and she just vanished on the spot. Poof. One moment she was there, the next, my old dad was cramming his useless arse into that chair and shouting about who the bollocks went and messed about with the remote control.

"Daddy, who was that lady?" I asked.

He blinked at me, looking, as he usually did, surprised at my existence. "What lady?"

"The lady who was sitting in your chair. Who is she?"

He squinted, like I was out of focus—which was likely, given the number of times he'd visited the fridge for another beer. "What's this nonsense, then? What are you on about?"

"There was an old lady and she was sitting in your chair just now. Who was she?" I repeated.

"Have you gone mad? There ain't no one but your ma home, and she knows better than to sit in this chair."

"She said to call her Nanny. Who's Nanny?" I asked.

Now, mind you, I was only four, but I knew what fear looked like. I knew what that widening darkness in someone's eyes meant. I watched the ruddy color drain from my father's face with interest, like I had pulled a plug and was watching the water funnel down the drain. It was a wizard trick, I remember thinking, almost like magic.

"What did you say?" my dad asked in a hoarse whisper.

As a little nipper who was usually ignored, this was all the invitation I needed. I launched into a long-winded explanation of Nanny—what she looked like and what she'd been wearing and what she'd said to me. By the time I was done, my dad's hands were shaking and his face was the color of porridge. He stumbled up from his chair, staggered into the loo, and spewed up all over the bloody place. Like any normal kid, I stood in the doorway and watched him, absolutely fascinated. I'd never seen my dad look like anything other than a great hulking brute, after all, and here he was, cowering and gasping on the floor in front of the bog. It was jolly good fun, I don't mind telling you.

Finally, after a few failed attempts, he managed to get himself up off the linoleum. He splashed some water on his face, dragged a threadbare towel across his mouth, and turned to glare at me.

"I don't know what you're playing at, girl, but I don't never want to hear a lie like that out of your trap again."

"But I'm not lying! I saw her!" I insisted, backing away and starting to cry with frustration that he was being so thick.

He pointed his fat sausage of a finger right in my face, so that

TALES FROM THE GATEWAY

I leapt back from him and whacked my head on the wall behind me. "You ain't seen nothing of the sort, you hear me? Now, sod off before I give you a thumping you won't soon forget!" he shouted. Then, he stalked back to his chair, popped the top on his beer, and settled into his usual pastime of pretending I didn't exist.

Naturally, I scarpered, seeing as I wasn't a fool, even at four years old. When my dad went off like that, you made yourself scarce, if you could manage it.

And then I found Nanny sitting right on my bed.

I opened my mouth to shout for my dad, but Nanny put a finger to her mouth to hush me.

"Don't push him, love. Some people just never understand. He's been that way since he was a lad, bless 'im."

"You knew my dad when he was a lad?" I asked.

"Oh yes, of course I did. Knew 'im better than anyone else, didn't I? I'm his mum."

My mouth fell open. I did a bit of mental calculation. "So that makes you my... my..."

"Grandmother, poppet. Yes," the woman said, and she beamed at me.

"But my grandmother's dead," I said, repeating what I'd been told.

"Dead but not gone, luvvie. Not gone at all," she replied, and winked at me.

"But my dad can't see you," I said.

"No, that he can't. Most people can't. But you can, can't you, you clever little thing?"

I grinned. I'm not sure I'd ever been called clever, but I enjoyed it, I can tell you.

At that moment, my mum opened the door to my room and Nanny just vanished from where she sat, leaving me staring at an empty bed.

"What are you playing at, upsetting your father like that?" my mum whispered in that whisper all mums have, the one that's mostly hissing and sounds worse than yelling.

"I wasn't trying to—"

"Don't get smart with me! You leave him be. He's had a hard day," she declared, then shut my door again.

My dad was always having a hard day, according to my mum. I supposed he didn't know how to have any other kind of day but a hard one, and that was why he was such a grumpy bugger all the damn time.

Nanny reappeared, just like that.

"How did you do that?" I asked her, eagerly.

"Do what, poppet?"

"Just disappear like that? It was a jolly good trick!"

Nanny smiled at me. "It's my own special magic. Most grown-up people don't believe in magic, do they? That's their loss, isn't it?"

I nodded wisely. As far as four-year-old Sav was concerned, this woman knew exactly what she was talking about.

"I don't want to upset your father, love, so don't mention me to him again, all right? It can be our little secret."

"All right then," I said, eager as you please. No one ever asked me to keep secrets—in fact, it always felt like they were keeping them *from* me. The world was one big secret, a place I had to live in while keeping my nose out of it. That's your lot in life when you're a measly four years old—just hoping someone somewhere will notice you and let you in on something instead of telling you you're in the way.

Armed with the power of a secret of my very own, I learned to keep my mouth shut after that, and when Nanny stopped by, as she did most nearly every day, I ignored her unless we were alone. She seemed to realize I was in a bit of a tight spot, being the only one who could see her, so she just vanished whenever anyone else came around. I think she knew it made things easier for me. I longed to be able to come and go as she did—to just disappear whenever I chose—and so I made a study of it. Consequently, by the time I was ten, I was a proper magician when it came to vanishing, just like that old woman. Poof.

Poof. "Where's Savvy? I turned around in the church pew and she was gone."

Poof. "Savannah Todd is absent from maths again. Has anyone checked the loo?"

Poof. "Is Savvy at your flat? I popped in to say goodnight and her bed's empty."

Honestly, it's a miracle I'm anything more than a puff of smoke at this point. It suited me, though. After all, the ghosts around me could come and go as they pleased, so why couldn't I do the same? In fact, I was in one of my transient states, neither here nor there, when my old dad walked out. I came home a good three hours later than I was meant to be home and found my Mum there, just sobbing with her head down on the kitchen table. When I asked her what was wrong, she didn't answer, just pointed to the bedroom. Drawers empty. Suitcase gone. Empty beer cans and a filthy ashtray still smoking on the bedside table.

Poof.

Sometimes I would feel right guilty after that, any time I disappeared for a bit. I mean, I lived in Council Flats for fuck's sake, not the cheeriest of neighborhoods. My mum probably thought I was lying dead in a gutter somewhere half the bleeding time. But then, I'd remind myself, I wasn't like him—my dad, I mean. I always came back, didn't I? Savannah Todd, the Amazing Disappearing, Reappearing Girl.

It was Nanny, really, who explained what I could do. See, she knew she was dead, not like some of these ghosts you get wandering around all confused, wondering why the bloody hell they can walk through walls all of a sudden. In fact, not only did she know she was dead, but she was right jolly about it.

"No bills to pay, no responsibilities, no aches and pains," she used to say, her voice all bright and cheery. "I comes and goes as I please, Savvy-girl!"

Nanny taught me how to tell the dead ones apart from the live ones. She helped me spot the way the light didn't seem to touch 'em, the way their movements were just a little too easy, like gravity had no hold on 'em. She also helped me learn which places and spirits to avoid—the troublemakers, so to speak. Some spirits will just nod at you and be on their merry way, after all. But then there are others—most of 'em were no good in real life, so they ain't about to start being any good once they're dead, see? And once they realize you can see and hear 'em, it can take a long time to shake 'em off.

Eventually, my mum figured it out—guess I wasn't quite as sly as I thought I was. She heard me, chattering away in my bedroom, and eventually she cottoned on that it wasn't just the idle, pretend chatter of a kid and her imaginary friend. I'll never forget, when I was twelve, she finally asked me about it. I suppose she wanted to sort it all out before me stepdad moved in, the blighter. Anyway, she sat down on the edge of my bed, which was no easy feat, seeing as she was pregnant with my twin sisters at the time, but once she finally managed it, she sighed, like she was steeling herself.

"Savvy, we need to talk," she said.

I caught sight of her face and panicked. "Look, mum, if you're about to give me a sex talk, you can just sod off right now. I've had it already at school, and the conversations in the girls' lav filled in the gaps, all right?"

My mum turned bright red, putting her hand on her belly as though she only just realized that I knew exactly how those two little buggers got in there in the first place. She recovered quick, though. "No, it's not about that. It's about you. I hear you... well... *talking* in here a lot."

I felt my heart flutter a bit but I played it cool. "Oh, yeah, well, you know me, mum. I'm always talking to meself out loud."

"Savvy, give me just a little bit of credit. I'm not completely clueless, love. I've... I've seen the programmes—they're all over the telly, you know, about haunted houses and psychics and that sort of thing. And I just... is that what you're doing, love? Cross my heart, you can trust me. I'll believe you. Are you a... a *psychic medium*?"

She said the last two words in such a slow, deliberate way, all serious, and twitching her fingers up in the air, making air quotes and all, and I just... I busted out laughing. I couldn't help it. Then she had to sit there, looking all offended and confused while I tried to get a hold of myself again, which admittedly took a long time.

"Mum, I'm sorry, I didn't mean to laugh at you, honest I didn't," I said when I finally managed to snort myself into silence. "But this with the fingers..." I imitated the air quotes, "I mean, do you even know what a bloody psychic medium is?"

My mum looked all offended, of course—if there's one thing she can't stand, it's being laughed at, which is probably why I do it so often. "Don't you get smart with me. I know enough to know that there's folks out there what can see... can see *ghosts*."

I felt the grin slide off my face, and suddenly I couldn't seem to remember what was so funny. "Yeah. Yeah, I know that."

"Come on now, love. You can tell me. I won't laugh. I'll believe you, I promise. I just want the truth, and to know if... if I can help you."

Bugger all, she was starting to cry! And that meant that I was probably going to start blubbering all over myself like a bloody great prat. "Mum, it's alright. Pull yourself together, will you? I'll talk to you, but you have to keep it under your hat, yeah? No blabbing to the girls down the pub. I'll tell you the truth, just... just stop leaking like some great bulbous hosepipe, all right?"

So, Mum pulled herself together and swore herself to secrecy and I told her everything, right from the beginning. And that was when I realized just how great my mum really was. I mean, her decision-making skills and taste in men were absolute rubbish, but she was alright, really, my mum. She believed everything I told her—asked me all kinds of questions, but not like she was doubting me. Just like, she wanted to understand—so that she knew me better.

After that, we were a damn sight closer, even if she did drive me absolutely mad at first, constantly whispering things like, "What about here? Are there any ghosts here? What was that? You just made a funny face. Did you see another one? Is it near me? It's near me, isn't it?" But she calmed down eventually, and things even felt... well, maybe not *normal*, but as normal as they were likely to get. We managed to keep a lid on my abilities around my sisters and that absolute wanker she insisted on marrying. Everything was all right, really, until the Durupinen turned up.

I was on my way to work when it happened. I'd just gotten hired at the local chip shop, which wasn't exactly what I had in mind, careerwise, but seeing as I'd failed most of my exams, there was no way I was going to sixth form, so my options were, as they say, limited. The pay was crap but it had its advantages—namely, free chips. I was running late, which my employers would later come to find as one of my less endearing tendencies, so I was turning the corner at a jog when a spirit stopped right in my path.

Unable to stop myself in time, I ran right through the bugger. "Blast it!" I shouted, shivering violently from head to toe before continuing on my way.

"Hey, come back here! I need to speak with you!" I heard the spirit call out from behind me, and a second later he was floating along next to me.

"No offense, mate, but I'm late and I don't have time for a chat," I muttered out of the corner of my mouth.

"But this is important!" the spirit insisted.

I stole a glance at him. He was young and nervous-looking, twisting a cap in his hands.

"It's always something important with you lot," I murmured. "Well, you want to know what I think is important? Not getting sacked before I even start my first shift, all right, mate? Good luck to ya."

"I have a message for you, Savannah Todd!"

I stopped and turned. The ghost, who was really just a kid now that I looked at him properly, was looking straight at me with wide, terrified eyes.

Glancing around and seeing far too many people milling about, I jerked my head in the direction of a deserted alleyway to our left, and the spirit followed me into it.

On the far side of a clump of rubbish bins, I rounded on him.

"How do you know me?"

"I don't," the spirit said.

"Then how do you know my name?"

"They told me."

"Who told you?"

"The people who want me to deliver the message."

"And who the ruddy hell are these people?"

He shrugged. "I don't know. I don't really know them either."

I threw my hands into the air in frustration. "Then what the blazes *do* you know, mate?"

"I know you're the same. You and… and them. You're the same."

I narrowed my eyes at him. "And what is that supposed to mean? How are we the same?"

The spirit shrugged. "Well, you can all see me, for a start."

That pulled me up short, I can tell you. Suddenly, my heart was pumping like I'd just run a mile. It took me a full minute to calm down enough to ask my next question, but the ghost didn't rush me. Honestly, he looked grateful for the break.

"Someone else who sees ghosts wants you to give me a message?"

"That's right," the boy replied.

"Well?"

"Well, what?"

"What do you mean, '*well what?!*' What the hell is the bloody message, already? Let's have it!"

"Oh, right," the boy said, twisting his cap so hard, he looked in danger of ripping the thing right in two. "The message is, 'The spirit world needs you. We can teach you how to use your gift. It is your destiny.'"

I blinked.

TALES FROM THE GATEWAY

"That's... that's it," the boy said, a bit sheepishly.

I snorted. "My destiny? It's my destiny to get stalked by the likes of you every place I try to go, is it? Not bloody likely. Tell your friends thanks, but no thanks. I'm managing this gift just fine on my own."

"They said you might say that."

"Say what?"

"That you weren't interested in talking to them. And if that happened, I was to tell you that they don't give up so easily."

"Is that so?"

"Um... yes. At least, that was the message. Please don't get mad at me, I'm just the poor sod they asked to deliver it."

I snorted. "Right, then. And is that it? Is that the whole message?"

The boy cringed. "There's a bit more, but I'm not sure I want to tell you anymore."

"Why not?"

"Well, it sounds just a bit... melodramatic, to be honest."

I rolled my eyes. "Come on, mate, you may as well come out with it. You've got me standing here, haven't you?"

The boy gave a great gulp and muttered. "They'll be watching you."

I just about busted a gut laughing. "Right. Well, that's just brilliant. Listen, run along then, will you, and tell them you've been a good lad and delivered their message, whoever the bloody hell they are. You can also tell them to blow it out their arse. Cheers, mate."

And with that, I turned and ran, an activity I never participate in on purpose, unless I'm being chased by an ax murderer, and got to my shift three minutes late, fresh out of breath but plum full of excuses.

I did not, at that particular moment, get sacked.

To be honest, I didn't think about the ghostly messenger much at all that day while I was at work. I had too much to learn, seeing as it was my first day and I had no bloody idea what I was doing. I mean, learning how to operate a fryer full of hot oil isn't really something you should do while you're distracted, and seeing as I didn't want to wind up in hospital covered in third-degree burns, I was on my best behavior. I blundered my way through making sandwiches, refilling sauce dispensers, and taking orders. Despite my general ineptness, I still managed to get two blokes' numbers for the purposes of future shenanigans, though this wasn't strictly part of my training. By the end of the night, after seven hours on my feet, I was absolutely knackered. Not too knackered to tuck into a huge plate of chips swimming in brown sauce, of course, and that's where the next ghost found me, sitting in the bus shelter and stuffing my gob.

I felt her before I saw her, and gave a huge sigh. "Not now, love, can't you see I'm weak for want of nourishment? Look at me, I'm wasting away!"

The spirit ignored my request, like spirits usually do, in my experience, and floated her way into the shelter, coming to rest on the bench beside me. If she'd been a living person, we'd have been rubbing shoulders. Instead, I just started shivering from the drop in temperature.

"Have you given any consideration to the message you received earlier today?" the woman asked. In life, she'd been tall, thin, and attractive, real put-together like. She was going to be harder to shake off than that first kid, I could already tell.

"Not a bit," I replied through a mouthful of chips.

"Really? I find that hard to believe," the woman replied, raising her eyebrows.

I shrugged. "You ain't never been put in charge of a deep fryer, then, I'm assuming."

"I should think not," the woman replied, looking scandalized at the very thought.

"Well, then, you'll have to take my word for it," I said. I held up my cardboard takeaway container and wafted it toward her. "Fancy a nosh?" I grinned at the joke, which was admittedly a bit below the belt.

Though I'm fairly sure she couldn't smell anything in her current state, the woman turned her nose up at it in disgust. "Not even if I was alive and starving."

I cackled and dug in again. "Suit yourself."

"Now, about the message from this afternoon..."

"Let me ask you something," I interrupted, plopping my food on the bench and turning to face the woman properly for the first time. "If this message is so bloody important, why don't these mysterious people come and talk to me themselves?"

TALES FROM THE GATEWAY

"They require a certain amount of anonymity. It's as much for their protection as for your own."

This was not what I expected her to say, and I had to chew on it for a minute before I could decide what to say next.

"Why would I need protection?" I asked, hoping like mad that my voice sounded like I wasn't bothered.

"Anyone with your abilities would be wise to tread carefully," the woman replied, and I could tell that she was trying to answer me without really answering me at all. It got my back up again.

"I'm always careful, and that includes not trusting ghosts who speak in riddles instead of just saying what they bloody well mean," I replied. I took up my chips again, but suddenly found I wasn't that hungry anymore. My insides were all churned up and my palms were sweaty.

"They don't want to alarm you," the woman said, and her voice was a bit gentler now, like she knew she was about to lose me. "Your abilities are not just a party trick, Savannah Todd. They are much, much more than that. It is crucial that you heed this warning and allow them to help you."

"Yeah?" I nearly shouted, standing up and letting all my gorgeous chips slide to the ground. "Well, I'm not much of one for heeding. And I don't need anyone's help, all right? I've managed this on my own my whole life, and I'll keep on managing it just fine."

I turned my back on the ghost, who did not follow me. But she did call after me. "They'll wait for you to come to your senses, but they won't wait forever. Tell a messenger when you're ready."

I flipped two fingers over my shoulder at her and started walking toward the next bus shelter on the route, but I walked right past it. In fact, I walked the entire way back to the flat, nearly two miles, just to avoid any other ghosts who might start harassing me. If I kept moving, maybe they'd take the hint and leave me alone.

When I finally peeled my sorry arse out of bed the next day and ran out to the offy for my mum, I found out quick that I was in proper trouble. The ghosts were everywhere. Three of them stood right at the front door. They lined the pavement on both sides of the street. There was one on every bench, under every lamppost, on every corner, and every last one of them was staring at me and calling my name. I don't mind admitting that I was half-mad with fear by the time I made it back to the flat, and knocked back a bevvy just to steady my nerves.

My little sister Maisie walked into the kitchen. "You ain't supposed to be drinking that in the house," she announced, as if I didn't already know it.

"Bugger off, Mais. I'm not in the humor," I grumbled.

"I'll tell Mum," Maisie taunted.

"Well, tell her then, and have done with it, you little twit!" I shouted.

Maisie seemed to decide, on balance, that maybe she should keep her little trap shut, which showed an unusual amount of sense for someone so closely related to me. "A lady stopped by to see you," she said instead.

I felt my heart speed up again. "When?"

"Just now. You only just missed her. You probably passed her on the pavement."

"I didn't see no one on the pavement," I said, which was a lie, of course. I'd seen plenty of people on the pavement—far too many of them for my liking—but as none of them were still living, they didn't matter for the purposes of our conversation. "What did she look like?"

"Pretty. Very posh. Dark hair. I liked her, she smelled good and had lipstick and high heels on."

I rolled my eyes. Maisie's standards of liking people had mostly to do with how closely they resembled her Barbie dolls. "And what did she say?"

"She asked if you lived here, and I said yes. Then she asked if you were at home and I said no. Then she asked when you would be back and I said I thought soon, and she said she would come back later," Maisie replied, without hardly breathing.

"Did she say when?"

"Nope."

"Well, did she tell you her name, at least?"

"Nope."

"A great bloody help you are," I muttered.

"Don't swear or I'm telling mum you left us alone," Maisie replied, before spinning and running back to our bedroom and slamming the door behind her.

I considered aiming a beer can at the door, but that would have been a waste of perfectly good beer, so I managed to talk myself out of it.

I started arguing with myself about what I should do next. Whoever this woman was, I didn't want to talk to her. Maisie said she was coming back, so if I wanted to avoid her, I should just disappear, like I usually did when I wanted to avoid something. Poof.

Trouble was, I couldn't avoid the ghosts. They were everywhere, more of them all the time. I fancied I could almost feel the chill of them, creeping into the flat, dropping the temperature, turning the air clammy and cold. I went to the window and twitched the curtain open so that I could peer down onto the street. There they all were, a crowd of spirit stalkers milling around, waiting to descend on me the next time I walked out my door. There would be no disappearing now. No poof-ing for old Sav this time.

Maybe I was being a fool, avoiding this woman, whoever she was. Maybe the thing to do was wait right here until she turned up again, and confront her. If I kept avoiding her, she'd just keep coming back. No, better to have it out, face to face, and let her know that I wasn't playing whatever game she was proposing. Yeah, that would sort it out. Then, I could get on with my life.

I went into the sitting room, sat down on the couch and flicked on the telly. I was hoping to distract myself, but I couldn't even focus on the screen. I kept jumping at the sounds of my sisters' voices, at every tiny noise from out in the corridor or in the street. When my mum opened the door coming home from her knitting club, I nearly had a heart attack.

"Bloody hell, woman, what the blazes do you think you're doing, sneaking up on a person like that?!" I shouted at her.

She just stood in the doorway, her keys still in her hands and a massive bag of yarn swinging off her arm while she stared wide-eyed at me. "Who's sneaking up, then? I just walked in me own front door, for the love of God!"

"Sorry, mum," I sighed, settling back onto the couch.

"I should hope so," my mum replied, before turning and gesturing out the doorway. "There's someone here who'd quite like to speak with you, though she mightn't anymore, now that she's heard the way you talk to your own mother."

"Who are you..." My voice trailed off, because I'd just spotted a woman standing behind my mother.

A tall woman. Pretty. Very posh. Lipstick. High heels. I couldn't get a sniff of her from where I was sitting, but I was willing to bet that she smelled damn good.

Fuck me.

The woman caught my eye quickly and then turned to my mother with a bright, friendly smile on her face.

"There you are, Alice," she said, in a voice smooth as silk. She reached out and handed my mother two more outsize shopping bags.

"Cheers, I really appreciate the hand, and all," my mother said, bunging her own bag onto the counter so that she could take the other two out of the woman's hands. "Hope it wasn't a bother."

"Nonsense, no bother at all," the woman replied, and turned to me at last. "Hello, Savannah. It's nice to see you again."

I almost asked her what the hell she meant by "again," but before I could even open my mouth, she had turned back to my mother. "I met Savannah at that quaint little restaurant she works at."

I snorted. Calling that greasy chippie a restaurant was stretching the boundaries of reality if you ask me, but my mum didn't seem to mind. She just beamed at the woman and said, "Oh, yeah, we've gotten our takeaway there for years. They've got the best chips."

"Indeed," the woman replied, as though she completely agreed. "Anyway, we got to chatting and I thought Savvy would be just ideal for an educational opportunity with my organization. I promised to stop by to tell her a bit more about it. Still up for a chat, Savannah?"

The woman smiled, looking for all the world as though we were best mates meeting up for long-standing plans.

"What organization is that, then?" my mother asked, looking skeptical. "I realize my Sav seems sharp enough, but school was never her cup of tea, if you get my meaning."

"Oh, I've no doubt she's absolutely brilliant when she applies herself, and of course, I can see where she gets it," the woman said, dodging the first part of the question smooth as you like. "Having a mother like you, who can so deftly juggle four girls, while running a household, and all the challenges that come with it? Savannah says you're quite the domestic goddess."

Now, my mum was a right sap for a well-delivered compliment, and this woman certainly knew how to dish 'em out. I would have been annoyed if I hadn't been so impressed to see a master at work, not to mention the fact that she gave me all the credit for it.

"Is that so?" my mum said, positively preening. "She said that, did she?"

"Oh, yes," the woman replied. "And on that note, we won't keep you another moment. Savannah, shall we?" She gestured down the hallway.

The presumption. The sheer cheek of the woman.

"Well, go on, Sav, don't be rude, now," my mum added, raising her eyebrows at me.

What else could I do? I slid right off the couch, grabbed my mac off the hook and followed her out the door without another word.

We didn't speak until we reached the bottom of the stairs.

"Clever of you, to get to me through my mum," I said grudgingly.

"Thank you," the woman replied. "I often find that the indirect routes are best. Usually, I employ spirits for that purpose, but that particular approach didn't seem to work with you."

"What one person calls indirect, another person might call dodgy."

The woman smirked and gave a shrug. "If you like."

"Am I allowed to ask your name, at least, or do you answer to 'Oi! You!'" I asked.

She held out a hand. "My name is Celeste Morgan. It's a pleasure to know you."

"Savannah Todd. I can't truthfully say the same, as yet." I took her hand to shake it, but pulled it away suddenly. Something odd, like a gentle current of electricity, had run through my fingers when I'd touched her.

"Ah, you felt that, did you? Good. Very good," Celeste said, and proceeded out the door and down the front steps.

The streets were still swarming with ghosts, but none of them were whispering to me anymore. They weren't moving either. On the contrary, they were dead silent, like statues of ice, and they were watching this Celeste woman instead. That was... interesting.

We turned and headed down the road just as the street lamps started to come on. Celeste waited until we had walked past a knot of young blokes messing about outside a pub before she spoke again.

"Have you considered what Hubert and Lavinia have spoken to you about?"

"Who are Hubert and Lavinia?" I asked.

She looked at me, puzzled. "The two spirits we sent to speak with you. Didn't you ask their names?"

I shook my head. "Why would I ask their names?"

"Don't you usually ask someone's name when you have a conversation with them? You asked mine," Celeste said. There was an edge of something in her voice that got my back up a bit.

"I don't tend to get... friendly with the ghosts I see 'round here," I said.

"Don't you wonder about them? About who they are? About why they might be here?"

I shrugged. "I might have, once, but these days I'm mostly just trying to steer clear of them."

"Haven't you ever wondered why you can see them when others cannot? Why they seem to seek you out? What they might want from you?" Celeste asked.

I shrugged again. "I dunno. Everyone's got their issues, haven't they? This is mine."

"And is that how you think of it, this ability you have? As an issue?"

"Well, how the hell else am I meant to think about it? I've got ghosts following me around like stray puppy dogs, and it's all I can do not to let on to the living people around me that I've got an unwanted entourage of the dead! What do you want me to call it, a party trick? A special talent?"

Celeste gave me a sad smile, a knowing smile, which honestly only aggravated me more. "I understand," she said.

"Like bollocks you do," I muttered.

"I assure you, I do. I've seen spirits all my life as well. Ever since I can remember."

"Oh, yeah? And how is it that you're so cheerful about it, then? How is it you haven't been chucked in the madhouse?"

"Because I know the purpose of my gift," Celeste said, her smile blossoming, "and now you will, too. I assure you it makes all the difference in the world."

"Is that so? Well, enlighten me, then. I can see I'm going to have to hear this whether I want to or not," I said.

"You are a Durupinen, Savannah: a living embodiment of the Gateway between the worlds of the living and the dead. It is your gift—your calling—to shepherd the spirits trapped here on earth through to the Aether and beyond. Spirits are drawn to you because they sense this gift running through your veins. They can sense that you have been put on this earth to help them, and they yearn for your guidance."

I'm not proud of what I did next.

I'm still not quite sure how it started. The laughing came first, I think. Yeah, I laughed until I couldn't hardly catch me breath and great fat tears started leaking out of my eyes. Once they started leaking out, though, I couldn't seem to shut 'em off, and they sort of turned into these great heaving sobs that took my body over. And then, even as I was crying, I could feel my anger at myself boiling over because I'd let myself cry in front of this woman I'd never met before, and then, before I knew it, I was ranting and shouting like a complete nutter, just screaming my bloody head off at this woman, at me, at the crowd of spirits who were gathering to see what all the fuss was about. And even though I don't remember deciding to do it, I found myself running as fast as I could back to my flat, nose dripping, eyes leaking, laughing, and crying and ranting all at once.

I suppose my mum must have said something to me as I charged through the door, but blast if I know what it was. My sisters took one look at me as I entered the bedroom and scattered like cockroaches. I crawled into my bed, pulled a pillow over my face, and screamed and screamed and screamed until I lost my voice. It's possible that I smothered myself into unconsciousness, because the next thing I knew, it was the middle of the night and I woke up to find the worst headache of my life bashing away at the insides of my skull like an enthusiastic collection of sledgehammers. It was hard to see—my eyes were swollen and my eyelashes were sticking together like I'd pasted them. My throat was raw and my mouth was dry. It was worse than the worst hangover I'd ever had, and I'd been spectacularly pissed more than once.

My sisters' beds were empty—they hadn't dared to come back into the room, even after I'd passed out. I squinted at the clock. It was 3:11 in the morning. The house was completely silent except for my stepdad snoring like an asthmatic rhinoceros in the next room. I peeled myself out of my bed and twitched aside the blind to have a look down into the street. I'm not sure what I expected to find—Celeste standing outside my window, throwing pebbles like a lovesick bloke desperate for a shag? What I didn't expect was the emptiness. For the first time in nearly a week, there wasn't a single spirit in sight.

I should have felt relieved. Instead, I felt desolate. That's just so bloody typical, isn't it? I spend my entire life trying to get away from ghosts, and the moment they finally scarper, I miss them.

I scrounged around for my slippers and padded out into the kitchen to see if I could knock up something to eat, and had just cobbled together a half-decent cold bacon sarnie when I noticed the envelope pushed under the door.

I just stared at it for a minute, kind of hoping it would vanish into the god-awful orange floral pattern on the linoleum. Poof.

It did not.

I already knew who it was for, and also who it was from, so I left it there until I was good and ready to deal with it. Who knew if I'd be able to eat a bite once I'd read it, and that would have been a waste of a perfectly good sarnie. Only when I'd devoured the whole thing, which didn't take long, did I shuffle over, pick it up, and have a look.

Blimey, even this woman's paper was posh—heavy, cream-colored, with a purple design on the back, kind of like three spirals put together. It even smelled good—like lavender. I unfolded it to see a few sentences written in penmanship neat as a pin.

Savannah,

Please forgive me for frightening you off. I know it wasn't easy to hear what I had to tell you, especially from a stranger, and I understand completely. But your role as a Durupinen isn't something you can run from. It isn't going away. And I'm not going away either.

I beg your forgiveness again, for though you have expressed that you have not appreciated my indirect methods of reaching you, I've taken the liberty of speaking to your grandmother. Nanny and I had a charming chat. She's lovely—and very protective of her "little poppet," as she called you. She told me all about you, and how she has been with you all these years, guiding your interactions with other spirits, and helping you to manage your gift. If only every sensitive was so lucky, to have such a loving and guiding hand from such a young age.

I have explained everything to her, and when you are ready she would like to speak to you about it. Perhaps she can convince you where I have failed to do so. But please, do not wait too long. The spirit world depends on you to commit yourself to your vocation.

I'll be in touch again soon. If you want to reach me, your Nanny can find me.

Yours in sisterhood,
Celeste Morgan

TALES FROM THE GATEWAY

I probably read the letter at least ten times before the words had really sunk in, and even then I found myself feeling like I was floating, like everything in the room had become immune to gravity and there was nothing solid to hang onto.

The thing is, everyone builds their scaffolding. Do you get my meaning? Over time you build up this structure of things you can hold onto, that keeps everything in place and from toppling over. The more rubbish life hands you, the more scaffolding you have to build to keep it all together, just so you can get from day to day. And here this woman came, with her fancy clothes and her sureness and her lipstick and started dismantling my scaffolding with a bloody crowbar and lavender bloody scented sticks of dynamite.

And I was supposed to be—what, exactly? Relieved? Grateful?

As I folded up the letter, I felt a creeping tickle of a chill up the back of my neck, and I knew that Nanny was nearby.

"Not now, Nanny," I whispered into the darkness. "It's late, and I'm knackered. Maybe tomorrow, yeah?"

The chill vanished, and I stumbled back to my waiting bed.

This is the part of the story where I ignore my own dead gran for a whole week, which makes me sound like a massive wanker, but there it is. She didn't mind. She knew I wasn't ready, and she didn't push me, which was one of the best things about Nanny—she'd leave you well enough alone when you needed it. It wasn't that I was trying to forget about Celeste and what she told me—you can't really forget something like that, can you, and you'd be a fool to try. I *was* trying to work up the courage to deal with it, and that meant shoving it away in the corner and not looking at it for a while, until I started to feel brave again. It also meant a number of poor decisions on my part generally, involving some blokes of a convenient nature and a fair few pints to soften the sharp edges of reality.

There was something I couldn't ignore though, and that was awareness. I couldn't unhear what Celeste had said to me—not that I didn't give it a damn good try. It's mad, because you'd think the thing that would nag me most would be the whole Durupinen thing. You'd think my head would be filled with a million questions—what the hell kind of word is that? What does it mean? What is a Gateway? Why the fuck did I need to be one? Why couldn't spirits just open the door and see themselves out? How did it all work? What came next?

The truth is, though, the thing I thought about more than

anything else was what Celeste called her ability: *a gift*. I laughed it off in the moment, but it stuck to me like a plaster and wouldn't go away. I'd never once, in my whole life, considered seeing ghosts a good thing. It has always been, at best, an inconvenience; at worst, a bloody nuisance. Why couldn't I see it any other way? I thought I knew who might be able to help me puzzle that one out.

"Nanny?"

"'Bout time, poppet. I was starting to think you'd forgotten about me." She was right there, of course. She always turned up, when I wanted a word.

"'Course I haven't, don't be daft," I said with a scowl.

"All right now, love, I'm only pulling your leg. I know you've been having a good, long think and I like to think your old Nanny knows when it's time to make herself scarce. Now, what do you need, love?"

I sighed. When I turned, there she was, in my dad's beat up old chair, the first place I'd ever seen her and the only thing left in the house that bastard ever owned. I wouldn't let my mum chuck it, God knows why. One time I dragged it back in from the curb and up three flights of stairs to put it back in its old spot.

"That woman, Celeste. She talked to you?"

"Yes, love. But you already know that."

I had about a million specific questions, but all that came out of my mouth was, "What d'you reckon?"

"I think you're too stubborn for your own good and you run away from things that you ought to face and give a good walloping," Nanny said, arms crossed.

I winced. "Ouch, Nan. I meant about what she said, not about me."

"But it is about you, Sav. It's always been about you, love. That's the trouble."

"I don't follow," I said.

"I mean, love, you've always thought that your seeing ghosts was about *you*. You thought about how it affected *you*, how it inconvenienced *you*, how it made things difficult for *you*. I don't think you ever once thought that it might not be about you at all—that it might be about the ghosts themselves."

"Gotta be honest, Nan, I didn't call you in to make me feel like utter shite. I was doing a pretty good job of that on my own," I said, raising my voice a bit.

Nanny didn't mind, though. In fact, she laughed. "I imagine you didn't call me in here to lie to you either, poppet. And the truth isn't that you're selfish, it's that you're young. All young people have to figure themselves out before they can turn their attention to the wider world. That's not selfish. That's just life."

"I'm... not convinced that makes me feel better," I said.

"I'm not here to make you feel better," Nanny reminded me. "I'm here to tell you the truth. And the truth is that it's time to stop looking inside yourself and start looking around you. Your purpose is larger than yourself."

I snorted. "My purpose. What a load of tosh. How am I supposed to know what my purpose is?"

"By stopping this vanishing nonsense. No more disappearing girl, Sav. No more poof."

"No more poof?" I asked. My voice sounded small, even to me.

"No, love. It's time to show up. It's time to ask yourself what you can do with these abilities of yours. Everyone has to ask what they can bring to the world, what they can make, or do, or be. And you're damn lucky."

"Lucky? How do you reckon?"

"Because most people have to figure it out for themselves. You've had someone knock on the door and point it out to you."

"You mean Celeste Morgan?"

"Yes. She's got the answer to the question you didn't even think to ask. She's handing you a chance to do something really important, love. And there's no running from it. It's inside you."

"You think it's true, then? All this bother about Gateways and Durupinen and Crossing spirits?"

"I do," Nanny said, and finally her voice softened. "Spirits aren't drawn to you by accident, poppet. They're drawn to you because you can help them. You've got what they need, badly."

A bloody awful thought struck me like a hammer. "Is that why you're here? Because I can help you?" I asked.

Nanny shook her head. "No, love. I'm here because I want to be, and that's all."

I heaved a sigh of relief. "But the others... you think they need my help?"

"Some of us choose to stay," Nanny said, gesturing to herself. "But others get a bit... stuck. Either they're confused, or lost, or maybe even just stubborn. But the truth of it is, they're here among the living and they shouldn't be."

"And I'm meant to do something about that?"

"They can't do it on their own. And they haven't just stumbled upon you, love. They haven't found you by accident. They're drawn to you, Sav. And that's because of this... this Gateway."

I swallowed. Hard. "I'm scared, Nan."

"Good. You should be. But there's nothing in life worth doing that doesn't scare the hell out of you at first."

"Right," I said, and for some reason, this made me feel a bit calmer. "Right."

The next day, when I walked out the door for my shift, the boy with the cap was there, standing against a lamppost, waiting for me.

"Hey, uh... Hubert, isn't it?"

The poor kid winced, like he was afraid I was going to hit him. "Yeah, that's right."

"You, uh... you still know how to get in touch with that woman? Celeste?"

His eyes went all round, and he stopped twisting his cap. "Yeah, I surely do," he said.

"Would you mind... don't suppose you could do me a favor, then, mate?" I asked him.

"I could try," he said, and he almost smiled.

"Go on and tell her I'm ready... when she is," I told him.

There was no question now. He was definitely smiling. "On my way," he said, and vanished.

And with him vanished a lot of other things, like my freedom, my independence, and any chance of a normal bloody life. Then again, though, I thought I could see, just for a moment, a path forward—something solid where I could put my feet down, one in front of the other, and actually get someplace.

And so, my fear vanished, too. Just like that.

Poof.

2

ANNABELLE'S STORY

THE FIRST TIME I MET David Pierce, I hated him.
Well, it's possible he hated me, too, I suppose, but for the sake of saving face, let's pretend our animosity wasn't completely mutual. It will give him something to yell at me about when I finally get to see him again, and we did dearly love a good fight.

Back when I first opened my shop, I supplemented my living at a mildly humiliating array of tacky fairs and occult conventions. You know the kind of thing—a bunch of Goth-inspired cosplayers, who mistook a fondness for vampire fiction for a personality, crowded into an overheated function hall, perusing teas and salves, crystals and amulets, all of little more than aesthetic value for those who did not know how to properly utilize them. Most of the vendors were harmless—middle-aged women peddling naturopathic remedies, artists with dark fantasy aesthetics, antiques dealers hawking wares ranging from the quirky to the disturbing. But occasionally, I would come across a real charlatan, someone preying on people's ignorance in ways I couldn't ignore.

It happened that day, with David, as I watched him set up his table in the church hall, erecting a banner that read, "Ghost Hunters of Central Massachusetts," and covering his tabletop with gadgets and laptops and photo albums. It was possible I actually incurred damage to ocular muscles from how hard I rolled my eyes. Shortly, he was joined by another man, a great hulking guy who wouldn't have looked out of place at a biker bar, and the two began fiddling with all of their cords, knobs, and buttons; setting their gadgets blinking, flashing and beeping.

Was I honestly going to have to endure an entire weekend with such bullshit in my periphery? I was just contemplating finding one of the convention organizers and begging a change of table location when I looked up and saw David heading my way, a curious smile on his face. I assumed my performative air of omniscient indifference; far be it from me to let my disdain lose me a paying customer.

"Hey, there! So, divination, huh? Excellent. What are your methods?" he said genially, his eyes scanning my table with what I can only describe as professional interest.

"Tarot, mainly," I replied with my well-practiced cryptic smile. "But I practice palmistry as well. Or I could read your tea leaves, if you prefer."

But he wasn't listening. His eyes had fallen on the deck of tarot cards I had just pulled from my bag and laid on the table. His eyes lit up like a kid at Christmas who just spotted his coveted new bicycle under the tree. "Oh, wow!" he breathed. "Is that a minchiate deck?!"

His use of the word pulled me up short, and for a moment, I almost forgot to look mysterious and unbothered. "Uh... why, yes. Yes, it is. You are familiar with tarot, then?"

"Oh, yeah! I've made a great study of mystical arts. It's unusual to see a traditional minchiate deck in modern tarot readings. If you don't mind me asking, how old is it?"

"I am unsure of the precise age. But it belonged to my grandmother," I replied, and fanned the deck out upon the table face up, so that he could see the artwork. His jaw dropped in a satisfyingly cartoonish manner.

"Are those... *hand-painted?*" he whispered. "Holy shit! Those must be at least a hundred years old! And in the traditional suits, too!" He looked up and narrowed his eyes at me. "If it's not too personal a question, what's your heritage? Italian?"

"Romany. Traveler," I replied a bit stiffly, assuming a judgmental response I rarely received but anticipated nonetheless. It was a Traveler tradition, assuming a defensive stance, and though I was several generations removed from true Traveler status, it was ingrained in me nonetheless.

But David merely nodded, that boyish look of genuine interest still splashed all over his features. "Right. Well, I should probably get back to my table. I'm Dr. David Pierce, by the way." He pointed unnecessarily at his name tag. "And that's one of my partners in crime, Iggy Kowalski." He waved over at the enormous tattooed man at his table, who returned the wave with a cheerful, gap-toothed grin.

"Pleased to make your acquaintance, David. I'm Annabelle Rabinski," I said, acknowledging Iggy over his shoulder with a flick of my hand.

"Good luck today. Maybe you could give me a reading later!" David said. And with one last, almost longing look at the cards, he turned and wandered off through the tables.

It was a busy morning on that first day of what would prove to be one of the better attended conventions I'd ever worked. I pressed through a steady queue of readings all morning, and by the time I put up my sign that I would resume readings after the lunch break, my voice was growing hoarse. I would have to pace myself if I hoped to last the weekend. Despite my preoccupation with customers, I did not fail to notice that the table beside me had also attracted a lot of traffic. Small crowds gathered to watch equipment demonstrations, video clips, and to flip through binders of "evidence," which, from what I could see, was nothing more than an assortment of nebulous, shadowy shapes caught in photographs. Still, I might have let it all go, and let them have their harmless fun, were it not for the couple who appeared just after noon time.

I noticed them right away, because they stuck out strikingly from the rest of the crowd. They were clearly out of their element, and they didn't stop to browse or peruse any of the tables they passed. They were consulting a map and staring around with wide, anxious eyes. It was with palpable relief that they spotted the sign for "Ghost Hunters of Central Massachusetts," and made a beeline for it. As they drew closer, I let out an audible gasp.

These people, whoever they were, were not alone: an intense spirit energy was attached to them. I felt it immediately, the shivers up my arms and into the roots of my hair, the way the very gravitational balance of the room seemed to shift to account for the spirit's pull on its surroundings. I could not make out a shape of any kind—the spirit had not manifested, and in any case, I would need a stronger personal connection before I could hope for a visual, but the emotional state was as loud and clear as though the spirit itself was shouting it through a megaphone.

Sadness. Frustration. Desperation.

Keeping my eyes carefully on my lunch, I shifted my chair closer to the edge of my booth, so that I could better hear what was happening.

"Hello, are... are you David Pierce?" the man asked. He was somewhere around fifty years old, though I had the distinct impression that grief had aged him considerably, so that he looked closer to sixty. The woman beside him—his wife, I was guessing—was clinging to his hand with a white-knuckled grip.

"Yeah, that's me," the man who I now knew to be called David replied, smiling genially and holding out a hand. "How can I help you?"

The man did not take David's hand. He looked down at it in bewilderment, as though he hardly knew what to do with it, before looking up and declaring in a hushed voice, "We're being haunted by our son."

The smile slipped from David's face instantly, and his hand dropped limply to his side. He threw a look at Iggy, who seemed to know instantly that David was dealing with a sensitive situation. Without missing a beat, Iggy gestured to a group of teenagers around the far side of the table, drawing their attention to a video screen, so that David could engage with the couple more privately.

"What's your name?" David asked quietly.

"I'm Lionel. Lionel Thompson. And this is my wife, Patricia," the man said, gesturing to the woman, who gave a weary nod but did not speak.

"And your son's name?" David asked.

"Reginald. Reginald Thompson," Lionel replied.

"Everyone called him Reggie," Patricia added, in a voice so quiet and hoarse I could barely make out her words.

I turned in my seat and pretended to be looking for something in the bag slung over the back of my chair, which allowed me a few surreptitious glances. David's eyebrows had drawn together thoughtfully.

"I'm so sorry, but the name sounds terribly familiar," he said.

"Probably from the missing person flyers. We've had them up all over the state since Reggie disappeared six months ago," Lionel explained and, reaching into the pocket of his coat, extracted a folded, dog-eared piece of paper. He unfolded it, pressed it smooth on the tabletop, and handed it to David, who peered down at what I could only assume was the face of Reggie Thompson.

"Ah, yes," David said, nodding his head. "I remember now. There are several of these flyers up around the campus where I work. I'm a professor at St. Matthews College," he added when he saw the puzzled expressions on the Thompsons' faces. "So, forgive me, but are you saying that your son's been found?"

Lionel shook his head. "No. The police have barely taken an interest in the case, because Reggie is a legal adult. At eighteen years old, he's free to come and go as he pleases, they say."

"Young men take off, stretch their wings, rebel a bit," Patricia added, in a voice clearly meant to be mocking the nonchalance of the police officer. "Give him some time, he'll find his way back." She snorted. "They don't know my son. He would never put us through this kind of heartache. Never."

"And what young man walks out his front door to stop by the corner market with nothing but five dollars in his pocket and never comes back? No keys, no wallet, no cell phone?" Lionel asked incredulously, then shook his head. "We've known from the start that something must have happened to him—something that was preventing him from coming home to us. And so, we've been on our own trying to track him down."

"And have you come up with any leads?" David asked.

Lionel shook his head. "The store manager says he never came in. It's only a few blocks' walk. Someone has to have seen something, but every person we've talked to claims ignorance. We've knocked on every door between our house and the store. We've canvassed pedestrians day and night. Nothing."

"And now you think Reggie is haunting you?" David prompted.

"It started about three weeks after he disappeared," Lionel said, dropping his voice to a whisper now. I leaned back in my chair, tipping it back onto two legs, in hopes of catching more. "At first, it was just strange noises around the house—knocking, footsteps, that kind of thing. I thought I was losing my damn mind. Sometimes I still think I am."

"That's a common reaction," David assured the man. "Don't question your sanity. Believe yourself. What else have you experienced?"

"Whoa, cool! Why's it doing that? It's like Ghostbusters!" One of the teenagers from the other side of the table was laughing and pointing to a piece of equipment in Iggy's hands. He had been showing them how it worked, pointing it in various directions when the thing quite suddenly went haywire. He looked up to see that the device was pointing directly at the Thompsons.

"Ah, too much electrical interference in here. It's all these damn cell phones," Iggy said dismissively, switching the device off at once. But he shot David a significant look which David silently acknowledged.

Picking up a small audio recorder from the table behind him, David held it up and said, "Do you mind if I record what you're saying? I'm afraid I haven't got a pen or paper handy, and it will be the easiest way for me to make sure I've got all your information. Totally understand if you'd rather not, of course," he said, and half-lowered it to the table again.

"No, please, go ahead," Lionel said in an almost weary voice. "It's nothing we haven't already told the police, private detectives, and anyone else who would listen to us."

"Excellent," David said, pressing a button so that a tiny red light flared to life on the recorder. "Please go on. You mentioned knocking and footsteps."

"That's right," Lionel said, picking up his thread again. "It usually only happened at night, when both of us were home. Then things started moving."

"Moving?"

"Yes. Like, we'd put something down in one place, and then when we went back for it, it was gone," Lionel said.

"What kinds of things?"

"Little things. Keys. Phones. Earrings. Hairbrushes. And they almost always seem to materialize in the same location."

"Which is?"

Lionel hesitated, as though he thought the answer too absurd to speak aloud. He glanced anxiously at Patricia who whispered, "The windowsill in Reggie's bedroom," before dissolving into tears.

At that moment, a burst of energy surged over me like a tidal wave and I saw, for a fraction of a second, the outline of a young man just behind her, waving his arms frantically. As quickly as the image presented itself, it was gone, nothing but a negative behind my eyelids, a darkened suggestion of a shape, like the sun was playing tricks with my vision. I shook my head to clear a kind of ringing that had begun in my ears, something akin to—but not exactly—a distant screaming.

By the time I recovered myself enough to tune back into the conversation, Iggy had shooed the teenagers away and David was pulling out his phone to exchange information with the Thompsons.

"Let me see if I can make some adjustments to our investigation schedule, since this is clearly a case that needs immediate attention..."

I felt a toxic mixture of panic and anger surge up inside me. How dare the man prey on grieving parents like this? Before I knew what was happening, before I could stop myself, I had risen from my chair and approached them.

"Excuse me, can I interest you in a reading free of charge?" I asked, doing my best to smile serenely. "You folks look like you could use some peace of mind."

Patricia opened her mouth as though to agree, but Lionel cut in sharply. "No, thank you very much. We've gone down that road before, and we will not be taken advantage of again." He turned back to David. "We'll be in touch, Mr. Pierce. Thank you very much for your time."

And with an utterly poisonous look at me, he put his arm around his wife's shoulder and steered her away through the crowd, their son's energy trailing behind them, leaving me light-headed. Before I was able to properly recover, David was confronting me angrily.

"What the hell did you do that for?" he hissed at me.

"Do what?" I asked, rubbing at my temples and willing my head to clear so that I could think straight.

"Couldn't you see that those people were vulnerable? You can't just swoop down on them when they're trying to—"

But I had recovered sufficiently enough now to let out a derisive squawk of laughter. "You can't possibly be lecturing me on taking advantage of vulnerable people. How you would even find the nerve..."

"Hey, they came here seeking me out, not the other way around!" David shot back. "And where do you get off telling me that I'm taking advantage of people? We don't charge for our services. Not a penny."

"What *services?*" I admit I actually placed air quotations around the word in a fit of sarcasm I couldn't suppress.

"Evidence collection! Analysis! Validation of their experiences!" David replied, ticking them off on his fingers.

"Oh, come *on*," I scoffed. "You don't really expect me to believe that all this crap is actually capturing ghosts, do you?"

"It captures a fair amount of evidence of paranormal activity, yes," David replied indignantly. "Photographs, EVPs, fluctuations in electromagnetic fields—"

"And how is any of that bullshit supposed to *help* those people?"

"It's not bullshit! We've been able to conclusively prove the existence of spirit activity in dozens of—"

But I wasn't interested in hearing about his Ghostbusters cosplay. I plowed on, speaking right over him. "So, let's say you go in there, you set up your equipment, and then you get a few blurry photos and inconclusive sounds on a recorder. Then what? How have you helped those grieving parents? How have you helped the boy that's clearly attached himself to—" I stopped suddenly.

David squinted at me. "What did you say?"

"I said how does any of this help those grieving parents?" I repeated, my face reddening.

"No after that," David pressed. "You said something about a boy being attached to them."

"I just meant..."

"Is that why you wanted to do a reading? Did you see something? Sense something?" he asked eagerly, his anger vanishing into thin air.

"I... I just didn't want to see them taken advantage of," I cried.

But David would not be deterred. "Are you a psychic medium? Is that one of your many tricks, *Madam* Rabinski?"

"I don't do *tricks*," I spat at him. "Which is more than I can say for you with all of this ridiculous—ouch!" I had picked up one of his gadgets, an EMF detector, according to the label. But I'd barely lifted it from the table when the thing lit up like a Christmas tree, emitted a high-pitched shriek, and sparked alarmingly. I dropped it to the tabletop and leaped back from it.

David didn't seem in the least concerned that I'd just short-circuited one of his expensive gadgets. Indeed, his eyes lit up exactly like the EMF detector now smoking gently on the table.

"Are you? A psychic medium? Did you sense a spirit around the Thompsons?" he asked eagerly.

"I have to go," I said. "My lunch break is over and I've got a queue forming."

And I turned away from him, my heart still racing as I sat down at my table and beckoned my next customer forward, hiding behind the privacy screen and trying to locate my usual air of mystical serenity. I need hardly say I failed miserably on that score.

TALES FROM THE GATEWAY

§

I bailed on the occult fair the next day, emailing the organizers and begging off with a fake family emergency. I had no desire to face David Pierce and his accusations again, and I resolved to put him out of my mind. Less easy to forget, though, was the Thompson family. I even pulled down one of the missing person flyers from a telephone pole near my shop, placing it by my phone on the counter, where I nearly dialed the contact number fifty different times, always hanging up before I could bring myself to complete it. I wasn't even sure what I would say to them if I did finally manage to complete the call.

It was the same issue I'd had all my life, and the same issue my grandmother had had before me. For most of my childhood, I had thought the stories my grandmother told me were nothing more than *paramicha*, fairy tales learned and passed down from the far-off days when she had traveled the world in a Romany caravan. Some nights while I slept, my dreams brought me back to her kitchen, where she made heaping platefuls of *bokoli* for me to eat, and I would burn the tips of my fingers stealing sizzling bits of sausage from the frying pan while she spun yarns of spirits who haunted forest groves and of the women who could speak to them. My mother would scold her for filling my head with such fodder for nightmares, but I loved every word, every rise and fall of her voice as she navigated my imagination on a vessel carved from old gypsy tales. It was not until much later, when I was a young adult, that my sensitivity to spirits revealed itself, a fact I could not hope to tell my mother without incurring her perpetual skepticism. Instead, I went to my grandmother with the news, and that's when she finally revealed the truth to me: All of the fanciful stories she'd told me hadn't been stories at all. They were our history, the history of the *mule-vi*: the Traveler Durupinen, though she did not call them by that name. They were also the most important secrets I would ever keep.

And now here I was, nearly twenty years later, plagued by the knowledge my "gift" had given me and utterly unsure what to do with it. This was how I'd fallen into the slightly ludicrous profession in which I now found myself. It was a compromise of sorts—a way for me to mask what I could really do in the guise of a Victorian parlor trick, and then leave it up to my customers whether to believe or not. And as was human nature, those who really needed to believe, did; while others laughed at the uncanny amusement and went on their merry way, unbothered by the undercurrent of the supernatural in their world.

I had finally decided to throw the flyer away and forget all about the Thompsons when the bell over my shop door rang and David Pierce walked in.

"Hello?" he called, glancing around.

For one absurd moment, I considered ducking behind the counter, but before I could send the message to my knees to bend, he had spotted me, and it was too late.

"There you are, Madam Rabinski! I was hoping I'd find you here," he said with a bit of a sheepish smile.

"I knew I shouldn't have put my name on the sign," I grumbled, slipping the flyer under the counter and trying to assume the air of a person who hadn't just considered playing hide-and-seek in her own place of business. "So, what can I do for you? Can I interest you in some teas? Crystals? Occult artifacts?"

"No, thank you. I actually, uh… I came to apologize to you," David replied, pushing his glasses back up the bridge of his nose like a nervous schoolboy.

My arms seemed to cross defensively across my chest of their own accord. This was definitely not what I had expected him to say. "I'm listening," I said.

"This past weekend, I cast aspersions on your abilities. I was… well, it's no excuse, but I was shaken as fuck over that encounter with the Thompson family, and I got pissed off because I thought you scared them off with your lack of tact."

"I'm not sure where you learned to apologize, but you seem to have missed some of the basics," I said dryly.

David shook his head. "Sorry, that's not what I… what I meant was, I misinterpreted your concern as lack of tact. I can see now that you were just worried that I was taking advantage of them because you don't understand what I do."

My right eyebrow arched like a cat. "I'm beginning to wonder if you even know what an apology is."

"Ah, fuck," David muttered, and ran his fingers back through his long hair, pulling several strands of it from his ponytail. "I suck at this, just ask my soon-to-be ex-wife." He took a deep breath. "Okay, what I meant was, you may have come across other people in your travels who fancy themselves paranormal investigators but who are no more than a bunch of assholes that enjoy scaring the shit out of themselves in the dark. I am not one of those people."

"Is that so?" I asked stiffly, though I felt my arms unknot themselves just a bit.

"It is," David replied. "I have a Ph.D. I am a real scientist doing serious work. I've written scores of articles and even a book on the nature of spirit activity. My presence at occult fairs aside, I am always striving for truth and verifiable fact in what I do. And I do believe that what I can do—with my equipment and my team—can really help people. And I think if you had proof of that, you might not think I'm taking advantage of people." He reached into his pocket and pulled out the voice recorder he had been using at the occult fair. "I brought something I think you might be interested to hear."

I looked down at the voice recorder with a vague kind of dread, like it might self-destruct at any moment. "What is it?" I asked.

"It's what I picked up during my conversation with Lionel and Patricia Thompson. I played it back so I could write down their contact information and heard more than I had bargained for."

Hesitantly, I stepped out from behind the counter and stood closer to the recorder, which David held out into the space between us. He pressed the playback button, and we both listened as the conversation we remembered replayed into the silent shop.

"Please go on. You mentioned knocking and footsteps."

"That's right. It usually only happened at night, when both of us were home. Then things started moving."

"Moving?"

"Yes. Like, we'd put something down in one place, and then when we went back for it, it was gone."

"What kinds of things?"

"Little things. Keys. Phones. Earrings. Hairbrushes. And they almost always seem to materialize in the same location."

"Which is?"

"The windowsill in Reggie's bedroom."

The voices were as I remembered them. But there was something else that could be heard beneath the voices: a sort of low, throbbing, periodic moan that had definitely not been audible in the room at the time. It was a heart-rending sound. And then, right at the end, as Patricia's voice broke and she succumbed to her tears, the moan stopped and four words could be heard, as plainly as though someone had whispered them in my ear.

"Please don't cry, Ma."

David stopped the recorder, letting the words hang in the air, so plaintive, so desperately sad. Before I could get a handle on myself, my eyes had filled with tears.

"He was right there with them," David said, his voice halfway between a statement and a question.

I nodded.

"You knew he was there?"

I nodded again. "I saw him. For just a moment, his form manifested right behind his mother. It was probably the surge of emotion."

"Why didn't you tell me?" Pierce asked.

"Because I didn't know if I could trust you!" I snapped. "There are a hell of a lot of people out there just trying to prey on desperate folks. Sometimes I have to assume the worst to protect myself—and people like the Thompsons."

"That's fair. Yeah. Yeah, I get that," David said. "But listen, you need to realize that we don't go into our process trying to prove that there are ghosts haunting a place. In fact, we do the opposite."

"What do you mean?" I asked.

"While we do believe in the existence of spirit activity, nine times out of ten, we are able to find logical, non-paranormal explanations for what families and businesses are experiencing. We look to debunk much more than we look to confirm, and that's the God's honest truth. More often than not, a haunting is just a plumbing issue or a bird stuck in the attic, or a baby monitor picking up errant frequencies. And we help people just as much by putting their minds at ease with a simple explanation as we do by confirming a spirit presence in their house."

"I see," I said, trying to conceal my genuine surprise.

"Look, I'm used to the skepticism," David went on. "I've grown a pretty thick hide when it comes to people who doubt what I do. I would imagine the same is true of you."

I nodded.

"I've developed my own healthy skepticism when it comes to anyone who claims to deal with the paranormal from a mystical standpoint rather than a scientific one. To be honest, so-called psychics and mediums and fortunetellers often make my life significantly harder. But I do believe that true mediums exist—sensitives. And I think it's pretty clear that you, Madam Rabinski, are the real fuckin' deal."

He grinned broadly at me. I scowled back.

"Thank you for your endorsement, Dr. Pierce, but I assure you I was not looking for it."

"Oh, believe me, I know you weren't," David replied, throwing up his hands in a kind of "*mea culpa*" gesture that was somehow endearing and therefore annoyed me even more. "But the fact remains that you picked up on Reggie Thompson in ways that my equipment didn't. You have a gift, and I need your help."

I raised my eyebrows. "You need *my* help?"

"Yes. My team and I are investigating the Thompson home this weekend. I want you to come with us—to work with us."

I blinked, completely blindsided. "I... no. I don't do ghost hunts."

"Don't think of it that way," David said encouragingly. "Just think of it as helping the Thompson family."

I bit my lip. "I don't... play well with others. Or so I've been told."

Pierce chuckled. "That's okay! I'm just going to stay out of your way and let you do your thing—whatever your thing is. The truth is, I've always hoped to find a truly legit medium to work with our team, and I've never found anyone who passed muster. But you... you're the real deal. I can tell."

I snorted. "How? Just because I claimed to see Reggie attached to his parents? How do you know I wasn't lying? What if I told you right now that I made the whole thing up? Would you leave me alone?"

"No," David replied with a knowing smile that was almost a smirk, which I would dearly have loved to slap off his beardy face, "because you weren't lying and you didn't make it up. And for the record, that EVP detector you touched was unsalvageable. Fried crispy. Anyone with that kind of electromagnetism is someone I want on my team."

"I'm not interested in being studied like a specimen. I'm not a science experiment," I warned.

"Well, that's good, because I'm not interested in studying you," Pierce said, crossing his arms and meeting the challenge in my gaze. "My only interest here is helping the Thompson family. I think you want to help them, too. That should make us allies, not adversaries. So, what do you say to joining forces, you working in your way, and me working in mine?"

I didn't answer at first, stalling for time as I fought an internal battle. My gifts were meant to be protected, like a precious treasure, my grandmother had always told me. But what good was treasure buried away? Shouldn't I be helping people—and I mean *truly* helping people, without all the crystal balls and smoke and mirrors to cheapen the effect?

"What do you expect from me on this… investigation?" I hedged, stalling for time.

"Nothing extraordinary, I assure you. Come see what we do. I think you'll be impressed. And we'll give you whatever time and space you need in the house to see what your sensitivities pick up. I'm not expecting miracles here. I just think we should bring in as many avenues of help for this family as we can."

Ugh. He looked so earnest. Like a Boy Scout. I couldn't say no to him. And hence, David Pierce roped me into his nonsense for the first time.

"Fine. I'll do it. But under no circumstances can you spring me on those poor people. Get their permission for me to come, or I won't do it. Tell them whatever you like, but just remember: I'm doing this for them, not you, and I am not joining your *team*."

David's smirk broke into a delighted grin. "It's a deal."

§

I sat in my beat up car outside of the Thompsons' house for a full twenty minutes, debating whether or not I should even go in, which was the same thing I'd been doing in my head for the last five days, since David had called and said that the Thompsons had given permission for me to join the investigation. I was scared. Scared that I would make contact with Reggie Thompson and scared that I wouldn't. Scared that my abilities would get exploited or worse, get discounted. All of it was selfish, but my brain wouldn't let it go. Finally, though, when the time came to turn off the engine and get out of the car, I did it.

"Annabelle! You came!"

David was sitting in the back of an open van, winding electrical cords around his arm, a cigarette dangling from his mouth.

"Isn't that a fire hazard or something?" I asked.

"Not till you plug 'em in!" he replied, grinning. "Come on inside, we're almost entirely set up. I'll introduce you to the rest of the team."

And that was how I met "the boys"—*my* boys, these days: Iggy, Oscar, and Dan. I've become as fiercely protective of them in David's absence as a mother bear of her cubs, even though both Iggy and Oscar were both considerably older than me. It's hard to imagine now that there was ever a time we didn't implicitly trust each other. But that day they regarded me as warily as I regarded them, though they welcomed me nonetheless. They walked me through a process for the first time that would become second nature to me in short order: the placing of cameras, the checking of batteries, the running of cables, the testing of doors, windows, switches, pipes, and appliances, all in preparation to spend the night investigating a dark and quiet house. Even though I was still skeptical at that point, I was impressed with the scale and professionalism of their operation.

Lionel and Patricia had left the house for the night already. Perhaps they had found it too unsettling to watch their home being overrun with equipment, or perhaps they didn't want to deal with the curiosity of neighbors who kept wandering out onto their front walks to gawk at the disturbance. Either way, I was grateful that I didn't have to interact with them yet—I was hoping to get a feel for the energy of the house without their grief and expectation weighing down on me. Over the years I've found that the stare of living eyes was often harder to tolerate than the eyes of the dead, and I don't think I've ever met a single seasoned sensitive who disagrees with me.

Once everything was in order, Dan ensconced at his tech table, Iggy and Oscar manned with cameras, and David armed with a toolbelt of gadgets, David turned to me. "Well?"

"Well, what?"

"What do you need? Where do you want to start?"

"I... I don't know. I've never done anything like this before."

"Well, do you want to go with one of us through the house? Or would you prefer to go alone? What's your process?"

"David, I've already told you, I don't *have* a process. I might be a sensitive, but this is a first for me. Just... can I have a few minutes to walk through the place? Alone?"

David looked disappointed for only a moment—I'm sure he probably wanted to go with me so he could wave gadgets in the air around me as I went—but he rallied almost at once, nodding encouragingly. "Go for it. We'll wait here until you're done."

As I set off through the house, the only thing I felt was... emptiness. The whole house felt like the acute *absence* of someone, rather than their presence. In truth, I had been expecting to feel something from the moment I had walked in the door, and the lack of energy, in itself, felt significant. How could Reggie have had such a strong presence around his parents and yet no detectable presence at all in his own house, the place to which he was most intimately connected? The only conclusion I could come to was that he was, at that moment, decidedly somewhere else.

I purposely saved Reggie's bedroom for last. Turning the knob, I peeked my head around the door like I might be interrupting someone. The room was as heavy with his absence as the rest of the house; perhaps even more so, as the room looked as though he was about to stroll in at any minute—his comic books on his nightstand, one sneaker peeking out from under the bed, a sweatshirt tossed over the back of his desk chair. I doubted his parents had moved even a single item from where he had left it six months earlier. I could feel the tears welling in my eyes as I eased the door shut again and made my way downstairs.

"I'm all done," I said, adopting as impassive an expression as I could muster and sitting back down at the tech table. "Your turn, gentlemen."

"What did you—?" Iggy began eagerly, but David held up a hand to silence him.

"I actually think it would be best for Annabelle to keep her impressions to herself, for the time being," he said. "It will prevent us from being influenced in our own personal experiences. Let's try to remain objective. We can compare observations after we've finished."

I had not expected this level of restraint from the guy who had gushed over an old set of tarot cards like they were winning lottery tickets, but I appreciated it. The rest of the team looked slightly disappointed but agreed to David's proposition. Then they all set off separately through the house, cameras aloft and detectors flashing. I sat at the table beside Dan, who acknowledged my presence only once in three hours by asking me to pass him a bag of potato chips. One by one, Iggy, Oscar, and finally David returned to the tech table. They set down their equipment, looking crestfallen.

All the eager energy that had been buzzing between them at the start of the night had faded.

"Anything from the stationary video cameras, Dan?" David asked, though without much hope.

Dan shook his head. "It's been dead all night," he said.

David looked at me. "I think I already know the answer to this question, but how did you make out on your walk through the house?"

I gave him a sad smile. "He's not here. I'd bet my life on it."

David swore under his breath. "Damn it. And I was so sure we were going to find something, after all the activity his parents reported."

"Can I ask... did you ask the Thompsons to leave, or did they choose to go while you were investigating?" I asked hesitantly.

"We always have the family vacate the premises," David replied. "It's standard operating procedure. There's far less interference with equipment when we don't have to keep track of the clients as well as our own team."

"There's also the possibility that the clients are manufacturing the experience themselves," Iggy said grimly. "Remember Sarah Spaulding?"

"Who?" I asked.

"Former client. Called us in. Swore her house was haunted, that the spirits in it were trying to kill her," Oscar chimed in.

"And they weren't trying to kill her?" I guessed.

"They didn't even exist," Iggy replied, shaking his head. "We caught her on camera scratching up her own back and turning crosses upside down. Since then, we've never allowed clients to stay in the house while we've been investigating."

"That makes sense, as a general rule," I said. "The problem is, I don't think Reggie is haunting his house. He's haunting his parents. And if you've sent them away, we may have ruined any chance we have of communicating with him."

David considered this. "That's a fair point. We've only been at it for three hours, though. It's not unusual for it to take most of the night before we get interaction. You don't think we should give it more time?"

He was asking the group at large, but he was looking at me. I shook my head.

"He's not here, David. I'm sure of it."

"Right. Well, that's good enough for me," David replied. "Dan, have you got the contact information there? I'm going to call the Thompsons and see if they'll agree to come back."

§

The Thompsons readily agreed to return, and within half an hour, they walked back through the front door. The moment they did, the cloud of spirit energy that surrounded them was so powerful that it raised the hairs on my arms and seemed to suck all the oxygen out of the room. I must have gasped because David gave me a sharp look. I nodded discreetly.

"Lionel, Patricia, why don't you come on in here and have a seat. Make yourselves comfortable. It's your home after all, and you certainly won't get in our way," Pierce said when Lionel and Patricia continued to hover in their own doorway. Still looking out of place in their own house, they walked around the tech table and sat down on their sofa.

Pierce looked at me, asking a silent question which I nonetheless understood: *what do we do next?* I took a deep breath and sat down in the chair opposite them.

"Mr. And Mrs. Thompson, my name is Annabelle Rabinski. I appreciate you trusting me enough to invite me into your home."

"Dr. Pierce said that you were sensitive... that you could sense ghosts, and that you thought you sensed Reggie around us at the convention last weekend," Patricia said, her voice cracked with emotion.

"Yes, I... I did," I replied. "I have had this sensitivity since I was about eighteen years old. My grandmother had it as well. She was the one who taught me how to cope with it. To be honest, I've spent most of my life trying to disguise it as something less... intimidating. The tarot cards and jingling bracelets and gypsy persona make talking to the dead less scary and more entertaining, you see—for them and for me."

Patricia's face twitched into a suggestion of a smile before falling again into lines of misery. "So you... you believe us? That Reggie is... is..." She couldn't bring herself to say the word. And damn it, neither could I.

"He's with you," I said instead. "And he's trying desperately to communicate with you. I think that's why we haven't had any luck making contact with him. He's not attached to the house. He's attached to you."

Patricia dropped her face into her hands and began to sob quietly. "I knew it," I could hear her saying, over and over again. "I knew it, I knew it, I knew it."

"It may just be that Reggie is trying to comfort you," I said, my voice shaking as I tried to stay professional while fighting a mad desire to burst into tears myself. David nodded encouragingly. "But there's also the possibility that he's trying to communicate something to you, something he wants you to know."

"You mean about where he is? Or how he... he..." Lionel couldn't finish the question. The word we all knew he couldn't bring himself to say hung heavily in the air between us.

"Yes," I replied, so that they knew I understood what it was they couldn't say. "And I want to be honest with you about what my abilities are. I have no interest in disillusioning you or building up your hopes. I don't see spirits walking around the world, as clear as living folks. For instance, I can't see him sitting there next to you on the sofa, even if that's where his spirit happens to be. For me, spirits always reveal themselves in bursts of energy. Sometimes that energy will manifest as a visual flash—almost like I'm watching someone's memory. Other times, it might simply be a wave of emotion that washes over me. Other times still, I might pick up on a word, or an image that provides a clue as to what the spirit is fixated on."

Out of the corner of my eye, I could see that David was as captivated by what I was describing as the Thompsons were. If he could have done so without seeming rude or unprofessional, I knew he would have whipped out a pen and paper and started taking notes like an overeager student in a college seminar. He managed to restrain himself, however, and when I caught his eye, he had settled his expression into one of calm attentiveness. Confident that he was going to allow me to finish, I went on.

"It's possible that I won't be able to get a completely clear message from your son. Even since you've walked in the door, the energy around you has faded considerably. That doesn't mean that he's not here," I added hastily, seeing the stricken looks on their faces. "But it may mean that he's not keen to communicate with the crazy tarot card lady." I tried to smile and was rewarded with a weary sort of nod in return. "But I think, if you stay here while we continue to investigate, we will have better luck understanding what's been happening to you, and what's happened to Reggie."

Patricia and Lionel looked at each other, engaging in the kind of silent conversation only truly connected couples can have. Then they turned back to David and me and nodded in unison.

"Of course," Lionel said. "We'll do anything to help. That's why we've asked you all here."

With the Thompsons now present and seated in the living room, the rest of the team reconvened at the tech table to come up with a new game plan—a plan which, as it turned out, centered around me.

"I think we need to give Annabelle the space to connect," David said at once. "But it would be foolish not to have equipment running at the same time, in case there is communication that might be documented in another way."

"Yeah, a two-pronged approach," Oscar said, nodding his agreement. "That seems the best use of our resources." He looked up at me, smiling sheepishly. "Not that I'm calling you a resource, of course."

"I've been called worse," I replied, smiling back.

"Where do you think you'd like to set up?" David asked me. "Do you want to do another walk-about? Or maybe stay with the Thompsons?"

I bit my lip, thinking. "The thing is, I think Reggie might be frightened of us—or at least wary. Otherwise, he would have stayed behind to try to communicate with us instead of following his parents out of the house. Even the initial energy I sensed when they walked in the door has faded—like he's trying to hide from us for some reason."

"Well, we are a bunch of strangers who have invaded his house," Iggy said reasonably. "And his parents said they've tried absolutely every avenue to get help, so he might be just as wary as they are at this point. Maybe he's trying to protect them by avoiding us."

"Huh," Pierce said, scratching at his beard. "I hadn't considered that, but you have a point. Not everyone believes in the validity of ghost hunting, and I imagine that even applies to ghosts."

"So how do we convince him we're here to help and not to take advantage of his parents?" Oscar asked.

"I... think maybe I need to try to make direct contact with Reggie," I said slowly. "Maybe if I can earn his trust, he will try to use the tools available to him to get his message across to his parents."

"That's a good idea," David said. "And like we said, we can wire the room from top to bottom, for redundancy. Where do you want to do it, Annabelle?"

"Let's get in his space," I replied. "His bedroom."

While David explained our plan to Lionel and Patricia, Oscar, Iggy, and Dan moved the bulk of the equipment to Reggie's room. They set up stationary video and thermal cameras to cover every angle, and left them recording. They placed voice recorders around the room as well, and left them on. They provided me with an EMF detector and showed me how to use it, though, as Iggy said, I was pretty much a human version of the thing to begin with. We also put a number of Reggie's parents' belongings in strategic positions around the house, documenting exact positioning, in the hopes that we might be able to catch the movement of objects to Reggie's room, as his parents had reported. Finally, when we had been as thorough as it was possible to be, they left me alone in the room.

I sat down on Reggie's bed and took a deep breath, realizing as I did so just how nervous I really was. I'd interacted with hundreds of spirits, sensed them effortlessly, but never with this kind of pressure, never with this kind of an audience. I knew my abilities were real, but here I was, suddenly wondering if they were all just in my head.

"Get a grip, Annabelle," I whispered. "People are depending on you." Then I raised my head, cleared my throat, and began.

"Reggie, if you can hear me, my name is Annabelle Rabinski. I'm not being paid to be here. I'm not using your parents for publicity or anything like that. In fact, I'll be happy never to talk about tonight again, to anyone, if it will put your mind at ease. The only reason I'm here is to try to help you."

A gentle whoosh of energy permeated the room, and I knew Reggie was listening.

"If you think all this ghost hunter stuff is bullshit, you're not alone," I said, making a mental note to apologize to the team later. "I was convinced of that myself, until tonight. But I sensed you at the convention last weekend. I sensed your energy around your parents. I even saw and heard you for the briefest moment, when you told your mother not to cry."

Another whoosh. The EMF detector in my hand lit up like a Christmas tree. Every hair on my head felt electrified at the roots.

I felt the question more than I heard it. It formed in my head as a thought, rather than echoing in my ears as a sound.

You heard that?

"Yeah, I did," I replied. "I could see you, too—the shape of you, just for a second. You were behind her, trying to put your hand on her shoulder."

The energy in the room intensified as Reggie's excitement grew. Again, his question reached me as though dropping into my head like a coin into a bank.

Help me. Please. You have to help me.

"That's what I'm here for. I know you're trying to get a message to your parents. What is it? What do you need them to know?" I asked.

A creeping feeling of numbing cold came over me, and a feeling of suffocating pressure. For a moment, the room had no air, just crushing weight and darkness. Then it was over, and I was left gasping for breath.

"Buried. You've been buried somewhere," I whispered. "Do you know where?"

Nothing. No coin into the bank.

"Okay, you don't know where you are," I deduced. "But can you tell me who put you there?"

A duality entered my consciousness. *Two. Two figures. Male.*

"Do you know them, Reggie? Can you tell me anything about them?" I whispered.

I heard a clinking sound and whipped around to stare behind me. There on the windowsill, which had been empty not a moment before, was a set of keys. I recognized it right away as the set that Oscar had carefully placed on the coffee table in the living room—it had the same braided leather keychain on it. Slowly, I leaned over and touched them with a single finger. The cold was radiating from them and the energy of it was so intense that I received an actual shock.

"I don't understand," I whispered. "What does this mean? Is it the keys? Are the keys the clue? Should we be looking for a key?"

And even as I stared at it, the set of keys trembled, vibrated, and with what I knew to be a massive effort on Reggie's part, fell from the windowsill and slipped down between the bed and the wall.

With my heart still hammering at having witnessed the keys move, I shoved my hand between the bed and the wall to retrieve them. My fingers fumbled around and finally closed not on the keys, but on what seemed to be a piece of paper wedged tightly between the boxspring and the wall. I tugged on it, but did not want to tear it, whatever it was. I slid off the bed, grabbed the leg of the bed and pulled hard, managing to slide the heavy oak frame an inch or so out from the wall. Then I peered under the bed and saw that the trapped paper, freed at last, had fallen to the floor beneath the bed. I slid my head and shoulders under the bed to retrieve it, and pulled it out into the light.

It was a photograph. A photograph of three boys posing in front of a sleek red car. One of them was Reggie, with an easy smile. I turned my attention to the other two.

All at once, I was mentally assaulted by a barrage of images. *Two boys rolling up to the sidewalk in that red car. An argument. Blinding pain. Confusion. Hands bound. Darkness. Fear. Cold.*

I slipped from the bed, overcome with nausea and dizziness. Somewhere I heard concerned voices and pounding footsteps, but I couldn't focus on them.

"They did this to you. Your friends."

The energy sang with relief that someone had heard him at last. *Yes. Yes. Yes. Tell them. Please.*

Suddenly, David was beside me, tugging at my arm, hurling frantic questions at me.

"Are you okay? Annabelle, what happened? Can you speak to me?"

I held the photo out to him and tried to speak. My voice sounded weak and slurred. "This was why he was leaving everything on that windowsill. He wanted his parents to find this photo. He couldn't move it himself because it was too tightly wedged between the bed and the wall— he didn't have enough energy. These are the boys. The police need to find these boys and search for this car. They did something to him. That's what Reggie's been trying to say."

Pierce stared down at the photo and then back up at me, wonder all over his expression. "Are... are you sure?"

"Yes!" I cried. "Yes. Go. Give this to the Thompsons. Tell them... tell them this is what Reggie wants them to know. I'm fine, just go!"

Without further argument, David took the photo from my trembling fingers and ran from the room with it. I sat on the floor, a feeling of wonderful release and calm coming over my body. And although I did not see or hear him, Reggie's gratitude sang in my bones, and I knew I had done what I could for him.

§

Over the next few months, our tiny moment of connection with Reggie Thompson rippled out into the world. I'm not sure how Lionel and Patricia convinced the police to follow the tip of the boys in the photograph, but somehow, they did so without dragging me into it. Within two weeks, the boys had been arrested for Reggie's murder. Within another week, Reggie's body had been recovered, buried in a construction site only a few miles from his house. And though the community had to endure the agony of a trial and the knowledge of what had befallen Reggie at the hands of two of his most trusted friends, it was at least more bearable than the agony of not knowing at all.

But even as Reggie's story faded from the newspaper headlines, my relationship with David and his team solidified into something lasting, and it was cemented at last when David walked into my shop four months later, a small cardboard box in his hand.

"Hey, I've got something for you. Well, two things, actually," he said by way of a greeting.

I looked down from my perch atop a ladder, where I had been restocking books on witch hunts and Wiccan spells. "Really? Should I be alarmed?" I asked.

"Just come down here and open it, will you?" David replied, rolling his eyes.

I descended the ladder and wiped the dust from my hands. "Okay, then. Let's have it."

David reached into his coat pocket and dropped a smooth, heavy something into my outstretched hand. I looked down and blinked in surprise at a round, clear, resin paperweight. Suspended within it were little paper squares painted with gold letters that spelled out, "Carpe Diem."

I looked up at David, bewildered. "What's this?"

"It was Reggie's. His parents wanted you to have it. They gave it to me after the memorial and asked me to pass it along to you."

My eyes filled with tears. "I just couldn't go. It was too..."

"I know," David said, his voice gentle. "They understood. But they still wanted you to have this. As a thank you."

I didn't know what to say. I placed the paperweight on the counter beside my cash register.

TALES FROM THE GATEWAY

"And these are from me. Well, from the whole team, actually." He held out the little cardboard box. I lifted the lid and extracted a business card from the top of the pile inside and read the tiny print:

Annabelle Rabinski

Psychic Medium

Ghost Hunters of Central Massachusetts

I looked up at him, my mouth falling open.

"It was presumptuous, obviously, to have the cards printed, since we haven't even asked you yet," David said quickly. "But it felt like a good way to demonstrate how much we really want to make you an official member of the team—you know, if you want to be."

"What were you planning on doing with them if I said no?" I asked, smirking.

David shrugged. "I dunno. Maybe I thought if I put it in print, it would come true. So, what do you think?"

I gazed at his anxious expression for a moment before allowing my smirk to break into a genuine smile. "I'd be delighted to join you, as long as it doesn't interfere with my ability to keep the shop running."

David's face split into a grin and he thrust out a hand, shaking mine so hard I nearly dropped the box of cards. "That's great! Oh, sorry. That's... that's really great. Thank you. And we understand—your business comes first. We'll be glad to take you whenever we can get you."

"Okay, then. It's a deal."

"Brilliant. You won't regret it," David said.

And he was right. I never did.

3

CARRICK'S STORY

I HEARD HER before I ever saw her.
Yes. I'll start there. That was the beginning, really. It began with a laugh.

The new Apprentices and Novitiates were arriving upon the grounds—a hectic and disorganized process that I detested. My training had taught me to be hyper-vigilant of excess noise, movement, and activity; and so move-in day was a headache from start to finish. I felt like every nerve, every sense was heightened beyond my threshold for tolerance. Finvarra looked down over the proceedings with her usual air of detachment and calm. As Deputy High Priestess, soon to be groomed as High Priestess, she had overseen many move-in days.

"You're on edge, Carrick," she said, and though I was not looking at her, I could tell that she was smirking at me. I could hear it in her voice.

"Yes," I replied, and left it at that. Far be it from me to complain, particularly about situations over which I had no control.

"Don't worry. We'll soon be settled from this chaos into our usual chaos."

"I'm not worried," I insisted. "And yes, normal chaos I can handle."

"I've yet to encounter anything you could not handle."

"You're too kind."

She moved away from the window. I remained, scanning the crowds below, on high alert for disturbances or disruptions.

"What are your thoughts, then, about this new crop of Novitiates?" she asked me a few moments later, when she had settled behind her desk. I turned to see that she was flipping through the roster and registration forms that I had brought up to her office at her request. "A rather large group, isn't it, that your men are taking on this year?"

"It is," I acknowledged, taking time to weigh my next words. "They are versed, though. Largely older bloodlines, with good role models. I am hopeful they will be competent in the basics, at least."

"Let us hope so, after last year," Finvarra said with a sigh.

I cleared my throat but did not reply. It had only been a few months since we had had to expel a Novitiate from the ranks, and the fog of scandal still hung over the barracks. It had caused quite the uproar amongst the Council as well, given that the young man was from a Council family and therefore very prominent. But I had argued my case, and prevailed. Exceptions could not be made for one who chose to flout the Code of Conduct simply because he was from a Council family. Indeed, his position was, in my opinion, a further strike against him. Who among the Novitiates, I insisted, could have known better what the expectations were? Who should have had a greater sense of duty than a young man of such a pedigree? His trespasses were, in my view, all the greater given his privilege and upbringing.

It was rare that a member of a Council family be met with true consequences. Many of their indiscretions were swept under the rug or else minimized and met with a mere slap on the wrist. But there was no such leeway in the Code of Conduct as it applied to the indiscreet relations between Caomhnóir and Durupinen. There could be no leniency there; upon that much, there was universal agreement.

"It was a shame," Finvarra was saying, interrupting my train of thought. "Still, he may yet prove honorable in his duties at the príosún."

"He may yet," I replied, not because I truly believed it, but because it was the proper thing to say.

"By any chance, has Eleanor Ballard sought you out?" Finvarra asked after a delicate pause.

I turned fully to face her now, a definite sense of dread settling over me. "No. Should I be anticipating that she will?"

"I'm afraid so," Finvarra replied.

I sighed, pulled myself away from the window, and settled heavily into a chair. "Come on, then. Let's have the worst of it. If I'm to face the dragon, I'd like to be prepared."

Finvarra laughed. "The dragon? Is that what she's being called these days? How fitting."

"I like to think I can settle on an apt metaphor when pressed," I replied dryly.

"Quite," Finvarra said, still chuckling. "Well, yes, I do expect you will be facing her soon, though to what extent she will be breathing fire, I cannot say."

"How so?"

"Her daughters are part of the incoming Apprentice class this year. It will fall to your committee to assign their clan their new Caomhnóir."

I managed to suppress a groan, but it was a close thing. "I hadn't yet made that realization."

"I realize that the assignments will not occur for several weeks yet, and so I felt it only fair to warn you that Eleanor will likely have a fair amount of... *input* to share with you."

"Input. There's a euphemism if ever I heard one," I replied. "Do you anticipate that our committee will have any say whatsoever, or are we just going to be handed the name of the lucky Novitiate in question?"

Finvarra gave a wry smile. "I cannot say for sure. It is, as I said, a very strong crop of Novitiates this year. I only know that she will have been making arrangements behind the scenes for months—doing her own assessments and making her own inquiries. She will likely have approached the clans from which her chosen candidates have come, so that you are pressured from both sides of the arrangement."

"Perhaps she would like to simply take over the running of the committee and have done with it," I suggested, "since she will have rendered our conclusions meaningless before we've even made them."

"An experience with which all of us in leadership are familiar, I assure you," Finvarra said. "Believe me, Carrick, I do deeply sympathize with your plight. That's why I felt it wise to put you on your guard."

"You have my undying appreciation on that score, ma'am," I replied. "Consider me on high alert for the foreseeable future. And on that note, if you've nothing further for me, I'd best head down to the entrance hall."

"There is one more thing, actually, and it is still on the topic of Clan Sassanaigh."

"Oh?"

"Eleanor's girls, Elizabeth and Karen... they're twins."

I froze. "Ah. I see."

"Which means the usual protocols will be in place," Finvarra said, her tone delicate. "And on that score, Calista would like to see you before you resume duties downstairs."

I just barely managed to suppress a hearty groan. The usual protocols. Of course. "Is she...?" I gestured toward the door which led to a larger, adjoining office.

"Yes, she's in. She's expecting you."

I turned toward the door, raising my fist to knock upon it, when a laugh floated up from the grounds like a snatch of music, and my breath caught most unexpectedly in my throat. I'm not sure I can adequately explain the effect it had on me—it was as though a melody had been played, a melody that reverberated in some deep intrinsic place—a melody that I *knew*.

So connected did I feel with this mere moment's laughter that, quite without conscious decision, I let my hand fall and hurried to the window, staring down into the grounds for the source of the sound. A second snatch of the laughter-song drifted up to me and my eyes fell upon the musician.

Two dark-haired young women stood apart from the milling crowd near the front doors, halfway down the gravel walk that led to the gardens. Even as my eyes found them, the shorter of the two threw her head back and laughed again, longer this time, a melody that rang with sheer and unspoiled joy. I felt the corners of my mouth twitch upward, and an almost irrepressible desire to join in the laughter burbled up from some deep, untapped place in me.

"Carrick? What is it?"

Finvarra's voice was like the breaking of a spell. As I pulled my eyes from the girl on the path, my sense of joy twisted at once into a knotted lump of confusion and horror.

Out loud, I replied, flustered. "Nothing. Nothing at all, ma'am. I just... I thought I heard a disturbance. I was mistaken."

Inside, however, I was reeling, my mind repeating the same question over and over again: *What the bloody hell happened there?*

"You'd best not keep Calista waiting," Finvarra told me, her expression mildly confused. "I shan't require you again until it is time to commence with the welcome address."

I pulled myself together. "Yes. Thank you, Finvarra. I'll see to the High Priestess, then."

"I know how unnecessary the protocols are, regarding Eleanor's girls, but just... just humor Calista, all right? She's not well." Finvarra sighed, and I knew she was dwelling, once again, on the health of the High Priestess. It was only natural, as her assumed successor, and she certainly wasn't the only one. We all worried about how much longer Calista would be fit to carry out her duties.

I knocked upon the door and heard a quavering voice reply, "Enter."

Calista sat in a chair by her window, watching the scene below with a vague preoccupation. Although she had both requested to see me and just bid me enter, she looked mildly surprised to see me standing there when she tore her gaze from the courtyard a moment later.

"Carrick," she said, and I could tell she was trying to remember why she had called me there.

"Good morning, High Priestess. Finvarra mentioned that you wished to see me, regarding the protocols."

"Ah, yes, that's right. Of course. Thank you for coming," Calista said, the confusion clearing from her face at once. She gestured limply toward the window. "Here we are again already. Can you believe it? Another academic year started."

"It is hard to fathom, madam," I replied. "Time marches on, as it were."

"Indeed, it does. But we must be on our toes as always. There is no room for complacency."

"Just so," I agreed.

"Each year we make sure to be alert to any threats to our security and stability. This year is no different, and our focus must be on Clan Sassanaigh."

Inwardly, I thought, "Given Eleanor Ballard's constant machinations, our focus is *always* on Clan Sassanaigh." Outwardly, though, I merely nodded.

"Her girls are twins, and they come from a powerful bloodline. Their abilities are, I believe, impressive already. I have heard no rumblings that either is a Caller, but, of course, Eleanor would never allow any such rumblings to circulate. It will be crucial, therefore, to do our due diligence and keep a watchful eye on them both."

"Of course," I said.

I had had this same conversation with Calista several times before. Any Gateway that continued its lineage through a set of twins was automatically subjected to intense scrutiny because of the Prophecy. Paternity had to be confirmed, and abilities had to be carefully determined, to ensure that the fabled subjects of the Prophecy had not come to Fairhaven at last to rain chaos down on us all. As the years passed, many in our leadership had come to consider this exercise a mere precaution, but recently, as Calista's mental state had begun to show subtle signs of decline, she had fixated upon the Prophecy as something of an inevitability, destined to come thundering down upon our heads at any moment. In fact, she seemed almost disappointed each time we were able to rule out a new Gateway as the apocalyptic pair of legend.

"As always, I will leave no stone unturned to ensure the Northern Clans are protected," I promised her, "and I will update you regularly on our findings."

"Be sure you do," Calista said sternly, before turning her troubled gaze back out the window. Her eyes scanned the milling crowd below as though she suspected the harbingers of the Prophecy would be wearing a sign identifying themselves to onlookers.

I interpreted this as a dismissal and took my leave at once.

§

The air in the barracks crackled with adrenaline—a unique sort of electricity composed of nervous energy, physical exertion, and mental tension. The young men there were highly strung—and likely would be for several months—as they navigated this alien terrain and found their place in it. There was a hierarchy to be built, and this process took time and competition. Once the rough boundaries were sketched out, they would begin to settle into a natural order, congregating around the obvious leaders and forming their factions and cliques. It was a tedious but necessary process that I loathed beyond measure.

Perhaps the worst part about it was the level to which most of the young men in our charge understood which skills were the most valued. The combat skills—along with the brute strength and the prowess it took to master them—while crucial, were hardly the most valuable asset in a good Caomhnóir's tool kit. A damn lot of good these boys—yes, *boys,* for that's precisely what they were—would be if they didn't master their Castings and hone their spirit sensitivities. Combat had its uses, but against spirits it was, of course, useless. Not that I could blame them for their misconceptions—some of my colleagues emphasized the physical training almost to the exclusion of all else. They saw themselves as soldiers first, a mindset that appealed greatly to the proclivities of youth. It was a much more literal, objective way to weed out the weak and establish a pecking order. It was nothing short of tiresome and oversimplified, and it was about to start all over again in the same, tedious cycle. Yet another reason I loathed the start of the academic year.

"Ah, Carrick! I was just about to send someone to fetch you," came a shout. It was Seamus, a Caomhnóir who had just been promoted into the leadership ranks. He was a competent Caomhnóir, eager to prove himself, and therefore louder and more insistent upon himself than he had any need to be, but that would mellow once he felt secure in his role, and overall I had been pleased with his work. He had excellent potential. I felt a kinship with him, as I, too, had been promoted to a desirable post over the heads of several older, more experienced candidates when Finvarra's Caomhnóir had unexpectedly died in a helicopter crash. Finvarra's confidence in my potential was not enough to convince some in the Caomhnóir leadership that I was the correct choice for the role, but none of their objections had been enough to sway the Deputy High Priestess from her choice. I had been constantly trying to prove myself ever since, and though I had long since proven myself in the eyes of most every member of our Brotherhood, I always harbored a soft spot for other young Caomhnóir who were called to rise to a challenge, and Seamus was certainly one of those.

"How goes it, Seamus?" I responded, as he handed me a roster on a clipboard.

"Shipshape, as it were," Seamus said, giving me a hearty slap on the back. "Bunks have been assigned and class schedules have been handed out. Tours of the castle will start in less than an hour, and all Novitiates have been assigned to a prefect."

I raised my eyebrows, impressed in spite of myself. "Well done. I must admit I did not expect things to be so far along."

Seamus smiled. "It helps that we've got so much old blood here. Much less riff-raff than a typical year."

I nodded, still looking down at the list. "And speaking of old blood, I feel it only fair to warn you that we should be expecting a full-frontal assault imminently."

Seamus's confident smile slipped from his face. "What do you mean?"

"I mean I've just been warned that Eleanor Ballard is on the warpath regarding Caomhnóir selection."

Seamus groaned. "Already? I mean, all right, I knew she'd have something to say about it eventually, but we've not even begun initial assessments! Surely, she can't have her eye on any one Novitiate yet?"

"I think you underestimate her… ah… initiative," I replied.

"Blast it. Blast it all to hell. Interfering old trout," Seamus hissed through his clenched teeth.

"Easy, now," I told him. "Remember your place."

Seamus closed his eyes and swallowed it all back—yet another underrated skill of an effective Caomhnóir. "Right, then. What do you propose we do about it?"

"Let me handle her," I said, looking over the list. "Eleanor Ballard isn't the only one who can take initiative around here."

The plan had started to form in my head as I walked down to the barracks, and by the time I had finished going through the student registration forms, it had shifted and cohered into something solid, and it might just kill two birds with one stone. If it worked, I would be able to head Eleanor off in her determination to disrupt our process, and forge an important inroad that would make it easier for me to carry out my orders from Calista. By the time I had finished the first round of placement tests and assessments on the Novitiates, I was ready. I marched myself down to the Council chambers with one goal and one goal only: beard the dragon in her lair.

Because there would be welcoming ceremonies that night, I knew that Eleanor would be preparing for her own speech—as the ranking member of the Council under Finvarra, it would be she who would address the new Apprentices after the Deputy High Priestess had made her remarks. It was no surprise, therefore, to hear a rather strident voice from behind the door when I raised my hand to knock upon it. What was a surprise, however, were the words that echoed out into the hallway.

"...can't believe you're trying to manipulate things before we've even had our first day of classes, Mum!"

"Elizabeth, don't be a fool. It is not a question of manipulation. It's a question of ensuring that our clan has the respect and position it deserves."

"Deserves? Do you even know what that word means? Getting something because you deserve it and getting it because you bullied people into it are hardly the same thing!"

"Am I to believe that my own daughter can't make the distinction between being a bully and wielding legitimate power?"

The second voice let out a screech of incredulous laughter, and, to my shock, I knew it was the same voice I had heard laughing on the grounds. The joy was gone from the sound, but the melody remained unchanged. "Not the way you do it, no. First, you demand changes to the class schedule to suit your preferences, sending all of the instructors scurrying to rearrange their lives—"

Eleanor scoffed. "They know we will sometimes be required to return to the States on short notice. It would make much more sense if the number of Friday lessons was—"

But the daughter, impressively, steamrolled right over her. "—and now you're trying to undermine the Novitiate selection, too! They have a process for that, Mum, and at no point does it involve Apprentices' mothers railroading other people's decisions! Why can't you just leave it alone?"

"Do you really think you understand this process better than I do? Do you really think that the Caomhnóir leadership will make a choice more fully in your best interests than I would?"

Another derisive laugh. "*My* best interests? When have you ever cared about anyone's best interests but your own?"

"Your best interests and mine are entwined, you foolish child. Do you really mean to tell me that you would prefer as your protector some scrawny, incompetent Caomhnóir who is incapable of expelling so much as a fly, is that it?"

"Better that than an overbearing nightmare for a mother!"

A resounding slap echoed behind the door. It took every ounce of my restraint not to fling the door open, and I'm not sure I could have held off a moment longer when footsteps pounded toward it and I leaped back just in time to be confronted with an arresting sight.

An angel of fury, framed in the light of the doorway.

The young woman who looked up at me was a thing of fire. Sparks danced in her dark eyes, electric anger crackled through her curls, and her very movements seemed fueled by ferocity. She held a hand to one cheek, and I could see that the skin beneath it was red and inflamed.

I opened my mouth to say something—anything—but not a single word could find its way to my lips. I was mesmerized—stunned that something so small and so lovely could be so powerful. From some long-buried school day memory, a line of Shakespeare rose up into my mind.

"And though she be but little, she is fierce."

Before I could speak, the girl threw a malevolent look over her shoulder and then glared back at me. "Enter at your own peril," she advised quietly, and stalked off.

I turned and watched her until she disappeared around the corner, feeling as though she had taken all the air in the corridor with her. Then I shook my head to clear it, and turned back to the door in front of me. I had nearly forgotten what I was doing there, what I had come to say. What the devil was wrong with me today?

I clenched and unclenched my fists several times before I trusted myself to knock upon the door and answer the terse summons to enter.

If I had not heard the row that had preceded my entrance into the room, I would never have believed that anything untoward had occurred. Eleanor Ballard looked as she always did—frigidly unflappable and utterly in control of herself. The only clue—and it was a minute one—was the fact that she was running a thumb over the palm of her right hand—the hand, I was quite sure, that had just delivered the blow that had still been glowing upon her daughter's cheek.

"Ah, Carrick," she said, her voice as smooth and cold as watered silk. "My apologies if you heard any of that. That was my daughter Elizabeth. She's a first-year Apprentice this year, along with her twin sister. A brilliant girl but very… spirited."

"Yes, ma'am," I replied, keeping my features utterly blank.

"How very fortuitous of you to turn up. Uncanny, in fact. I had planned to make my way down to the barracks after this. You've saved me a trip."

"Very good, ma'am," I said. "I had my own agenda in coming to see you, however, and I hope you'll forgive me for addressing it directly, as I view it as a matter of great import. I wished to speak to you regarding the upcoming Novitiate assignments."

Eleanor clapped her hands together, creating a much less ominous sound. "The very topic I wished to discuss with you, Carrick. Although I had hoped that Seamus might also—"

"You will pardon me for getting right to the point, Councilwoman Ballard, but time is of the essence. I am concerned, as I am sure you are, about ensuring that the right Novitiates are matched to the right clans come next month, and naturally, Clan Sassanaigh is at the top of our list."

As I knew it would, Eleanor's face broke into a wide, satisfied smile. "Is it, indeed?"

"Of course, ma'am," I said, trying to look mildly surprised that she didn't already know this. "It is well known that the oldest families, who hold the most sway within the system, find themselves more commonly to be targets of attack. That's just a statistical fact."

She nodded as though she had not yet thought to play that angle, and was slipping it into her back pocket for later. "Is that so?"

"Quite," I replied. "And as such, we must ensure that due deference is made when Caomhnóir selection is completed. Now there are those who would suggest that this gives the Council families undue privilege, but I strongly disagree. The priority of the Caomhnóir leadership has always been to strategically place the protection where it is most needed, and that placement has nothing to do with privilege and everything to do with risk assessment."

Eleanor looked like a cat with canary feathers around its mouth, and I almost hated myself for handing her such powerful arguments to defend her own entitlement, but desperate times, and all that. Anything to keep that woman clear of the barracks and out of our hair.

"I think it fair to warn you that some of the young men in my charge who may seem like appealing choices have not actually tested as such. I would hate for you to set your sights on a prospect who turns out to be... less impressive than advertised." I added this last phrase delicately, both to let her know that I was well aware of her conversations with other clans, but also to lay any misconceptions resulting from those conversations solely at the doorstep of the other parties. It seemed to work; Eleanor's usually confident expression faltered just a bit, her eyebrows pulling together as she considered this for the first time.

"Do you have reason to suspect that some clans have... *misrepresented* their Novitiates in hopes of a more favorable alliance?"

Seeing my opportunity, I went on. "I cannot say, madam, not having participated in any such conversations myself. I only know that politics can sometimes override good sense in these proceedings, and we must be practical, for the good of the Northern Clans. The initial assessments will soon be completed, and at that time, I will have a much better idea of who would make the ideal protector for your daughters, as well as every other clan. I want to assure you that I am personally overseeing the assignments," I said, almost conspiratorially.

"I understand, and I appreciate your candor here, Carrick," Eleanor said, eyeing me with an interest she had certainly never shown before, as though she was assessing my possibilities. I could see I would have to tread carefully from now on. "Perhaps we can discuss this matter further when you've had time to get to know the Novitiates better?"

"An excellent suggestion, ma'am," I replied, inclining my head respectfully. "I will keep you informed. I would also appreciate it if you didn't speak of this conversation to anyone. I wouldn't want anyone to think I am not being completely objective in this process, and I fear others will see this as a matter of favoritism or privilege rather than one of practical risk assessment."

Eleanor's smile widened. "Of course, Carrick. You can count on utter discretion from me. Oh, and one more thing." She reached behind her onto the desk and picked up a folder of papers from the desktop, which she handed to me. "I imagine Calista has already spoken with you. Here is some documentation regarding my girls, just to help make your job a little easier."

I took them, feigning a smile of gratitude. How was it, after all these years, that I still managed to underestimate Eleanor Ballard? She knew perhaps better than anyone the precautions we took to ensure the Prophecy could not sneak up on us. Of course, she had come prepared to cast suspicion away from her own daughters. How had I not expected it?

"Very good, ma'am," I said and, with one last bow, excused myself from the room.

§

"You sly bastard," Seamus said, roaring with laughter.

We stood watching the morning combat training on the lawns the next day. I had only just had a chance to alert him to my conversation with Eleanor, and his resultant laughter was so raucous that several of the Novitiates were distracted from their tasks and received a jolly good thumping as a result.

I swept into a sarcastic bow. "I'll take that as the compliment you so clearly intended to pay me," I said.

"I suppose this means I can't intentionally assign her the bottom of the barrel candidate now," Seamus said, still laughing.

"No, you bloody well cannot," I agreed. "But let's be honest, you never could have. They're twins, after all, and the family is almost universally feared. We'd have been required to protect them accordingly, regardless. But at least this gives us the room to assign at our discretion. I'll feed her which candidates we already intend to consider, so that when she expresses her choice, she can think she's made the decision."

"Brilliant," Seamus said. "Well sorted, that."

"Cheers," I said, handing him a clipboard. "Duty calls. Make sure you put them through their paces in expulsion before lunch. They've got their first joint session with the Apprentices this week, and they've got to be prepared."

"Consider it done," Seamus said, and set off across the lawn, correcting stances and grips on weapons as he went.

I headed back to the castle, attempting to shake off a fog of distraction that had settled over me since the previous afternoon. Try as I might, I could not stop thinking about my encounter with Eleanor's daughter.

Elizabeth. Her name was Elizabeth.

On the one hand, I would have been filled with admiration for any person who had the fortitude and sheer cheek to stand up to Eleanor Ballard. My own passing interactions with the woman had been trying enough—I could not fathom actually being raised by such a domineering, unyielding woman, and my own upbringing had been no picnic. On the other hand, there was something more to it—a strange, immediate connection I could neither identify nor shake off. I had felt, upon being confronted with her, ablaze with fury, an almost overwhelming urge to protect her. Had I been a less disciplined man, I may not have had the strength to quash the instinct that rose in me, an instinct to storm the room and shout down the woman who dared to strike this girl.

Even as I scolded myself for such a thought, a second thought overtook it—a thought I will forever remember each and every time I remember Elizabeth, and it was this: I had never seen a person who was so equally and gloriously incandescent in both rage and joy, and my soul would not let go.

I was uneasy—uneasy that such a brief encounter with her had managed to overtake such a disproportionate space within my head. This was exactly the kind of behavior I made it my priority to warn young Novitiates about, and the fact that I was engaging in it was beyond reproachful—it was hypocritical, and if there was one thing I despised, it was a hypocrite. And so, I did what any Caomhnóir worth his salt would do, finding himself in such a position: I denied the existence of any such feelings, stuffed them away whenever they surfaced, and threw myself headfirst into my work. Most unfortunately, my work involved engaging with both Elizabeth and her sister much more than I would have liked.

Over the next two weeks, we carried out our assessments of the Novitiates, focusing, as we always did, on a wide array of skills and relevant character traits, and inevitably, the cream began to rise to the top. Before very long, we had a short list of highly competent Caomhnóir who showed great promise in all areas of their training. Any one of them would have been easy to sell to Eleanor as the best choice for her clan's Caomhnóir, and yet, I found myself thinking not of Eleanor at all, but of Elizabeth. Which match would suit her best? Which would provide the best protection? The most consistency of skill? The most desirable clan connections? Then I berated myself. Why the blazes was I doing Eleanor's work for her? Why was I giving far more consideration to this assignment than I had any other in recent memory? What in the name of the Aether had come over me, and why couldn't I master it?

Eventually, the committee agreed upon Liam Shea as the appropriate assignment for Clan Sassanaigh. In order to keep up the appearance of her influence over the process, I brought Eleanor down to the barracks to observe a bit of sparring practice, as well as an expulsion lesson. Liam, having performed admirably in both (and given his standing in another Council clan with whom Eleanor had shared interests), was given her stamp of approval, and the rest of the assignment process went forward without difficulty. It was with a great sense of relief that I watched all the Novitiates pledge their fealty to their assigned clans, a feeling marred only by the grim expression on Elizabeth Ballard's face, like she was facing a firing squad. Perhaps she thought the assignment had been entirely engineered by her mother, and thus disapproved of it on principle? It seemed the sort of thing she might do, given the argument I'd overheard between her and her mother. Well, if that was the case, I told myself, she'd just have to go right on believing it. I could certainly never admit my part in the manipulation of the process, or every Council clan would be banging down my door demanding preference in the next round of assignments, and I'd never know a moment's peace again. No, the girl would just have to swallow her indignation and get on with it, like the rest of us who had any sort of regular dealings with Eleanor Ballard. Besides, she would see, in time, that Liam Shea was as fine a protector as she could have hoped for.

I would gratefully have disengaged my brain from Elizabeth Ballard at that point—it would have been an immense relief not to be confronted with her every day, and if she had been any other Apprentice, I would have been able to steer clear of her entirely. But most unfortunately, she and her sister were the subject of my assignment from Calista, and so it was with great reluctance that I oversaw their training with regularity. Naturally, I had to make it appear that I had an equal interest in all the Gateway pairings, and that my hovering presence was to oversee the Novitiates and how they began to work together with their assigned Gateways. Under cover of this, I was able to gain a complete picture of the Ballard girls and their abilities.

They were both extremely intelligent, well-spoken, and well-versed in all Durupinen culture, including Castings and history, though I would have expected little else, given who had raised them. But there was a rebellious streak in Elizabeth that became more and more apparent as the weeks went on. Her class participation often challenged or questioned the underpinnings of the teachings. And while her sister seemed content enough with their designated Caomhnóir, it soon became clear that Elizabeth was not.

About a week after the Caomhnóir assignments, in the central courtyard, Elizabeth's independent streak met Liam's Caomhnóir pride in a head-on collision in a very public fashion, and I realized for the first time that her issues with her Caomhnóir assignment might be more deeply seated than her issues with her mother.

The Apprentices and the Novitiates were working together in the central courtyard on Summoning and Expulsion, two skills which went hand in hand so perfectly that it seemed almost foolish to practice them separately. All was going smoothly, when a sudden disturbance at the end of the courtyard caught my attention. Voices rose in argument, growing louder all the time.

"But I told you he wasn't within the boundary of the Circle yet!"

"What does that matter? If he was having that kind of effect on—"

"What does it matter? You've Expelled through the boundaries, which means they've been altered by the application of another Casting! You've weakened the circle, and that leaves both of us vulnerable!"

"Vulnerable to what? It's just a practice exercise!"

"What's happening here?" Melisande, the instructor, had reached the squabbling pair before I had made my way to the other side of the courtyard.

"A spirit just wandered through our circle, which means our boundaries are compromised!" Elizabeth was saying, clearly trying to maintain a respectful tone, despite her edge of frustration. "I told him earlier I thought the first Expulsion was premature, but he won't acknowledge the mistake, and now our protective Castings have been rendered ineffective."

"What mistake?" Liam asked, reddening around his collar. "I'm not to blame if you've miscast the Circle!"

"You know damn well I haven't miscast the Circle!" Elizabeth shot back, gesturing behind her, where her sister still sat, wide-eyed within the boundaries of the chalk. "The Circle worked perfectly until you let your nerves get the better of you and jumped the gun!"

"Lizzy, calm down, it's not a big deal," Karen murmured, blushing violently as all eyes turned to stare at the altercation.

"It shouldn't be a big deal, but he's gone and made it one!" Elizabeth replied. "If he can't admit to even the slightest mistake, how can we possibly work together? If we can't listen and communicate and learn from each other, why are we even here?"

"What is the meaning of this, Shea?" I asked, arriving at last beside my Novitiate, whose face was darkening with a sinister mixture of embarrassment and anger.

"Nothing, sir," Liam mumbled. "Everything is under control."

"You mean, *I'm* under control, I suppose?" Elizabeth spat.

"That's not what I—"

"Look, if I screw up, I'll be the first person to admit it," Elizabeth said, her teeth gritted together now. "It doesn't benefit me in the long run to sacrifice my competency to my pride just to save face. I'm not interested in working with a Caomhnóir who doesn't feel the same."

Before anyone could so much as muster a reply, the girl had picked up her bag, slung it over her shoulder, and stalked off.

"Elizabeth get back here at once! You have not been excused from this class!" Melisande called, but she might as well have stayed silent for all the response she got. The entire class watched her retreating back, whispering behind their hands and looking scandalized. My attention, however, returned to Liam.

"Is there truth in what she said? Did you mistime an Expulsion?"

Liam lifted his chin defensively. "No."

"Right. Well, that's easily determined, isn't it?" I replied, and approached the Circle. Liam's entire body stiffened as I passed him, as though my very questioning of him was some kind of betrayal.

A quick examination of the Circle was all it took to confirm that Elizabeth had spoken the truth. The marks of the Castings—where they had clashed and how they had affected each other—were written in the very energy in the air. I probed against them carefully with a simple Revelation Casting upon my fingertips, identifying the traces of the original unbroken Circle, as well as the path of the first Expulsion. I could see from the expression on Liam's face when I straightened again to face him that he knew full well what I would find, and I felt my ire rising.

"She was right," I stated bluntly. "The Expulsion was premature and ruptured the boundaries of the Circle. What have you to say?"

Liam did not reply, his chin still thrust defiantly in the air.

"Arrogance protects no one," I told him. My voice was quiet, but he flinched as though I had shouted in his ear. "Humble yourself or you will fail in your duty."

At first, he seemed incapable of replying. Then, as though the movement cost him dearly, he nodded his head, once. "Yes, sir."

I turned to Karen, who still sat looking mortified within the boundary of her now useless Summoning Circle. "Go find your sister and bring her back to class, please. Liam will re-Cast the Circle properly in your absence, so that you can resume work as soon as you both return."

Karen nodded once, jumped to her feet, and hurried out of the courtyard while I oversaw Liam's stony, grudging re-Casting of the Circle. But when twenty minutes had gone by and she hadn't returned, I found myself growing unaccountably anxious. Making my excuses to Melisande, I left the courtyard and turned in the direction of the castle. I spotted Karen almost at once, walking out of the front doors and onto the walkway.

"I can't find her anywhere," Karen said, sounding both contrite and heartily annoyed. "What should I do?"

"Return to your class and work as best you can," I replied. "I'll keep an eye out for her."

Karen looked mildly surprised at this offer, but nodded her head and turned off in the direction of the courtyard where her classmates were still gathered. And I, with no real inkling of where I was going or what in the blazes I was doing, set off across the grounds. I had searched the entire garden fruitlessly and was just wondering if I ought to bother walking the perimeter of the lake or give up entirely when the first scream reached my ears. The sound echoed up from the far northern corner of the grounds, growing in desperation as I listened. I did not think. I simply acted. I took off like a shot, sprinting toward the sound, my heart pumping with terror.

As I ran, the scream became a sort of wailing sob, leading me through the grove and toward the graveyard tucked into the far corner of the grounds. I could not think what would draw a person here—modern Durupinen and Caomhnóir had an almost universal loathing of tombs and graveyards—a collection of grisly monuments to the moldering physical bodies with little regard for the souls that had once inhabited them. The traditions of

TALES FROM THE GATEWAY

Durupinen cemeteries had died out with the Victorian era, and the cemetery on the grounds lay largely forgotten. Nevertheless, I was sure now, as I approached the rusty gates, that the sounds were emanating from the place, an assumption supported by the fact that the ancient gate had already been forced ajar. I slipped through it and began pelting between rows of tombstones and dodging behind mausoleums, until I staggered to a halt at the scene before me.

Elizabeth Ballard knelt sobbing uncontrollably within a Summoning Circle drawn upon the stone top of a sunken mausoleum, a piece of chalk still clutched in her hand. Inside the Circle with her, a pale wraith of a spirit in trailing white garments was clutching at her own long hair, throwing back her head, and keening toward the sky. The wails were not coming from her mouth, though—they were coming from Elizabeth's.

A single, stunned moment to absorb what I was seeing, and then my Caomhnóir instincts kicked in. Neutralize the threat. I leapt into assessment mode. The spirit was within the boundaries of the Summoning Circle; that meant that the girl had invited it in—or else mis-Cast the Circle. I dismissed this possibility— in the first place, the Circle looked, upon cursory inspection, to be correct; and in the second place, hadn't I just verified her Casting competency in the courtyard? The spirit, therefore, needed to be Expelled. I wasted no time.

A whispered incantation, a centering of my mental acuity, and a powerful thrust of my arms, and the spirit was thrown backward out of the Circle with such force that it blurred out of sight beyond the far boundary of the graveyard.

The heart-wrenching cries faded at once into silent sobs. Elizabeth keeled over onto her side, curling herself into a fetal position, and I raced forward, breaking the boundary of the Circle as I did so. I placed a tentative hand upon her shoulder, and when I spoke to her, I found my voice cracked and weak with fear.

"El— Miss Ballard... are you alright? Are you hurt?" I asked.

Though she continued to sob, she shook her head and brushed my hand away with surprising force. Having satisfied myself that she was at least uninjured, I stepped hastily back out of the Circle and waited for her to recover. After what felt like an eternity, she fell silent and pushed herself up onto one elbow and then, shakily, to a seated position. When she turned her gaze on me, I was taken aback to see how fierce it was.

"You shouldn't have done that," she said, her voice hoarse but stern.

I blinked. "I'm... I'm sorry?"

"I said, you shouldn't have done that. I was handling it just fine on my own."

I very nearly let out an incredulous laugh in my shock, but managed to check the impulse. "You'll forgive me, but that was not my assessment of the situation. I acted accordingly."

"You acted without asking me," she replied.

"Pardon?"

"You didn't ask me if I needed or wanted your help."

"I confess I thought you incapable of answering such a question," I replied, trying to remain calm even as my frustration rose. What had she expected me to do, allow her to keep making those awful sounds? Stood by and done nothing?

"You could at least have given me the chance to try," she said, picking up a black Casting bag that had been lying on the tomb beside her and pulling it open.

"Fair enough," I said, though if truth be told, I was humoring her. "May I be so bold as to ask what you're doing here when you ought to be in class? Your sister has been scouring the grounds for you. How did you come to be in this... situation?"

Her lips twitched at the word, as though she knew perfectly well that I would much rather have called it something much more dire. "I'm sorry to have stormed out of class like that, but I just couldn't work with Liam Shea anymore today."

"I see. But then how did you..." I let the sentence trail away, gesturing at the Summoning Circle.

"Liam's behavior made me realize I need to be able to look out for myself. I'm an Empath, you see, and a very sensitive one at that. Spirit emotions affect me dramatically, and it leaves me particularly vulnerable."

I knew this already, having been keeping careful tabs on her abilities at Calista's insistence, but I did not inform her of this. Instead, I replied, "All the more reason, if you'll forgive me, not to attempt Summonings alone," I replied.

"Besides being an instructor, you're Finvarra's Caomhnóir, aren't you?" she asked, looking me squarely in the eye.

"Yes."

"And where is she right now?"

The question pulled me up short.

"In the castle, working in her study," I replied, wondering, as I did so, what bearing Finvarra's whereabouts could possibly have on the conversation at hand.

"And what happens if she's attacked while you're down here on the grounds?" Elizabeth asked, crossing her arms.

"Attacked? In her own study?" I asked, unable, this time, to repress an incredulous chuckle.

"Yes," Elizabeth replied in a very serious voice that caused the laugh to die in my throat. "What if, somehow, a spirit managed to attack her within her own walls?"

"The space is Warded. There's no way that…"

"No possible way? Are you absolutely sure of that?"

I hesitated, my mind reeling at the thought.

"You assume she's safe. She assumes she's safe. So, you part ways, temporarily. But what happens if, while you are apart, something were to happen to her? What would she do?"

I felt heat rising in my face. Was this girl suggesting I could not do my own job? "She… in such an *unlikely* eventuality, is very capable of implementing any number of Castings that might keep her safe."

"Exactly. She's prepared. I'm sure she knows all kinds of skills you would never teach to a lowly Apprentice like me. You are, however, teaching them to the Novitiates."

I hesitated. It was true that the early Novitiate training had a heavy emphasis on defensive and protective skills, while the Apprentices were focused much more upon communication and the nuts and bolts of conducting Crossings. I nodded.

"Well, I'm sorry, but I think that forcing us to rely on a near stranger, and an inexperienced one at that, as our sole source of protection is short-sighted and limiting, and never has that been more apparent to me than in the courtyard today," she announced, trying to stand up. Her legs trembled violently and she collapsed onto her knees again. I started forward automatically, offering an outstretched hand, but was met with such a ferocious glare that I withdrew it at once.

"Did anyone bother to examine our Circle after I left?" she asked.

"Yes," I replied. "In fact, I examined it personally."

"And?" she asked, an almost triumphant note in her voice, because she knew exactly what I would have found.

"And you were correct. Liam mistimed an Expulsion and compromised your Circle. But surely you do not expect perfection from a Novitiate? After all, you are both learning."

"Of course, I don't expect perfection. But I do expect honesty."

"I do not wish to make excuses for Liam, but admitting a serious error in front of a courtyard full of people is not an easy thing to do, especially when you haven't gotten to know any of those people yet. Liam may be a near stranger now, but in time, as you work together, that will change," I said.

"Work together?" Elizabeth scoffed. "When have we ever worked together?"

This pulled me up short. "In your classes. In your practicums. I've seen it for myself, you've had many opportunities already to—"

"I'm not sure what definition of 'together' you're using, but we couldn't be more separate. I mean, for heaven's sake, you've drawn a line down the middle of our classrooms and forbidden us to cross them. We've been conditioned to mistrust each other, and many of the Caomhnóir are so terrified of overstepping their boundaries, they will barely deign to speak to us. You could cut the mutual disdain in the air with a knife. What kind of way is that to build trust?"

I ought to have had a real smashing answer to that question. The Code of Conduct, after all, was the set of rules by which I'd lived my entire adult life. And yet, when I opened my mouth to reply, the answer was nowhere to be found.

"I'm not trying to devalue what you do," Elizabeth said, perhaps mistaking my silence for offense. "Believe me, that's not my intention. I know how crucial the Brotherhood is to our safety and security. But I have no interest in being a sitting duck every time my Caomhnóir is not within a few feet of me," Elizabeth continued, stretching her legs out in front of her and massaging them vigorously. "I've dealt all my life with the sudden onslaught of spirit emotions, and have always had to rely on someone or something else to help me deal with it. My mother, who allows not even the smallest aspect of my life out of her control, has always seen to it that I was sheltered in this way."

TALES FROM THE GATEWAY

"I'm sure she was only trying to protect you," I offered, finding my voice at last.

Elizabeth scoffed. "Oh, you're sure, are you? What she's done is left me without the skills I need to protect *myself*. She has always relied happily on Caomhnóir to do the job. I, however, have no intention of placing my safety solely in the hands of another person who must shadow me every waking moment of my life. I am more than capable of learning to Expel a spirit, and since no one will teach me how to do it, I intend to teach myself."

I could hardly believe what I was hearing. "You're... you're teaching yourself how to Expel spirits?"

"Yes. Or rather, I was, before you rendered my practice quite unnecessary," she replied, trying her legs again. This time, she was quite steady. I must have looked rather indignant, for her expression softened when she looked at me again. "I'm sorry, that wasn't at all the right thing to say. I am grateful to you for the help. You had no way of knowing what I was doing, and to be honest, I wasn't *entirely* in control of the situation."

I could see this was all the concession she was going to make, and I allowed it to pass with a nod of my head. "You are most welcome. And I suppose I was hasty. I ought to have... consulted you before jumping in."

She raised her eyebrows, clearly surprised at this concession of my own. "Your apology is entirely unnecessary but greatly appreciated, and I accept it," she said. "Now, would you indulge a professional question?"

I hesitated, but after a moment, gave a cautious nod. "Very well."

"How would you have graded me, if I was your student?"

I hesitated again. "Honestly?"

"Honestly."

"Abysmal. Bottom marks."

And that was the second time I heard the laugh, that jubilant song, soaring like a bird over the graveyard, breaking into a joyous chorus of echoes in the grove behind us. "Well, I asked for honesty, so that serves me right, I guess," she said, still chuckling as she replied. "What could I... I mean, could you tell what I was doing wrong?"

Again, I hesitated. This wasn't territory I had ever navigated before. My interaction with Apprentices had been transitory at best, and I had certainly never attempted to teach one before, let alone a Casting that was not considered part of her curriculum. Exactly how many rules was I breaking here?

"I'm sorry," she said, sensing my hesitancy. "That's not your job, is it? I guess, I'll just…"

"The Summoning Circle was well Cast," I said, blurting it out before I'd really decided whether to answer or not. "I could sense the boundaries of it, and they were strong. You've definitely mastered that part of it."

"Okay," she said, with an encouraging smile that caused my heart rate to speed up.

"The issue for you, I imagine, is the summoning of mental clarity required to Expel. Not that I'm casting aspersions on your intelligence or focus," I added, seeing her expression cloud over. "It's simply that another spirit's emotions have invaded you, and it's clear that they affect you powerfully. It will be a challenge to clear them for long enough to complete the Expulsion."

She nodded, looking thoughtful. "Yes, that's true. The emotions can be overwhelming, especially when they blindside me. You probably noticed that was a particularly tortured spirit I had in here with me."

"I did indeed notice," I agreed solemnly. "But, I suppose, the more powerful the emotions, the more important it is for you to be able to Expel them."

She smiled again. "Precisely. So. Any tips?"

I considered this. Expulsions were second nature to me now. It had been a long time since I'd really thought about the internal process. "Well, I imagine a box."

Her eyebrows arched in confusion. "A box?"

"Yes. One of my elder brothers suggested the analogy to me once, and it has always stuck with me. I imagine a box—like a big, empty trunk—inside my head. When I have to focus on the Expulsion, I imagine gathering every stray thought in my head and shoving them, all together, into the box. Then I slam the lid on them."

"And that works?" She sounded skeptical.

"You won't find it in a Caomhnóir textbook," I admitted, perhaps a bit sheepishly, "but it certainly worked for me. Other analogies might suit you better, of course. Just find a mental image that will allow you to thrust those new emotions aside."

"Hmm." Her brows pulled together and deep lines creased the space between them as she gave this careful consideration. "A rubber band," she said at last.

"Sorry?"

"A rubber band," she repeated, sounding more confident this time. "A rubber band that I could gather all the emotions against, and then pull it back and let it go."

I smiled as the image clarified itself in my mind. "Ah, I see. Rather like a mental slingshot."

She grinned broadly. "Yes, exactly! A slingshot! I think it would be more effective for me, imagining the emotions flung as far from me as possible, as opposed to being bottled up inside me."

"Well, there you are, then," I said, returning the smile. "So, once you've settled on the image, you must use it to clear your mind. Play it out, like a film, and clear the mental space you need to do the work. It will take some practice, but…" I cut myself off before I completed the thought out loud.

But I've no doubt a woman of your strength and spirit can do anything she sets her mind to.

"Thank you," she said. "I'll definitely try that next time."

"Would… would it be too much to ask that you carry out this… training… with your Caomhnóir around? Just in case it goes poorly?"

Elizabeth raised one of her eyebrows skeptically. "Let me ask you something. Do you honestly think Liam—or any Novitiate, really—would dare stand by and allow an Apprentice to subject herself to such an exercise on his watch?"

I wanted to offer a different answer, but I could not. "No. He would be too afraid of being reprimanded. And, truth be told, I'd probably be the one doing the reprimanding."

"You see my predicament, then," Elizabeth said with a shrug.

"What about enlisting the help of a spirit?" I asked, the idea coming to me out of the blue.

"A spirit?" Elizabeth repeated, looking skeptical.

"Yes! Find a spirit willing to assist by offering himself up as the target for an Expulsion."

Elizabeth frowned. "What spirit would possibly want to do something like that?"

I gestured broadly to the grounds. "Fairhaven is full of spirits who remain here out of loyalty to the Durupinen. I am quite sure you would have no trouble at all finding a willing volunteer."

Elizabeth considered this. "Huh. That wouldn't do me much good for when a spirit ambushes me."

"That may be true, but you could at least get some practice doing Expulsions first, without worrying that emotions will overwhelm you."

Elizabeth looked extremely skeptical, so I went on. "Look, the way I see it, you've got two challenges here. The first is learning to Expel a spirit. The second is learning how to Expel a spirit when in the grips of an Empath-related emotional takeover. It seems to me that you ought to learn how to deal with the one, before you attempt to tackle the other. A volunteer spirit could help with that."

Elizabeth looked thoughtful. "Yes," she said, much more to herself than to me, it seemed. "Yes, perhaps I am going about this in the wrong order. Although, eventually, I am going to have to try Expelling a spirit whose emotions have overwhelmed me."

"By that point, you may have developed enough of a relationship with your Caomhnóir that the two of you can—"

"A relationship with Liam Shea? With a person who, in three months of training, has yet to look me in the eye or address me by my actual name? A person who would lie and risk my safety rather than allow himself to look bad in front of his classmates by admitting to and correcting a simple error? I find that suggestion bordering on ludicrous."

"Very well then, perhaps… perhaps I could help you." The words were out of my mouth before I'd even thought them consciously and I couldn't take them back. They hung there in the air between us, surprising us both as we acknowledged them.

Elizabeth stared at me, eyes wide. "*You?* Help me to Expel a spirit?"

I hesitated, wanting to smack myself for being so forward. What the devil was I doing? But even as I reprimanded myself, I plunged on recklessly, having, it seemed, completely lost control of my own mouth. "Well… that is to say… you are a student. I am an instructor. It's true that your training does not strictly fall under my jurisdiction, but I see no reason I could not oversee your extra-curricular Casting practice, if you truly believe Caomhnóir Shea unequal to the task."

TALES FROM THE GATEWAY

Elizabeth's face broke into a smile so bright, so genuinely full of gratitude, that I felt my breath catch in my throat. "Thank you so much, Carrick! I really appreciate the offer." She quickly composed her face. "I mean, I'm not saying I'll definitely need help. Because I really do think I can do this on my own. But I'll take your advice about the slingshot thing, and if I need help… well, I may just take you up on your kind offer."

"It's not kindness. It's my job. Durupinen safety is the pinnacle of our duty, and I take my duty very seriously," I replied, forcing myself into the most aloof and professional of tones.

It seemed to work. A little of the light seemed to fade from Elizabeth's eyes, and I instantly hated myself for extinguishing it. "Yes, of course. Well, I'm grateful all the same. Good day, Carrick."

"Good day, Miss Ballard," I replied with a respectful nod.

She dropped her eyes and hurried past me, tying her Casting bag to her waist as she went. I waited until she passed, then turned to watch her go, the breeze snatching at her hair and flinging it out behind her, like the tail of a kite. Within me, a kind of war was raging, and I felt dizzy with the disorder of it all.

Part of me, the part who was a Caomhnóir and an instructor and a member of the leadership, was ready to take myself out behind the barracks and dress me down for my weakness and my lack of discipline. Another part of me, a part I must confess I had never known existed, seemed to be awake and alive and breathing for the very first time, thrust into existence by the very presence of Elizabeth Ballard.

This was dangerous. This was bloody dangerous and I knew it, and there was sod all I could do about it.

I spent the next few weeks desperately hoping that Elizabeth would forget all about my offer to help her. She was clearly a force of nature—surely, she could learn the skills she desired on her own without interference from the likes of me. I paid close attention to the way she and her sister Karen interacted with Liam but, as I would have expected, their exchanges were always short and tense. In fact, the more I watched, the more I became convinced that we had rendered trust between Durupinen and Caomhnóir nearly impossible. How had I never seen it before?

"Deputy High Priestess, do you trust me?"

The question came in a quiet moment as I waited for Finvarra to finish a written proclamation to the rest of the Council. The surprise I felt in asking it was nothing to the surprise on her face when she heard it.

"Why, Carrick, what kind of a question is that? Of course, I trust you. I would never have chosen you as my Caomhnóir if I did not trust you."

"Yes, ma'am," I said at once, dropping my eyes and hoping that she would let it go.

She, of course, did no such thing.

"Where did that question come from all of a sudden?" she pressed.

"Nowhere, ma'am. I'm sorry to have—"

"Is there something you're not telling me?" she went on.

"No, of course—"

"Some reason I should not trust you?"

I lifted my eyes to hers, horrified. "No, ma'am, of course not! That's not at all what I meant."

"Well, then, what did you mean? Explain yourself, Carrick!" Her gaze was both stern and concerned.

I hesitated, trying to choose my words carefully. "As you know, I've been overseeing Prophecy protocols on Clan Sassanaigh, and that means I've spent a good deal of time in the classrooms watching the students work. I've been... preoccupied when watching the Novitiates and the Apprentices working together in classes. It doesn't feel as though they are connecting with each other."

"I don't follow. Connecting in what way?"

"They don't seem to be establishing the proper kinds of bonds with each other."

Finvarra looked slightly alarmed. "Bonds? I should certainly hope not."

"That's not what I... I just mean... it doesn't seem as though they... *trust* each other very much."

Finvarra gave a dismissive wave of her hand. "That will come with time. They are mere children, most of them."

"And yet they are being tasked with adult responsibilities. Do you ever wonder if we are doing them a disservice, training them the way that we do?"

Finvarra put down her pen and looked at me with the kind of penetrating gaze that seemed to go not only through me, but to burn a hole in the wall behind me. "Carrick, what in the world are you on about? What's brought this on?"

"I'm not sure, ma'am. I suppose I've just been thinking."

"It seems out of character for you, questioning the Code of Conduct," Finvarra said. "Is there someone—or something in particular that you've—"

"No!" I said, entirely too quickly. "It's simply... perhaps it's just this particular group—the pairings and the way they work together—but I just worry how functional some of them will be, moving forward."

"Do you doubt the Novitiates' abilities to properly protect their charges?"

I shook my head. "No, no, it's not that."

"The Apprentices, then? Are they failing to meet their required—"

"No," I replied. "They're all quite capable, all working very hard."

"Then I'm going to take you back to the topic with which you first opened this discussion: *trust*. Trust in the system, Carrick. It has served us well for hundreds of years, and I do not anticipate that it's in any serious danger of breaking down imminently simply because you've witnessed the growing pains of early training. These things have a way of working themselves out, Carrick. Look at us. We have an exemplary working relationship. I have no doubt that, with time and patience, our younger counterparts will attain the same."

"Yes, of course. You're right, ma'am. Please forgive me. We've experienced quite the shake-up in our leadership ranks of late. I think it's rather thrown me for a loop."

"Perfectly understandable, Carrick. But let's hear no more of this questioning our Code of Conduct. I would hate for your seeds of doubts to plant themselves in younger, more impressionable minds."

"Of course not. I have spoken of this to no one but you, and it shall remain that way."

Finvarra gave a satisfied smile. "Very good, Carrick."

In that moment I understood my relationship with the Deputy High Priestess as I had never fully understood it before, and it did absolutely nothing to quiet my mind. In fact, I was more full of doubt than ever. How had I lived my entire life in a world the boundaries of which I had never even thought to question? And why had such a fleeting acquaintance with Elizabeth Ballard acted as such a sudden and violent catalyst to the upheaval of that world?

It was at this time I began to panic in earnest. Perhaps I ought to go to Finvarra and demand another assignment—the furthest outposts of Northern Clan territory—Skye Príosún, perhaps, or even as a gifted Guardian to Havre des Gardiennes. But at almost the same moment the impulse seized me, I stamped upon it violently. Chased from my life's work, from the pinnacle of Caomhnóir leadership and rank, by some... some *girl* with whom I had only ever had one real conversation? I heard the contempt in my own thoughts and hated myself for it. For all my recent questioning of the Code of Conduct, it could not be clearer that I had been poisoned by it. That "girl" was a young woman, not a child. How could I revel in my own assertion of my youthful abilities and influence and in the same breath, scoff at hers? The answer to that question rose in my throat like bile, and I choked on it.

What was worse, I turned my frustrations on the Novitiates, pushing them harder, raising my expectations, demanding standards students could never meet. It was Seamus who suggested I step back and let him take the reins, and though he pretended it was because he was eager to prove himself, I knew the real reason. I was failing my charges. Willingly, I agreed that it was time for Seamus to oversee more of the training. It was with great relief that I handed over my comprehensive assessment of Clan Sassanaigh to Calista, having been able to conclude that the Ballard girls were not, in fact, the twins of the Prophecy, and that they needed no further observation. That done, I stepped back into the shadows, spending more and more time away from classrooms, retreating both within the castle and within myself, all the while terrified that somehow, someone would figure out why.

It was nearly spring before I spoke to Elizabeth Ballard again. She caught me as unawares as on that very first day she arrived, with a laugh like a siren song, and me, dashed upon the rocks like a bloody fool.

"Carrick! Hey, Carrick!" She was running along the path behind me as I made my way to the barracks. She must have been in the gardens as I passed, but I had not seen her.

"Miss Ballard," I said, cringing internally at the sound of my own voice, so flustered. "What are you... that is to say, how are you?"

"I'm well," she replied. "I just wanted to take the opportunity to thank you."

I blinked. "Thank me?"

"Yes," she replied. "I did what you said. I used the tactic you suggested for me, about compartmentalizing spirit emotions, and it worked!"

"Is that so?" I asked, trying to hide the relief that sprung up inside me like a geyser.

"It's true!" she said, as though she doubted I believed her. "I found a spirit—she used to be a maid here, and she still hangs around the Apprentice sleeping quarters quite a bit, out of habit, you know. I explained what I was trying to do, and she practically fell over herself to volunteer before I even properly asked her! Of course, she's not the kind of spirit likely to overwhelm me emotionally, but I used your trick, and I did it! First, I Expelled her emotions from my head, and then I Expelled her from my Summoning Circle!"

She was positively glowing, elated with her victory. It was utterly disarming, and I smiled before I could stop myself. "I am very glad to hear it. Well done. No small feat for an Empath of your sensitivity."

"Thanks," she replied, although her face fell almost before the word had left her lips. "I also think I owe you an apology."

"An apology? To me? Whatever for?" I asked, genuinely puzzled.

"I think I may have offended you, that day that you found me in the graveyard," she said, biting at her lip and no longer able to meet my eye. "You helped me—rescued me, really—and all I could do was scold you and complain about Caomhnóir. I was just so angry at Liam, and I'm afraid I took it out on you."

"There's no need to apologize," I replied, unable to bear the look on her face. "I was in no way offended. You were justified in your anger toward Liam, and I was only too glad to be of assistance."

"Are you sure? Because it seems like..." she began, and then a rose-colored glow splashed across her cheeks and she dropped her eyes again.

"Go on," I urged her, feeling my heart begin to pound inexplicably.

"It's just that… you've barely been to classes since it happened. You haven't looked at or spoken to me…" Her whole face was scarlet now, and she twisted her hands together in front of her. "I thought maybe it might be because you were angry or…"

"Please put that out of your mind," I replied, barely able to catch my breath, my voice escaping my lips in a hoarse kind of whisper. "How could I be angry with such strength… such passion? You said nothing wrong. You did nothing wrong. I am only sorry that I gave you such an impression."

She lifted her eyes to mine and I was nearly lost. "Do you truly mean that?" she asked quietly.

"I do."

A smile bloomed over her face—a sunrise just for me. "Thank you."

She turned and walked away, and I knew, from that moment, that no matter how hard I battled, how fiercely I fought to escape the pull of Elizabeth Ballard, I would lose.

I had already lost.

4

KAREN'S STORY

CAMBRIDGE, MASSACHUSETTS WAS A RIOT of warm fall colors, and I was a riot of tumultuous emotions. (That's a pretty way of saying I was a mess, by the way. An absolute mess.)

On the one hand, I'd realized my greatest ambition: my sister and I were starting our very first semester at the school of my dreams. On the other hand, it was Harvard, and now that I was here, getting what I had always wanted had suddenly become terrifying and overwhelming.

"Karen? Are you okay?" Lizzy was looking at me, a knowing smirk playing at the edges of her mouth.

"Huh? Yeah, I'm fine," I lied, although I'm not sure why I bothered. She was my twin—she knew me better than I knew myself. She let it slide, however.

"Did you hear what I said?"

"No, sorry."

"I said, do you want to grab a coffee or something before class? We've got plenty of time."

"No," I replied, my stomach roiling at the thought. "I don't think I can handle caffeine right now. I might explode."

Lizzy chuckled, reached out and squeezed my hand. "Just keep breathing. You're meant to be here. You'll be fine."

I tried to return her smile, but all the muscles in my face seemed confused. I'd have felt better about starting at Harvard as a transfer student if my transcript hadn't been a total lie. As far as the admissions staff knew, I'd spent the last two years at Fairhaven Hall, a prestigious and highly selective private university in Cambridgeshire, England, reading for pre-law. In reality, I'd spent the last two years at Fairhaven Hall, a secret epicenter of Durupinen power, learning how to Cross trapped spirits into the Aether. And though I had kept up a rigorous workload with a private tutor to ensure I wouldn't be behind when I arrived, I still felt like an imposter.

"What if I'm not meant to be here?" I whispered, the wave of my fear cresting and breaking at last. "What if the only reason we got in was because Mom pulled strings and used her Durupinen influence to get us to the top of the admissions application stack?"

"So what if she did?" Lizzy asked, crossing her arms and glaring at me.

"What?" I gasped, my mouth hanging open.

"Oh, come on, Karen. She's Mum. Of course, she did. She pulled every string she could get her interfering fingers on and you bloody well know it."

"If you're trying to make me feel better, it's not working," I muttered.

"Do you want me to lie to you? What's the point? We'll both know it's a lie, and you'll go on worrying because you haven't faced up to things as they are. Mum did what Mum always does. So what? Are you going to pack your suitcase and go home with your tail between your legs, or are you going to prove you're Harvard material on your own merits? She only got us through the door, she can't do the work for us. Not that I think that would stop her from trying," she added with an exasperated roll of her eyes. "I'm still not convinced she submitted the essay I actually wrote."

"She ought to have. It was brilliant," I replied.

Lizzy narrowed her eyes at me. "We both know the brilliant one here is you. I'll be clinging to your coattails for the next two years. Just make sure I don't fall off, okay?"

Secretly, I thought Lizzy was the brilliant one. I'd always gotten better grades than she had, but not because I was smarter—it was merely that I was better at following the rules. We both had our strengths, of course. I was the logical, practical one, memorizing facts and figures and whizzing through research and equations and committing whole textbooks to memory. Lizzy, on the other hand, was extremely perceptive. She could read between the lines, dig beneath the surface, unearth new ideas. She was creative in a way I could never be, but this flare often landed her at odds with her teachers, especially the ones who disliked being questioned. I hoped Harvard would be the kind of place that would nurture an intellect like Lizzy's, rather than squash it, but that remained to be seen.

"Where is this student guide anyway?" Lizzy muttered, glancing down at her watch.

"I'm not sure, but the welcome packet said this was where we're supposed to meet, so... oh, wait, I think this might be him coming now," I said, looking up and pointing to a figure who was approaching down the walkway.

He was tall and trim, with blonde hair and a square jaw. He had a bag slung over one shoulder and his hands thrust casually into the pockets of his jeans, until he extracted one of them and raised it in welcome.

"Elizabeth and Karen Ballard?" he asked, though he was already smiling and nodding as though he'd answered his own question. "Nice to meet you. My name's Michael Chandler. My friends call me Mike." He thrust out a hand, his confident smile broadening. His mouth was just a bit out of proportion to the rest of his face, his teeth just a little too square and white, so that what was meant to be a friendly smile felt like an invasion of personal space. I took a tiny, involuntary step back even as I reached out to take the handshake, which threatened to pull my arm from its socket.

"Quite the handshake you've got there, Mike," Lizzy said, hitting the "k" in his name just a little too hard. I nudged her in the ribs, but she ignored me.

Mike didn't seem to notice. "Thanks," he replied, clearly taking her comment as a compliment. "My father always told me you can size up a man by his handshake."

"Your father is bang on," Lizzy replied. I suppressed a mad urge to giggle.

Mike squinted a bit. "Whoa, are you from England?" he asked, in an awed kind of tone that implied England might be on Mars. I jumped in before Lizzy could say something snide.

"No, we're from Boston. But our mother is English and we've spent a lot of time there recently, so the accent sneaks in sometimes," I said.

"That's wicked cool," Mike replied. "My mom never mentioned..." He stopped as though he'd caught himself saying something he shouldn't.

"Your mom?" I asked, confused.

"So, I bet you're wondering how to get around the campus, huh?"

Mike asked, ignoring me. "I thought we'd start with a quick tour of the academic..."

"Actually, we were hoping you could start by showing us where you keep the coffee," Lizzy interrupted.

"Oh, yeah, sorry," Mike replied. "Of course! I'll show you."

Mike escorted us to our assigned dining hall, which was Eliot House; and then, coffee in hand, we set off on a whirlwind tour of the campus, during which Mike barely seemed to need to take a breath as he rattled on in a constant monologue full of historical facts and personal anecdotes. It might have been interesting if I hadn't been so busy trying to memorize the locations of all the buildings and making notes for myself on the crumpled map I kept folding and unfolding. In fact, I was so wrapped up in my attempts to get my bearings that I hardly noticed the way Mike was walking closer and closer to me, how he directed more and more of his conversation toward me, so that by the time we had arrived at the building where Lizzy's first class was located, we were practically shoulder to shoulder.

"I'll see you back in the room later, Karen," Lizzy said, a laugh in her voice.

"Huh?"

"Have fun," she whispered, arching an eyebrow at me and winking.

"What are you talking ab—"

But she had already disappeared through the door and I turned to find Mike almost offensively close to me.

"Alone at last," he said with that too-wide grin.

I smiled weakly. "Ha."

"Shall we?" He offered me his arm, which I stared at like I'd never seen an arm before. After a few seconds of silence, he shrugged, still grinning, and gestured up a tree-lined path to the left. "Your first class is just up here. So, pre-law, huh?"

"Yeah," I said, tucking my map back into my bag and attempting to engage properly. "I find legal studies fascinating."

"It's a great profession. So many possibilities. I'm pre-med myself," he said in what could only be described, even charitably, as a self-satisfied tone.

"Oh, that's... that's wonderful. Very, um... selfless," I said, scrambling to find the response he seemed to be fishing for.

"Self had nothing to do with it," Mike said with an offhand

chuckle. "My father is head of cardiology at MGH. My grandfather was head of general surgery at New York Presbyterian. I didn't choose medicine so much as medicine chose me."

"Mm-hmm." It was a ridiculous cliché, and yet, in a way, I could relate, given my Durupinen history, though I could hardly tell Mike that.

"I've never minded, though. There's room to make your own way in medicine. Harvard Medical's really the only choice for med school, of course, but after that, I can branch out anywhere, find my own calling."

"Of course, you've got to get *into* Harvard Medical first," I said. "It's very competitive."

"Not for a third-generation legacy, it's not," Mike replied with an almost salacious wink.

For the second time that morning, I found myself incapable of returning a smile, though this time nerves had nothing to do with it.

We arrived outside the building where my "Ethics and Public Policy" class met and came to a sudden stop. Unsure what to do, I stuck out my hand again.

"A pleasure to meet you, Mike. Thanks for the tour," I said, trying to sound genial.

He took my hand but did not shake it. He held it instead, and leaned in a little closer. "This tour was just an excuse, you know," he said quietly.

"An excuse for... what?" I asked, feeling my hand begin to sweat. I wanted to pull it from his grip but was afraid to be rude.

"To meet you both. Talk with you. My mother said you were charming, but..." he let out a low whistle that made my skin crawl.

"Your mother? I'm sorry, do I know your mother?" I asked, flustered.

"She met you at the Chilton Club Charity Auction last year," Mike replied, looking mildly surprised that I didn't remember. "She and your mother are on the board together. You didn't recognize my name?"

Something clicked, and a spark of anger ignited somewhere deep in my chest. My mother. Of course.

"Anyway, after spending the morning together, I quite agree with your mother. It couldn't be plainer we'd make an excellent pair, which I'm sure will only become clearer after dinner on Friday night."

"Dinner? Friday night?"

"Yes. I've already got a reservation at my family's table at The Palm. Your mother's suggestion. I'll pick you up at your dorm around 6 o'clock?"

The conversation was charging ahead of me as I struggled to keep up.

"You... made a reservation for dinner before you'd even met me?" I asked blankly.

"Well, of course. I mean, I knew I'd be bound to hit it off with one of you. As I said, your mother and my mother are—"

The spark caught flame now.

"You made a reservation for dinner before you decided which twin you would be bringing with you?" I asked through clenched teeth.

Mike scented danger, bless him. His smile slipped a little. "Well, I thought—"

"You thought you'd take the Ballard girls out for a little test drive around the campus and see which one you liked better before honoring her with an invitation to dinner you'd already assumed she'd accept?" I asked. My voice was rising now, but I didn't care.

"I didn't realize—"

"You didn't realize what? That I was a human being? That I have free will? That I might have something resembling an opinion about being trotted around like a show dog by a guy who lets his mother pick his dates the way other mothers pick out their sons' clothes?"

Mike's ridiculous grin faded completely. "Well. It looks like I picked the wrong twin, didn't I?"

"No, you picked the right one, trust me," I said with a snort of derisive laughter. "I'm simply going to walk away from you now. If you'd tried this with Elizabeth, she'd have left you bloodied on the pavement. Thanks for the tour, Mike, but you'd better cancel that reservation, unless you want to eat alone. At least your sense of entitlement will have a seat all to itself."

And leaving him spluttering on the sidewalk, I charged through the front doors, determined to leave my fears about Harvard, much like Mike's pride, in shreds on the classroom floor.

§

Two hours later, I burst into our dorm room like a tornado.

"I hate you!" I announced to Lizzy, flinging my bag onto my bed.

"No, you don't," she replied, not even looking up from the battered copy of *Pride and Prejudice* she was reading for the five hundredth time. "You love me. But I can see how you might get those two emotions confused. When it comes right down to it, they're sometimes indistinguishable."

"That doesn't even make sense," I shouted.

Lizzy shrugged. "Maybe not to you."

"You knew, didn't you? You knew he was going to corner me like that."

"I recognized him from one of Mum's charity things," Lizzy admitted, and then, seeing the confused expression on my face, clarified. "We didn't actually meet him in person. His mother had pictures she was flashing around and I was roped into ooh-ing and ahh-ing over his sailing exploits for at least an hour."

"Why didn't you warn me?" I asked.

"Because I thought it might just be a coincidence," Lizzy replied. "After all, the ivy leagues are swarming with country club spawn, aren't they? It's a pretty small fishbowl Mum floats around in. Anyway, once he started throwing himself shamelessly at us, I figured it out. I thought for sure you'd caught on too, but apparently you were too busy trying to commit the entire campus to memory. Did he actually ask you out?" A grin spread over her face, and I knew she already knew the answer.

"No, he didn't ask me out. He told me what a great time we were going to have on the date he'd already planned. It was a simple case of 'insert less hostile twin here.' He's lucky I didn't smack him."

"Aw, come on, let's be fair. It wasn't Mike's fault," Lizzy said, finally deigning to put the book down. "If anyone needs a good smack, it's Mum."

"She can't keep doing this. She just can't keep doing this," I sighed, flopping down onto my bed, all my anger deflating into despair.

"She can and she will," Lizzy said. "I've gotta say, I expected a bit more subtlety on her part. I mean, come on. The first guy we meet on the very first day? What is he, a future Senator?"

"Doctor," I said dully. "Third generation Harvard Medical School, or so he seems confident enough to announce two years before he can apply." I turned to look at Lizzy, whose face was now a storm cloud. "It's only going to get worse, you know."

Without a word, Lizzy stormed across the room, picked up the cordless telephone from its cradle on the desk and dialed furiously.

"Lizzy, what are you—" I began, but she held up a hand to silence me, and we both waited for someone to pick up on the other end of the phone. When they finally did, Lizzy jabbed her finger at the speakerphone button, so that I could hear both sides of the conversation.

"Tracker office," came a bored voice from the other end.

"Trina, is that you?" Lizzy asked.

The voice brightened. "Yeah. Elizabeth? I thought it might be you, from the area code. What's going on?"

Trina had been a year ahead of us at Fairhaven. She'd been taken on as an assistant in the Tracker office over the summer, hoping to get hired as a full-time Tracker once she'd gotten some experience.

"I need your help," Lizzy said. "It's my mum."

Trina groaned sympathetically. "What's she done now?"

"It's the scouting, Trina. It's absolutely out of control. She's driving us mad."

Trina laughed. "I'm not surprised. She calls here at least once a week. How many has she flung at you so far, then?"

"Too many," Lizzy replied. "Look, I'm more worried about who she's going to throw at us next. Can you do some digging around? Get me a list?"

Trina hesitated, then spoke in a voice so low I had to lean in to hear her. "I... I'm not sure that's something I can..."

"Oh, come on, Trina, you owe me a favor and you know it," Lizzy pressed. "Who covered for you that night in the library with—"

"Okay, okay! Blimey, is that what you call never talking about it again?" Trina hissed, and Lizzy's face broke into a satisfied smile. She winked at me.

"So, come on, then," Lizzy went on, sensing weakness and going in for the kill. "I'm not asking for files or anything. Just some names, so Karen and I can prepare ourselves. We're getting ambushed over here, and it's only going to get worse as she gets more desperate."

"Why don't you just go on a date or two?" Trina suggested. "It might calm your mother down if she thinks you're playing along."

"No."

"They can't all be bad!"

"They can if my mother's approved them!" Lizzy cried. "My mother would marry me off to a crash test dummy with a trust fund if she thought it would improve her social standing. Please, Trina. I'm not above begging, but it would be great if you didn't make me."

"All right, all right, give me the day, I'll find something," Trina snapped.

"Thanks, Trin, you're the best," Lizzy said.

Trina's reply was less of an answer than it was a mumbled string of curse words before the line went dead. Lizzy looked up at me with a grim smile on her face.

"There. That's probably the best we can do for now."

"Mum will be furious with me when she finds out about Mike. And you know she will find out."

"She probably already knows," Lizzy said with a snort. "Mike's probably already gone crying to Mumsie."

I groaned. "Like this wasn't going to be hard enough, being here."

"Forget about all that. How did your first class go?" Lizzie asked, sliding onto the bed and curling up next to me. I put my head on her shoulder and sighed, feeling a tiny bit of the tension leave my body.

"It was really good, actually. Ethics and Public Policy. It's going to be fascinating."

Lizzy laughed. "You have the quaintest ideas about what's fascinating."

I shrugged, ignoring her. "How about you?"

"Victorian British literature seminar. The professor is going to hate me."

I rolled my eyes. "Don't they all?"

Lizzy laughed. "Usually."

"You know what bothered me the most about that Mike kid?" I asked suddenly.

"What?"

"We got here exactly the same way he did. No wonder he thought I'd lap up his dinner invitation—we both walked up the same red carpet to get here, didn't we? I really, really hate that."

"It's not about how we got here. Damn how we got here," Lizzy said, squeezing my arm. "It's all about what we do next. We're not under her roof anymore, Karen."

"We'll always be under her roof. She just keeps expanding it to hover over wherever we happen to be."

"That's because she's panicking," Lizzy said. "She can feel us prying ourselves out of her grip, and she can't stand it. It's why she's been so insufferable lately."

I laughed. "Lately? Lately?"

"Oh, you know what I mean. Even more insufferable than usual. She can feel us slipping away, and so she's holding on tighter. But we're almost there, Karen, I promise."

"If you say so."

"I *do* say so. And we both know I'm always right," Lizzy said, kissing me on the cheek and rolling away off my bed. She stood up, took one look out of her window, and groaned. "Oh, no."

"What is it, now?" I asked.

"It's that spirit. The one from the alleyway."

I hopped off my bed and went to stand behind Lizzy. If I hadn't been expecting to see her, she would have scared the daylights out of me. The figure of a young woman, her morose expression half hidden behind long, straight, damp hair that clung to her face. She was dressed, as she had been every time we'd seen her, in a ribbed yellow turtleneck, a wide belt, and white bell-bottomed pants. Her lips were swollen and bruised, and the side of her head was matted with blood.

"Thank God for Wards," Lizzy whispered, her whole body shivering, and I knew she was remembering the first time we'd seen the spirit, crouching in the shadows of a brick alleyway between two stores in Harvard Square. Or rather, *I* had seen it. Lizzy had felt it before anything else.

We'd been exploring the area around the campus, checking out the shops and restaurants. Liam had just vanished around the corner to feed the parking meter when suddenly, in the middle of a debate about where we should go for lunch, Lizzy gave a shuddering gasp and burst into hysterical sobs.

For one insane moment, I thought she was actually *that* upset about my refusal to try a pizza joint we'd just walked past, and then it clicked. There was a spirit nearby, and we had walked straight into a wall of disembodied emotions that Lizzy hadn't expected.

I stared wildly around for the source of the aura while Lizzy tried desperately to calm herself. I spotted the spirit within seconds, her form faintly luminous against the grimy bricks of the alley walls.

TALES FROM THE GATEWAY

As though I had shouted her name, whatever it may have been, the spirit's head snapped up and locked eyes with me.

I was no Empath, but the wave of terror, sadness and rage that washed over me almost took my breath away. Some spirits were like that—hitting you like a freight train upon first contact, unlike the gentle prickling sensations that announced when other, more settled spirits were nearby. It was tied directly, in most cases, to the nature of their passing, and it took only a single glance to see that this spirit had suffered things no human soul should be put through. And now she was dragging Lizzy straight down into the yawning abyss of it all.

I threw myself between them, even though I knew logically that physical barriers meant little, but it worked. I watched as the spirit's eyes lit up with understanding, as she realized there were two people who could see her, two people who might offer some kind of remedy for her torment. And in the moment it took for her to connect with me, Lizzy's breath eased up behind me. I heard her murmuring something, felt a tingling rush, a gathering of energy...

Whoosh. The spirit disappeared from the alleyway with an almost violent speed and with her, the heavy cloud of her sorrow lifted, too. It was like watching the sun explode through cloud cover with the force of a bomb. I spun around, expecting to see Liam running up behind us, but the street beyond us was empty, with the exception of a few curious pedestrians. I grabbed Elizabeth by the shoulders and steered her down the sidewalk, away from the murmurs and prying eyes of onlookers.

"Are you okay?" I whispered as we walked. "What happened? Did... Did you...?"

"Expelled her. I Expelled her," Elizabeth gasped, still swiping at the tears that continued to stream down her face.

"You can't be serious?!"

But her tearstained face, as she raised it to look at me, had broken into a triumphant smile. "I did it. I actually did it."

I threw myself onto her in a hug that almost knocked us both to the ground, but I didn't care. I'd known Lizzy had been practicing Expulsion, had even had success at it in controlled settings, but as far as I knew, she'd never been able to do it while in the throes of such a powerful emotional takeover.

But her elation had been short-lived. The spirit, now that it had found us, had appeared numerous times, even within the boundaries of the campus. Between Liam, Lizzy, and myself, we had surreptitiously Warded half the buildings on campus so that Lizzy could function, but the process had only made the spirit more insistent. Now she hovered just outside our bedroom window, and I could practically feel the waves of her despair slamming like storm-driven waves against the glass.

"We've got to try to Cross her," I said, staring out at the figure, hovering silently like a ghastly hummingbird just beyond the boundary of the Ward.

"I know. But she's gone mad with grief over what's happened to her. I'll never be able to get through a Crossing if she's emotionally accosting me," Lizzy replied.

"Well, back to the library tomorrow night then, huh?" I said, rubbing Lizzy's arm as she continued to stare at the spirit. "We're bound to find out who she is eventually. If we have a name, we'll have more options to keep her contained until we can get her Crossed."

Pucey Library, part of the vast network of library resources on campus, was home to the Harvard Archives, and it was here Lizzy and I hoped to find the identity of our tormented spirit stalker by searching digital copies of local newspapers. We had very little to go on, but based on the style of the spirit's clothing, we narrowed the window of time down to the decades of the 1960s and 1970s. We didn't have a name, of course, but the emotions that radiated from the spirit every time we entered her presence left no doubt as to how she died.

We were searching for a murder victim.

Over the course of our first few weeks of classes, whenever we weren't in class or tackling massive homework assignments, we were to be found in Pucey Library, poring over old newspaper headlines, desperate for a clue that might help us identify the spirit and ease her suffering.

On one such night, my eyes were drooping and itching with tiredness, and I was just about to suggest to Lizzy that we call it a night when my gaze fell, finally, on an eerily familiar face.

"Lizzy! It's her! I found her!"

"Thank God," Lizzy muttered, sliding her chair noisily across the floor so that she could read over my shoulder.

It was a miracle I was even able to recognize her, so carefree and joyful was the expression that graced her features. Her dark hair, parted down the middle of her head, hung in two straight curtains on either side of a luminous smile, a lightly freckled nose, and wide, dark eyes fringed with thick lashes. The caption beneath her photo read, "Lesley College student Janine Saunders, missing since Thursday."

As my lips formed the name, something indefinable clicked into place, a surety that the face staring up at me and the spirit haunting our steps was one and the same. And as I met Lizzy's gaze, I knew she felt it, too. We leaned our heads together to read the article.

The body of missing Lesley College student Janine Saunders has been found, according to Cambridge Police. Miss Saunders, a junior at Lesley College majoring in education, had been missing for nearly a week when her body was discovered in a dumpster near the outskirts of the Harvard University campus in the early hours of Monday by a restaurant employee. Miss Saunders disappeared after leaving a friend's apartment to walk back to the subway.

It is clear that Janine Saunders was a victim of foul play, but we are not releasing the details of her death to the public at this time. If anyone has any information regarding her death, we urge them to contact the Cambridge Police Department as soon as possible.

"Not making the details of her death public at this time? How the hell is that supposed to help us?" Lizzy asked in an exasperated hiss.

"It's not supposed to help us," I reminded her. "It was supposed to help them. Her death would have been a big deal—a big story. I'm sure they didn't want to release too many details so that they could tell the fake leads apart from the real ones."

"Yeah, that's true," Lizzy said grudgingly. "This kind of crime always brings the crazies out of the woodwork. I bet they were flooded with fake tips."

"So, we've got a name. Janine Saunders. That ought to be enough to give us a little Casting help in keeping her at bay, at least until we can get her to communicate."

"Hey, it's Elizabeth, right?"

Startled, we both spun around to find a young man smiling down at us, a backpack slung over his shoulder and a stack of books tucked under one arm.

"Uh, yeah," Lizzy said warily. "Do I know you?"

"Sort of," the boy admitted, holding out a hand. "My name is Dave Miller. We're in British Lit seminar together."

"Oh," Lizzy replied, stalling for time as she closed the cover on the newspapers we were looking at before taking the boy's hand a bit reluctantly. "Nice to meet you, Dave."

"I thought you might have recognized me from The Country Club. My family has been members there for three generations now. We also took a sailing lesson on the Charles together once when we were like ten," Dave went on.

"Oh, for God's sake here we go," Lizzy muttered faintly under her breath as she bent down to retrieve her own backpack from the floor.

The Country Club in Brookline was so elite that it literally just called itself "The Country Club," as though daring other country clubs in the area to justify their very existence. The power, prestige, and money that circulated like lifeblood within its walls was a who's who of East Coast royalty, and the criteria for acceptance was so nebulous that objectively rich and famous people frequently found the doors being shut in their faces. But of course, The Country Club—and clubs like it all over the world—were simply crawling with Durupinen. It was our mother's favorite place to wield her social and financial influence—and as a result, Lizzy and I had avoided the place whenever humanly possible.

"So, um, how've you been?" Dave went on, rather bravely, I thought, given the way Lizzy had begun to scowl.

"Busy," Lizzy said bluntly. "It's Harvard, after all."

Dave laughed as though she'd just cracked a hilarious joke. He paused for a moment, as though giving her the chance to help him out and move the conversation forward. When she just sat in silence, he plowed on, unperturbed. "Look, I heard through the grapevine that you'll be attending the fall homecoming gala at The Country Club next weekend. Any chance you'd like to meet up? Maybe save me a few dances?"

His face looked so bright, so optimistic. It was almost a pity Lizzy was about to snuff every spark of hope within his being.

"What grapevine?" Lizzy asked.

Dave's smile slipped. "Huh?"

"You said you heard through the grapevine that we would be attending. What grapevine would that be?"

"Oh, uh..." Dave looked a little sheepish. "Well, to be honest, my mother is on the social functions committee with—"

"Let me guess: *my* mother. And she just happened to mention to *your* mother that I was at Harvard and also inexplicably wanting for a boyfriend at the present time."

"I... well, yeah..."

"And then, when you couldn't catch me on my own after class, because I always bolt out of there to make it to a seminar across campus, my mother told your mother where you might be able to find me in the evenings," Lizzy went on.

Dave gave a nervous chuckle. "Did... did your mom tell you that?"

"Oh, no," Lizzy replied, smiling. "My mother never warns me when she's about to interfere in my personal life. But believe me, I'm used to it."

"So... is that a no?" Dave asked, his face falling comically.

"Decidedly," Lizzy said. "But be a chum and don't tell my mother, all right? I do so love to see the look of seething disappointment she gets when I've disrupted one of her well-planned bouts of meddling, and I'd like to break the news to her face."

Dave just sort of stood there, his mouth opening and closing uselessly as he tried to figure out how to respond. We gathered our things and walked past him. I sort of patted him on the shoulder on the way out.

"Chin up," I whispered. "It's not your fault, really."

Hardly missing a beat, Dave turned hopefully to me. I raised my eyebrows and he seemed to think better of it.

"Okay, well... I'll see you around, then," he mumbled before turning tail and fleeing between the stacks.

"You didn't have to be so hard on him, Lizzy," I said as I caught up to her.

She turned on me, incredulous. "Me? Hark who's talking! Was there anything left of Mike Chandler, M.D. when you were finished with him?"

I waved my hand dismissively. "That was different, he was a jerk. Dave was just... well, in the wrong place at the wrong time."

"Wherever our mother is, is always the wrong place at the wrong time," Lizzy replied, tossing her hair and resuming her walk across the library reading room. "The sooner Dave and the rest of the eligible Country Club bachelors learn that, the better off we'll all be."

"Maybe we should post a warning notice in the men's locker room at the Club," I suggested.

Lizzy laughed too loudly, earning a reproving look from the student manning the circulation desk as we passed.

"Let's forget about Mum, for the moment," she said, when she had recovered herself. "We've got a name for our ghostly stalker now. Let's do some more research and see if we can't put this spirit to rest properly, huh?"

But forgetting about our mother's romantic machinations would be easier said than done, as we were leaving the next morning to go home for the weekend. I should have known something wasn't right from the moment the car picked us up. It did not drop us at the Club, where we were meant to have lunch with Mum while Dad golfed. Instead, our chauffeur told us there had been a change of plans, and that our mother had instructed him to take us home instead. When we arrived home, the house was empty except for the housekeeper, Mrs. Bryant, who set out lunch for us on the back patio and said in a nervous voice that our father had been called into work and that she didn't know where our mother was, or what time she'd be home.

The emptiness in the house deepened as the afternoon went on. I wandered from room to room, flicking around on the television but unable to settle on something to watch, then trying to do some homework, but unable to focus my brain, reading the same sentences over and over again without absorbing any information at all. Giving up entirely on studying, I fell instead to researching Janine Saunders on the internet. We were in luck: her name was all we needed to unlock the secret of what had happened to her. I read article after article about her disappearance, the discovery of her body (in the very alley in which we had first spotted her), the arrest of her killer after a second attack, and his eventual conviction and imprisonment. I printed out the information and brought it down the hall to Lizzy's room, so that she could read through it as well.

"I wonder how much of this she knows," Lizzy said, flipping through the pages and shaking her head.

"I'm betting not much of it," I replied. "She appears very locked in the moment of her attack, don't you think?"

"Definitely," Lizzy replied with a delicate shudder. "Everything she's projecting is visceral pain and confusion and fear. I'd be surprised if she even realizes she's dead. She drags me into the very heart of the experience the second she approaches. I don't think she's probably ever managed to climb out of that abyss since it happened. She just pulls people in with her instead."

The thought of it made me want to cry. Decades spent in a spiral of horror and pain and confusion. This girl had suffered more than any one soul should ever have to suffer.

"When we get back to school, we'll have to find a way to tell her all of this," I said. "Once she knows that her killer was caught and that justice was served, she may finally stop projecting long enough for us to Cross her."

"Let's hope so," Lizzy replied. "I don't want to spend the rest of the semester worried about her stalking us across campus and ambushing me with emotions I can't handle."

Darkness fell and still, the house remained empty, which felt like an ominous sign. By the time the dinner bell rang, the knot of tension balled up in my stomach had erased all desire for food. Even Lizzy looked grim as she met me in the hall and we began our descent to the dining room.

Our family's dining room contained one of those long, polished tables that seated about thirty people, the kind that people sitting at the opposite ends of would have to shout to hear each other. And there sat our mother at the head of it, her back poker-straight, her face impassive as she dissected her chicken into tiny pieces. She did not speak as we entered the room.

I threw a nervous glance to Lizzy, who gave a minute shake of her head that I understood to mean, "Don't rise to it. Make her speak first." Then she lifted her chin, walked to her seat, and placed her napkin in her lap. Feeling like I'd much prefer to slip straight through the floor into the basement than endure an entire meal in this silence, I reluctantly did the same.

It was a battle of wills, that much was clear. Mum seemed determined not to acknowledge us, and Lizzy would rather die than give her exactly what she wanted—for one of us to dare to ask her what was wrong. But as determined as our mother could be, this was one battle she would undoubtedly lose. Lizzy would have been pleased as punch to eat her food in peace and vanish upstairs again without ever giving Mum the satisfaction of a single word. Mum, on the other hand, would not allow this meeting to pass without asserting her authority. I knew it was only a matter of time and, about twenty minutes into dinner, she finally reached her breaking point.

"You've really nothing to say for yourselves?" she asked at last, her voice sounding like a gong-strike in the silent room, though she spoke quite softly. I jumped, my fork clattering to my plate. Lizzy gave me a quelling look before turning to reply.

"You set the tone, Mother. We've simply been following suit," she said calmly.

"After everything I've done for you, after everything I've given you both, I little expected this kind of ingratitude."

"Ingratitude?" Lizzie repeated. "For trying to manipulate our lives?"

"INGRATITUDE!" Mum's voice rang out, echoing off the walls. Somewhere outside the room, the servants were running for cover in anticipation of the storm that was about to hit.

"How do you expect me," Mum went on, "to show my face at the Club after you've humiliated me in this manner?"

"Humiliated you?" Lizzy cried with a blast of incredulous laughter. "Humiliated you?! Oh, this is rich, Mother, even for you."

"Are you suggesting that I've humiliated you by setting you up on a date with a handsome young man?" Mum asked, her tone dripping with condescension. "Oh, you poor, poor thing, however shall you cope?"

"It *was* humiliating, Mother," I replied, finding my voice for the first time.

Mum turned and looked daggers at me. "Yes, I've already heard how you turned down Michael Chandler. Such a handsome, successful boy, and you treated him like some riff-raff at a fraternity party."

"And do you care at all about how he treated me?" I asked, firing up. "About how he could have cared less which of us actually went out with him? About how he didn't even bother to ask me out, assuming already that I'd be so flattered by the invitation that my accepting it was a foregone conclusion? About how he preened and bragged and strutted about like a peacock while showing not the slightest interest in me other than who my mother is?"

Mum laid down her fork. "It is my duty as your mother and the matriarch of our Durupinen bloodline to see that you are properly matched with a young man whose connections and pedigree advance our standing and expand our influence."

I opened my mouth to argue, but Lizzy had already jumped in. "And it's our duty to... what, exactly? Accept it? Smile and nod at every bloviating egomaniac you throw across our path? Marry someone simply because he's ticked all the boxes on your wealth and privilege checklist?"

"Yes, you foolish girl. Where is your sense of duty, both of you? How could daughters of my own flesh and blood be so completely lacking in self-preservation and pride? For Aether's sake, how do you think this family, this clan, was built? Certainly not on the sentimental daydreams of schoolgirls or the petty hormone-driven rebellions of youth. It was built on our ability to adapt, thrive, and climb, higher and further and more successfully than those around us. It has taken generations to shore up our position and our power, and I will not stand by and watch it leveled because you feel the need to engage in some juvenile teenage temper tantrum."

"Power isn't everything, Mum," I said.

"The only people who believe that are the powerless." She flung the words at me, then flung her napkin on the table. "Now, if you'll excuse me, I've quite lost my appetite."

Lizzy and I continued sitting at the table, our food going cold in front of us, saying nothing. What was there to say? She was our mother and she was never going to change. Ever. What was the point of trying to make her see reason? She had no use for reason when she had control.

"Well, hey, there, you two!"

We looked up to see our father standing in the doorway, an expression of mild surprise on his face. His briefcase was clutched in his right hand, his hat held in his left.

"Hi, Dad," I said, attempting to hitch a smile onto my face with less than successful results.

"Welcome home!" he replied, looking back and forth between us. "I'm sorry I missed our lunch today—and dinner tonight. There was a crisis at the office, and I had to..." He glanced at his watch. "Dinner was over an hour ago, wasn't it? Did Mrs. Bryant serve you late? Where's your mother?"

"No, everything was fine," Lizzy said. "It was just Mum being... Mum."

"Uh-oh," Dad replied, setting down his briefcase and hat with a resigned sigh before taking Mum's seat at the table. "All right. Let's hear the worst of it."

And so, we told him the whole messy story, glossing over absolutely nothing, especially our own role in it. There was no point in being anything other than completely straightforward with my father—after all, we were keeping such a huge secret from him regarding the Durupinen that maintaining our sanity required total and complete honesty in all other aspects of our lives. Stacking secrets upon a foundation of secrets was a recipe for disaster. This way, the teetering tower of falsehoods never got too high, never exceeded our ability to manage it. It was my mother's cardinal rule and, unlike her other rules, we never broke it.

Dad listened with an expression that grew stonier and stonier with every word we spoke. By the time I had finished, he might have been carved from marble, so set was the grim anger on his face. I braced myself for the coming lecture.

"Dad? I... look, I'm sorry we weren't more... polite to those boys, but..."

But Dad raised a hand to silence me. "Stop apologizing. You've nothing to be sorry about. It's your mother who should be apologizing," he said, sighing deeply. "How many times? How many times is she going to try to sabotage your education with this marriage nonsense?"

He stood up, pacing the length of the table. "No matter how many times we discuss it, no matter how many times I implore her that there is ample time to get you girls properly settled, she insists on meddling in this matchmaking foolishness. You're barely twenty-one, for heaven's sake! What is the rush?"

"Apparently, in Mum's eyes, we shrivel into unloveable spinsters by the time we're twenty-five," Lizzy grumbled, stabbing at a piece of cold carrot with her fork and then mashing it into a pulp.

"It was the same when you were accepted to Harvard!" Dad went on, ignoring the comment. "I told her it was the best place for you, insisted you could get no finer education anywhere, but she had her heart set on that infernal boarding school of hers. Half your classmates came out of that place with one foot down the aisle! I attended more weddings last summer than I've attended in my entire adult life!"

I winced as I thought of the closet full of bridesmaid dresses I'd already racked up, each one of them another brightly colored stripe in the rainbow of my mother's shame that it was not yet us sauntering down the aisle in white.

"I realize things are... different, where your mother grew up, but I will not have her stifling your opportunity for a good education with this marriage foolishness. There will be a time and place for all of that, but you shouldn't be dodging boys like landmines while you're trying to focus on your studies. Speaking of which," he looked down at us, suddenly stern, "how are your classes going?"

"They're going great," I said at once. "We're working hard, Dad, I promise."

He turned to Lizzy, who smiled ingratiatingly. "Very stimulating."

"Excellent. I'll not have either of you slacking off so that you can flounce around with boys. Put it out of your mind, now. I will speak to your mother."

He kissed us both on the head, picked up his briefcase and hat, and left the room. I followed Lizzy to the kitchen, where she made each of us a bowl of Lucky Charms, which she called her "specialty," and which she had convinced Mrs. Bryant to keep hidden for her behind the saucepans. We carried our bowls quietly upstairs and shut ourselves in Lizzy's room just as the shouting began from the direction of our parents' rooms.

"She's going to be furious that we told him," I said between mouthfuls of stale marshmallows.

"Good. If she's not speaking to us, she can't set us up on any more surprise dates," Lizzy said.

"She set the last two up without talking to us," I pointed out.

"But she won't. Not after this row with Dad. At least, she'll have to be much more discreet about it."

"Of course, this just opens the door for Dad to start throwing boys from church across our path," I pointed out. Our father's commitment to our education was rivaled only by his commitment to religion. We'd been dragged to services every Sunday since we were born and going away to college had not loosened that stricture. You'd think, given the patriarchal roots of religion, our father would have welcomed the idea of marrying his daughters off to good Christian boys before educational institutions could start filling our heads with dangerous ideas; but our father was one of those rare men of his generation who saw the benefit of both religion and strenuous education.

"God gave us free will and the capacity for knowledge. What kind of servants would we be if we wasted those gifts?" he was fond of saying. "Faith cannot exist in a vacuum. Only true faith can stand tall in the face of questions. Challenge it. Challenge it every day and watch how it sustains you." Lizzy and I both knew that speech by heart now.

"Yeah, but at least he probably won't start doing it until graduation," Lizzy pointed out. "And in the meantime, we just need to—"

Lizzy stopped speaking. She was staring across the room at the bow window on which she had not yet pulled down the blinds.

There hovered Janine Saunders, staring in at us with wide, haunted eyes, her mouth open in a silent, perpetual scream.

"Christ, she followed us home," Lizzy whispered. "What are we supposed to do? It's not the full moon for another two weeks. I don't think she's going to wait for another lunar Crossing."

"She might back off if we name her," I suggested tentatively.

Naming was a technique taught at Fairhaven. Using a spirit's name often gave the Durupinen a kind of power over them. Well, power was perhaps too strong a word. But there was something about using a spirit's living name that connected them to their humanity. It often helped to ground them, to make them easier to communicate with. It was also a good reminder for Durupinen as well—sometimes, spirits could feel like "others," when in reality, they were people. Just people, in their purest form.

Lizzy looked sharply at me. "We'd have to leave the Wards and expose ourselves to her to do that. That leaves me too vulnerable. We can't risk it, not with Dad home."

"Why don't I do it myself?" I suggested.

"Alone? No way," Lizzy said, crossing her arms and looking truculent.

"Come on, Lizzy, it's the only way. She's going to keep accosting us like this until we find out what she wants, and we can't do it if you're going to go to pieces every time she approaches. She needs to know that we understand, that she doesn't need to project so much emotion just to be heard. If she realizes we know what happened to her, she won't shove it down our throats every time she sees us."

Lizzy still looked skeptical. "You have to take Liam with you," she said. "And use the pool house, so no one spots you."

"Good idea," I said, draining the milk from my bowl and shrugging into my bathrobe. "I'll be right back."

It was only nine o'clock, but the house was quiet. Liam's room was on the first floor near the back staircase, and I knew he would still be awake. I knocked softly on the door and listened to the hurried shuffle of his footsteps on the other side. He pulled the door ajar, squinting at me.

"Everything all right?" he asked.

"Yes, but I need your help," I told him, and quickly explained the situation. He listened intently, nodding his head, then grabbed his Casting bag and pulled on his boots. Without another word, he followed me outside.

Liam had proven, after a bit of a rocky start, to be a competent Caomhnóir. Though Lizzy didn't like to admit it, he'd grown up considerably since those first few months when they'd clashed so openly in the central courtyard. I'd always thought that Carrick, the new High Priestess's Caomhnóir, had more than a little to do with it. It was clear he took great interest in Liam, though I didn't really know why—perhaps he saw him as a sort of protégé. In any case, he had taken him under his wing and our training had progressed smoothly from then on out. Lizzy really didn't give Liam enough credit. He had never failed us since, and I trusted him implicitly. I couldn't call him a friend—but then, what Durupinen could call her Guardian her friend, really? The system didn't allow for such intimacy.

We crept out into the back yard, taking the path around the left side of the house, as far from my parents' bedroom as possible, Liam taking care to disable the automatic security lights so that they wouldn't give us away. Our footsteps fell muffled on the carpet of leaves that October had strewn over the yard, and a fine mist fell over us, so that we glistened with a million tiny beads of it by the time we reached the pool house and slipped inside.

Janine was nearby—I knew it as soon as we shut the door. She had probably followed our progress from the house, drawn like a moth to the light of the Gateway.

"Stand right where you are, please," Liam whispered the second we shut the door, and wasted no time in Casting a protective Summoning Circle around me, reinforcing it with rose quartz and salt and a number of runes scrawled swiftly in chalk. The pool house had been left intentionally Unwarded, the only space on our property to be left so, with the exception of a small dressing room of our mother's chambers. It was important, Mother said, to protect the house from being overrun, and yet allow ourselves spaces from which we could conduct Durupinen business and interact with spirits when we chose. My father, who detested swimming, never set foot in the pool house; and of course, my mother's perfume-drenched inner sanctum of eye creams and pantyhose inspired a similar aversion.

I felt my breathing ease as the protection of the Circle rose up around me, and so it was with only a mild burst of anxiety that I watched Janine Saunders materialize before me outside the boundary of the Circle.

"Hello, Janine," I said quietly.

As I had predicted, the initial, violent burst of her emotions faded at the sound of her own name. Her face went curiously rigid, her expression blank. She actually retreated a few inches, looking warily at me.

"What did you say?" she whispered.

"I said your name. You are Janine. Janine Saunders. Do you remember?" I asked.

"I..." I watched as she searched inside, digging through the horror of her trauma for this tiny shred of herself. I saw the light kindle in the deep wells of her eyes as she found it. That, right there, was the magic of naming. "Yes. Yes, I remember. That is my... my name."

"You haven't thought about it in a long time, have you?" I asked.

The specter shook her head, dark hair swinging. "No."

"I know that it seems like no one can see or hear you, but I can, so please don't project your emotions at me, okay?"

"Project my... what?" she asked dazedly.

"Your emotions. You may not realize it, but you've been accosting people with them, shouting with your experiences because no one can hear your voice. But I can hear you. Okay?"

The girl blinked again. "I... okay." I was reminded that she had been almost exactly the same age as I was now when she died, and it sent a shiver up my spine.

"Do you know what I am? Do you know why you're drawn to me?" I asked.

The girl nodded. "I can feel it. I'm supposed to... to go."

"That's right," I said, trying to inject some encouragement into my tone. Behind me, I felt the tautness of Liam's presence, his second-by-second reading of the exchange, poised to react at the slightest sign of animosity. "But I'm not going to make you go, okay? It's your choice."

"None of this was my choice," she said with a wail, her eyes darkening again.

I put both my hands up in front of me, in a gesture of surrender. "You're right. Please forgive my insensitivity. You're absolutely right. You did not have a choice, and that is terrible. I'm speaking only of what happens next, and it is your choice and yours alone. I promise you this, Janine."

The girl's face twisted for a moment, but then she gave a curt nod.

"I want to help you," I went on.

"No one... no one can help me. I scream and scream. No one comes. No one," she said, her voice breaking.

"That was a long time ago," I said gently. "Do you realize that? That was many, many years ago, the screaming."

She stopped, and again, I watched as she dug in her memory for some hold on time and place. When she raised her eyes again to mine, she looked devastated. "Oh."

"Yes," I said, keeping my voice gentle, a lullaby. "And you've been screaming since. But I'm here now. I want to help you. Tell me what you need."

"I don't know," the girl gasped. "I... I don't know."

"Do you know who did this to you?" I asked.

She did not have to stop and think this time. After all, this was the moment in which she had been existing for years. She shook her head. "No. A stranger. A man."

"They found him," I told her. "The police. They found him and arrested him."

Her eyes went, if possible, still wider. "They... they did?"

"Yes. He tried to attack another girl, but she got away, and the police caught him. He confessed to your attack, to try to lessen his sentence. He's in prison. He's been given a life sentence, with no possibility of parole. He will be there until he dies. I've been researching it ever since you first appeared to us. We found all of the records from the newspapers."

The darkness of her eyes threatened to swallow me. "What is his name?"

Why did I have trouble saying the name? It was as though my mouth did not want to let go of it for some reason, perhaps because I knew the power of naming. "Donald Malone."

"Where is he?" the girl whispered.

"Souza-Baranowski Correctional Center. It's a maximum-security prison. He's not getting out, Janine. He can't hurt you or anyone else ever again."

The girl smiled, a smile that did not reach her eyes. Then she was gone.

I released a breath I did not realize I had been holding and turned to Liam. He looked exceedingly troubled.

"I shouldn't have told her, should I?" I asked him, my heart still thundering in my ears.

"I'm not sure. No. No, perhaps not," he replied, and I read in his face the same fear that had lodged deeply in my chest.

§

For the next two weeks, our lives settled into a kind of normalcy that it would have been all too easy to get used to and was therefore much too good to last. Mum, chastened by her argument with Dad, had stopped hurling eligible boys across our path—or at least, she seemed to, as they stopped appearing out of the blue. I wasn't foolish enough to think she'd truly stopped trying to engineer our matrimonial prospects; but at the very least, she seemed to be regrouping, coming up with a new strategy, which meant that Lizzy and I could breathe again, if only for the moment. And, thanks to Trina's convenient lack of scruples, we soon had in our possession a list of the boys whose names had surfaced as a result of the initial scouting request, which meant we were forewarned if any other suitors decided to try their luck.

Not only had the string of boys left us alone, but Janine Saunders had as well. From the moment she vanished from the pool house, we hadn't seen a single glimpse of her, not a whiff of an errant emotion that didn't belong to us. And though it was in many ways a relief not to have her floating around like a gruesome shadow, I was still uneasy. It felt ominous that a spirit so persistent should disappear so completely. Still, I managed to mostly push it from my mind, throwing myself into classes with reckless academic abandon, and was finally starting to feel like I might just belong at Harvard when my nebulous fears about Janine materialized at last.

Lizzy burst through the door of our dorm room and, without so much as a greeting, flung a slightly damp newspaper onto our bed.

"Have you seen this?"

"Seen what?" I asked, picking up the paper. She didn't need to reply. The answer was splashed across the front page of the paper:

TALES FROM THE GATEWAY
NOTORIOUS CAMBRIDGE COLLEGE STALKER FOUND DEAD IN PRISON CELL

I felt the bile rise in my throat. I looked up at Lizzy, whose expression was twisted with disgust. "Lizzy..."

"I know."

The article went on for pages, but I was only able to absorb a few scattered details. *"Donald Malone... reports of screams in the night... moved to psychiatric watch... apparent suicide... troubling security footage shows him carrying on conversations in his empty cell... unexplained marks on his body..."*

"Oh, no," I finally managed.

"I guess we know where Janine has been the last couple of weeks," Lizzy muttered.

"What do you think we should... should we *do* something?" I whispered.

Lizzy raised her eyebrows. "Like what?"

"I don't know... like, *tell* someone that..."

"Tell them what? That a ghost was responsible for this? How would we even begin to substantiate that without dynamiting the entire Code of Secrecy? We'd be up in front of the Council before we could even blink."

"So, then what do we do?"

"We don't do anything. Janine's done enough."

"But... can we really just... it's our fault, isn't it? Well, *my* fault! I'm the one who told her where he was!"

Lizzy grabbed me by the shoulders as my voice rose in a hysterical sob. "This part is not our job. We're not here to decide what's right and what's wrong, okay? Life and death are too messy, too complicated. Somewhere beyond the Aether that will all get sorted out. You are guilty of nothing but trying to help a spirit get past her pain. That is it. The rest was her choice, and I'm not even sure it was the wrong one."

"Meaning?"

"Meaning Donald Malone was damn lucky I wasn't a ghost who could get to him."

I stared at my sister, and she stared calmly back at me until I felt my breathing return to normal. Finally, I nodded. We didn't fully understand what happened in the Aether or beyond it—only those who had been there could fully comprehend what was to come. But in my heart, I thought there must be some sort of accounting—some sort of reckoning, not exactly of the sort my Dad believed in, but still—some sort of karma that balanced things. Lizzy nodded as she saw me come to my senses.

"We Cross them, Karen. That's it. We don't judge them. Let the universe sort it out."

"Right. Okay."

"We'll open up our lunar Crossing tonight when we get home, and with any luck, Janine will feel the pull and find her way back to us. Now that I've seen this," she tapped on the newspaper, "I have a feeling her unfinished business is officially finished."

"Unfinished business" was one of those terms that Durupinen didn't often use. It sprang up from mainstream culture, a way to rationalize the existence of ghosts among us and, sometimes, to encourage the mind to believe in the presence of a spirit who had departed for the Aether the moment it had parted ways with its body. The truth was, that there were as many reasons for a spirit to stay behind as there were spirits lingering, and even those who Crossed at once rarely did so with the sense of having done and said everything they hoped to in their time on earth. More often, it was confusion or attachment to someone in the living world that left a spirit in need of a Gateway. In some cases, though, a spirit's reason for staying behind was singular, powerful, and destructive. Janine, it was clear now, was one such spirit. My pity for her was twisted up with a kind of fear now, and it was with definite relief that I considered the prospect of Crossing her safely out of our world and into the Aether where she belonged.

Mother always made sure that Father was out of the house on the occasions of lunar Crossings. Because it was one of the few things in the spirit world that happened on any kind of predictable schedule, it was one of the only things we could truly plan for. And because my father had never paid proper attention to anything so pagan as a lunar calendar in his life, he never caught on that the random outings, dinners, and events that always sprang up on Crossing days were part of a larger pattern. And so, when we arrived home that evening to an empty house, everything was as it should have been.

Even though it was only the two of us, Mrs. Bryant fixed us a gorgeous dinner—coq au vin, one of her specialties, because she detested the idea of us living on "institutional food," as she called it. After we had devoured it, with many compliments and hugs for the chef, we slipped upstairs to get ready for bed and prepare for the Crossing.

We chose Mother's dressing room to perform the Crossing—she had all of the necessary candles and Casting equipment in her vanity drawer amongst her perfumes and makeup, as well as a Circle inlaid into the floorboards beneath her expensive Oriental rug, and it was a simple matter of rolling it back and lighting the candles to get started. Liam stood just inside the door, on alert, as always, for any issues with the ceremony.

"Ready?" Lizzy asked. She looked pale, anticipating, as she always did, the onslaught of emotions we were about to endure as spirit after spirit used us as their conduit. She would be exhausted when we had finished and likely sleep all the next day.

"Ready," I replied.

We joined hands and began.

"Téigh Anonn. Téigh Anonn. Téigh Anonn."

I felt the connection open, the flood of energy, the gathering of souls at our gates.

"Téigh Anonn. Téigh Anonn. Téigh Anonn."

Flash.

The first spirit, a woman, aching for a reunion with her husband, her mind full of him in his military uniform, kissing her goodbye.

Flash.

A man, lamenting all of the things he'd never done, the places he had never traveled, because he had put it off too long.

Flash.

Another man, practically weightless with joy that he no longer felt the relentless pull of addiction, but wishing he'd seen his daughter one last time.

"Téigh Anonn. Téigh Anonn. Téigh Anonn."

Lizzy's hand jerked slightly in mine as we both felt Janine come rocketing into the connection, her mind a heady, swirling tornado of grief and anger and triumph and guilt and regret and pain and other emotions too tangled to understand, though the weight of it all took my breath away. I knew a single moment of relief that she would now be safely on the other side, and then...

Chaos.

Vague shouting and banging somewhere in the mental distance. A strange breeze and the familiar whiff of cologne. A rippling scream of energy—the Circle being broken—and then something knocking into me hard in the shoulder, startling me, a rough grasp on my wrist, and then...

Agony. The connection was in turmoil. A second energy had inserted itself where Janine had been a moment before, thrusting itself in, but something was wrong with it. It didn't whip through in a stream of colors and emotions and images. It was like a radio frequency full of feedback and static. All I could make out was confusion and fear and blinding pain and, cutting through the static, images of my own and Lizzy's faces over and over again.

And then it was over.

I lay panting on the floor, my head pounding, my body aching, my fingertips still buzzing with the spark of the connection. Somewhere nearby, I could hear Lizzy moaning. And there was another sound, a kind of guttural, animal sound that I couldn't quite place. I peeled my eyes open.

The first thing I saw was one of the candles, tipped onto its side, the wick extinguished but still smoking, streaks of clear wax turning white as they hardened onto the floorboards. Beyond it, a huddled shape with many arms and many legs, from which the strange moaning sound seemed to be emanating. Even as I watched, trying to focus my eyes, a form detached itself from the shape and crawled toward me, patting my cheek, grasping at my wrist to feel my pulse.

"Karen?! Are you all right? Can you hear me? Speak to me!"

It was Liam. His voice was clipped and harsh, a sure sign that he was afraid.

"I'm okay," I managed to reply. "I'm... I think I am, but... what happened? Lizzy, where's Lizzy?"

But the moment he had satisfied himself that I was alive, Liam had crawled away from me, and I could hear him making the same assessment of my sister, heard her voice, cracked and feeble, reply that she, too, was all right.

"But Dad..." she was saying. "What about Dad?"

Dad? What was she talking about Dad for? He wasn't even here... was he? My memory thrust forward the passing smell of familiar cologne and my heart seemed to freeze mid-beat. It had been his cologne I had smelled. But why?

I rubbed at my eyes and squinted into the corner, where the many-limbed shape continued to moan and rock. And then I heard a single word that sliced through me, that sent my frozen heart into frantic, galloping beating once more.

"John! John! John!"

The shape resolved itself into my mother and father, huddled together on the floor. My mother's voice was the low, constant, sobbing moan I had taken to be some kind of animal, and she had her arms wrapped around my father's shoulders, rocking him like a child. My father's face was a frozen mask of desperate longing, eyes bulging and moving rapidly back and forth, mouth moving silently, limbs shaking and twitching incessantly. As I watched with growing horror, she took his face in her hands and tried in vain to get him to look at her.

"John! John, speak to me! Look at me, darling! Look at me!"

But he wouldn't. He couldn't. Ever again.

§

I remember so little of the next few weeks. "Stroke," I murmured over and over again to curious and concerned relatives and neighbors. "Debilitating stroke. Loss of function. Heavily sedated." This was the official story put out by the Council who had arrived to clean up the mess that our lives had become. Finvarra, half the Council, and a slew of Caomhnóir descended on our house, assessing the damage, and arranging for the proper medical and financial arrangements to be made that would hide the truth of what had happened to our father—a truth which, when fully explained to us by Finvarra herself, would send us spiraling into grief and despair.

"When he broke into your connection, his soul was pulled partially from his body," she told us, sitting calmly on our pristine white sofa, hands folded in her lap. "It made contact with the Aether, and that has altered him indelibly. In a way, he has already left you. His soul, having seen what lay beyond, is not of this world anymore, and yet it is trapped here. I am so very sorry. I'm not sure there is anything we can do. What is done cannot be undone. It is a terrible tragedy."

Mum was inconsolable. For all their disagreements, she worshipped our father. She always prided herself in a strange way on insulating him so completely from the Durupinen legacy. But the world she had so carefully crafted around him, one built of lies and deception and manipulation, had crashed down around us, and we had lost him in the rubble. She kept vigil by his side day and night, not eating, barely sleeping, a living monument to her own grief. As for Lizzy and me, we took a month's leave from school while arrangements were made for Dad's care, and while we struggled to come to terms with what had happened.

Over the first few days, we slowly learned the details of how it had all come to pass: how our parents' dinner had been cut short by yet another argument over Mum's matchmaking; the way he stormed out of the restaurant; the ensuing ride home, during which Mum desperately tried to contact us, to warn us they were coming home, but we were already immersed in our preparations, oblivious to her warnings. He'd entered their bedroom to find Liam standing there, then heard our voices coming from the dressing room. What he thought was going on, what terrible conclusion he had leapt to, we would never know, but having found his good little Christian daughters engaged in some kind of ritual with candles and chanting and circles upon the floor, I'm sure he panicked into visions of Satanism and witchcraft. Mother and Liam had been unable to stop him from rushing forward... from breaking the Summoning Circle... from wrenching our hands apart...

Worst of all, Lizzy retreated from me and into herself. Once the Council contingent had left, she spent days locked in her room, ignoring my pleas to let me in, to speak to her. I could only imagine that she felt as consumed with guilt as I did. The difference was that I wanted to console each other from it, to shore ourselves up against it, not let it consume us separately. We had always faced everything together, hadn't we? Why should this be any different?

Finally, on the eve of our return to school, I felt her crawl into my bed in the middle of the night. Her arms folded around me, and I sighed with relief.

"There you are," I said.

"Sorry," she whispered. "I'm sorry I shut you out. I was just..."

"I know," I said, although I really didn't. "It's okay."

"I'm sorry, Karen. I feel like this is all my fault."

I rolled over to look at her. "How? How could this possibly be your fault?"

"I don't know," Lizzy replied, her face buried in my pillow. "It's just what my brain keeps telling me."

"Well, if it's your fault then it's my fault, too," I said. "And Liam's fault. And Mum's fault. And Janine Saunders' fault. And the Council's fault. And the whole damn universe's fault. But it can't be everyone's fault. What happened to Dad was just a horrible accident."

"You sound like Carrick."

"Carrick?" I asked, surprised.

"Yeah, he... he said something similar to me, when he was here with Finvarra." Lizzy said.

"I'm surprised he said anything at all," I said, frowning. "He's not really the consoling type, is he?"

Lizzy didn't reply—just gave an odd sort of shrug.

"Look, my point is that we can't just give up. I'm going to do what Dad would want me to do—make my mark at Harvard and get into a really good law school. And I'm going to keep faith—keep faith that somehow everything will be okay."

"Do you really think everything will be okay?" Lizzy whispered.

"It's up to us," I said. "We have to make it okay."

"But how? How do we do that?" Her voice was so small. So sad. I'd never heard her like that before.

"We do what we've always done. We do what's right for each other. We protect each other."

"Protect each other," Lizzy repeated.

"That's right."

She was silent for so long I wondered if she had fallen asleep. Then, just as I began to drift off...

"I love you, Karen."

"I love you, too, Lizzy."

And I knew that she meant it. And I knew that she wanted to protect me. And I wish I could have known, in that moment, what she was thinking, so that I could have said or done something to change her mind.

Because the next morning, when I woke up, she was gone.

5

MILO'S STORY

HERE'S THE THING ABOUT HUMAN MEMORIES that most people will never find out for themselves; they fade. I don't mean the kind of fading they naturally do while we're alive—into the rosy colors and vague impressions of a past we don't have room in our brains to remember in detail. I'm talking about the fading they do the instant we die. There's a wall that goes up, between the life you had and the half-life you've chosen to cling to. The memories are there, but separate from you, on the other side of that wall, and no amount of thinking and feeling and dwelling can haul them over clearly to the other side. Dying is the equivalent of cutting the cords that link them to you, so that you seem to have no real connection to them anymore.

This is true of every memory I have—my childhood, my family, my school days and summer vacations—each one an image that means less and less with every passing day out of my body. But not the memories I have with her. Every moment I spent with her is as sharp and clear as though it happened a moment ago. And I think that that must be what it means to be Bound; our story has become the only true part of my story.

And this is how it started.

§

"Welcome to Prison, You Screwed Up Little Fairy." That's what the sign said outside the building. Okay, that's not what the sign said outside of the building. It said, "Welcome to New Beginnings." But I maintain that's what I saw when I looked at it.

I glanced over at my mother, who was sitting in the driver's seat. She was also staring at the sign as though it said terrible things. For a second, I thought about asking her what she was thinking, but then I remembered that I was pissed off at her and didn't actually care.

"Well, here we are," she said after a few more seconds of listening to the engine run. It was exactly the same thing she'd said every time we pulled up to one of these places. It was the ultimate expression of the obvious except for one, glaring inaccuracy. She wasn't really here. Neither was my sister, sitting in the back seat, sucking on her long, shiny braid, so that the end of it looked like the tip of a paintbrush. Neither of them was really here. They were going to turn around and drive home in a few minutes, free from whatever lay on the other side of that sign. No, I was the only one who was here, and we all knew it.

When I didn't reply, she plowed on through the sea of awkward silence now filling the car, handing me a large manila envelope as she talked. "We did all of your paperwork ahead of time, and faxed all of your records over. It should make everything nice and easy when you get in there."

Translation: I did everything in my power to avoid walking into this place with you, because my crippling maternal guilt can't handle the reality of where we're sending you. Again.

"Nice and easy," I repeated, looking at the envelope. "Yeah, right."

"Now, Milo, don't start. You know what I mean," she said, wearily, like I was the one making this difficult.

"So, what's the cover story this time?" I asked, tucking the envelope into my bag.

She looked me in the face for the first time all day.

"Cover story?"

"I mean, what's Dad telling everyone? It's not as though he's actually admitting that he's locking me up to medicate the gay away."

"Don't talk like that in front of your sister," she hissed through clenched teeth, the way that parents do, as though pressing your teeth together will render your children miraculously deaf. Seriously, you would have thought I'd dropped an f-bomb. But no, I'd dropped the g-bomb, and that was clearly much more damaging to a seven-year-old psyche.

I looked into the rearview mirror at my sister, who was watching us intently. I winked at her and she smiled. I turned back to my mother, who was not getting off the hook that easily.

"You still haven't answered my question. What's the lie this time? Math camp? Future Doctors of America Conference? You're going to have to let me know so that I stick to the official line when I finally get paroled from the joint."

"I'm not having this conversation with you right now," she said, pinching the top of her nose as though my attitude was bringing on a spontaneous nosebleed.

"Now or never," I muttered.

"Do you want us to come in with you?" she asked, because she had to.

"Of course not," I said. "I don't want Phoebe to see that place, and neither do you. That's why you brought her, isn't it? A sweet little ready-made excuse not to get out of the car."

Without waiting for her lame protests, I opened my door and slid out of the car. I leaned into the back seat to pull out my bag, and kissed Phoebe on the nose. Her mouth was quivering at the corners.

"Stay cool, dancin' fool," I told her.

"Stay hot, tater-tot," she said tremulously.

I shut the car door and turned my back on her quickly, before she could see that I was teetering on my own verge of tears.

§

I don't recall much about the whole "Welcome to New Beginnings" bullshit, except for a few random details. The woman at the front desk had a mole on her lip that was like a whole other face sprouting under her nose, and I couldn't concentrate on a single word she said because I was staring at it. The nurse gave me a welcome packet with, I shit you not, a smiling sunshine peeking over the top of a hillside on the cover. Then she swiped an ID card to open the door from the lobby and pointed me in the direction of my room. She told me that she'd come and get me in an hour for my first group therapy session, but to "make myself at home" in the meantime. I may or may not have laughed in her face.

It was obviously a guys' hall; it smelled like body odor poorly masked with cheap body spray. I put a hand on the door handle to my assigned room and pushed. It turned easily, but wouldn't open. I leaned my shoulder against it and shoved, throwing my body into it. Still nothing. These places were always full of locked doors. The nurses had probably forgotten to get it ready for the new head case. I looked again at my ironic, sunshiny welcome packet and checked the room number. I was in the right place, according to the paperwork. I was about to turn and head back to the front desk to tell mole-lady when I heard something that made me stop in my tracks.

A voice was just audible on the other side of the threshold. It was speaking in low, urgent tones, but I couldn't make out what it was saying. There was a small window near the top of the door, and I stood on tip-toe to peer through it. The bed had been pushed up against the inside of the door, which explained why it refused to open. But more interesting than that was the fact that a girl was sitting on the end of said bed, carrying on one hell of a conversation with absolutely no one.

I groaned. Over the last few years, I'd decided that there were four kinds of kids in these places. And screw medical terminology, I guarantee you that any doctor would agree with me, even if he didn't admit it out loud; in his head, he'd be saying, "Well, shit. I spent a small fortune on my medical degree and this kid has gone and nailed it without a single day of med school." Seriously. Here's how it breaks down. First, you've got the Fixer-Uppers. These are kids like me, whose families are unhappy with something about them. A lot of these kids don't even realize there's anything wrong with them until other people start pointing it out. "Oh, that's not normal. Should he be doing that?" "Oh, that really isn't typical behavior. You should really have that looked at." The Fixer-Uppers are hardly crazy. They're just dealing with the repercussions of being told that they're wrong in some way. In fact, if people would just accept them, or at least leave them the fuck alone, they could go pretty happily through life. But no one ever leaves them alone. The world bullies and harasses and beats their square little selves into the socially acceptable round holes, and when they don't fit, they end up in places like this.

Then, you've got the Look-At-Mes. The Look-At-Mes need attention as badly as the Fixer-Uppers DON'T need it. They thrive on drama, and will do just about any crazy shit they can think of to get someone's sympathy. Their behavior escalates and escalates with each new level of attention until they wind up someplace like this. And they're actually proud of themselves for making it in, like this place is some kind of reward. They see it as validation. "See? I told you I was crazy! Look at how crazy I am!" They're the ones the rest of us want to bitch slap. Repeatedly.

Next, you've got the Periodics. As in Table. Chemistry. These kids aren't crazy either. They've just got to find the right cocktail to keep their chemistry balanced, and then stay on that cocktail long enough to function normally. These are the depressives, the bi-polars, the kids who can do just fine on the outside if they play by the meds. Of course, a lot of the time they don't. Sometimes they convince themselves they're better and don't need the meds anymore. Sometimes they just don't like the side effects or the way the meds make them feel. Sometimes they just want to flip-off their doctors or their parents, or the world, and won't take them on rebellious principle. Either way, they are usually in and out a lot-periodically, in fact. I've flirted with Periodic status, but so far, I maintain my Fixer-Upper label.

Finally, you've got the Foxes. As in, "crazy as a." These are the lifers, with no chance of functioning outside the walls. They start in places like New Beginnings, but that's usually just a stop on the way to someplace that makes New Beginnings look like a spa getaway. I hadn't met many of them, but the few I had met scared the crap out of me.

One look through that window and I knew that girl was the craziest Fox I'd ever seen.

And she was in my room. Of course. Because that was just my freaking luck.

I hovered on the spot for a minute, trying to convince myself to go find a nurse, but also weirdly fascinated by what the girl was doing. The conversation, if that's what it was, was escalating quickly. The girl's hands were gesticulating wildly now, and she kept pointing to the door, where I stood gaping at her. Finally, she stood up, stamping her foot in frustration, and said, loudly enough so that I could actually understand her, "It's not your room anymore! You have to leave!"

She looked towards the door this time and froze. We stared at each other, neither of us moving a muscle, neither of us sure what to do. I was fighting an impulse to run. She looked like she would have jumped out the window if it hadn't been barred. Finally, after a long, tense moment, she dropped the hand she had been pointing with. Her face fell into a perfectly serene expression, and she walked calmly towards me.

I backed away until the opposite wall bumped gently against my shoulder blades. There was the sound of the bed being pulled away from the door, and then it opened. The girl turned and closed it carefully behind her before she spun around to look at me again.

She was tiny and frail looking, with long, thick brown hair, a pale face, and enormous eyes; the kind of eyes you could fall into and not find your way back out of again. Her hands were clasped demurely in front of her, and her voice, when she spoke, was a fluttery thing.

"I'm sorry about that. I think you should ask the nurses for another room," she said. Then she walked away down the hall without another word of explanation and disappeared around the corner.

§

She was there an hour later, in my first group therapy session, or as I fondly called them, the feelings circle. Group therapy is probably the most awkward thing you can imagine; a dozen kids who don't know each other being prodded and coerced into a forced conversation, each trying to say as little as possible while still getting credit for participation, with the exception of one or two over-sharers who can't shut up. The good part about being the new kid on the block was that I could usually get away with telling them nothing but my name and a few bland getting-to-know-you details, unless the therapist on duty was a real prick. Luckily, Dr. Mulligan was the bleeding heart type, and I launched into my well-rehearsed introduction.

Hi, my name is Milo Chang. My favorite subject in school is math. In my free time, I like to read fashion magazines and sketch. My favorite snack food is barbeque potato chips. My favorite color should probably be pink, but actually it's the dreary black of my misunderstood soul.

Once my intro was out of the way, I could size up my fellow inmates as they did the obligatory round robin introductions for my benefit. I had a bad habit of inventing names and backstories for them instead of actually listening to what they were saying, purely for my own amusement, but that day I didn't even do that. I couldn't seem to force my focus onto anyone but the creepy little Fox I'd found in my room. She didn't look up at all as the others spoke, but examined with a detached sort of interest the pattern of scars on her forearms. When it was her turn to speak, I had to lean forward to hear her.

"My name is Hannah. I like to read and listen to music. I haven't been to school in a while, so I don't have a favorite subject anymore."

I looked around the circle. None of the other kids seemed to want to look at Hannah. One boy had actually gotten up and moved his seat away from her when she sat down. She couldn't have been paying them less attention, though. Her eyes, when not fixed on her own hands, had a strange tendency to dart suddenly one way or another, like she was reacting to sounds that only she could hear. At one point she jumped as though startled, her face twisted into a knot of annoyance, but I didn't see or hear anything that could have brought on such a reaction. Yes, this girl wasn't just on the crazy train: she was driving it.

A sudden scraping of chairs against the linoleum signaled the end of the session, to which I had been paying zero attention. I vacated my seat just in time for a large, surly-looking girl to pull it out from under me and carry it to the stack in the corner.

"So Milo, that's the general format of our group sessions," Dr. Mulligan said with a smile that made her look like she had twice as many teeth as a normal person. "Topics are fairly patient-led, and you should feel free to jump in any time that you have something you would like to add. Do you have any questions that I can answer for you?"

"Uh, no, thanks," I said, attempting to smile back. "It seems pretty straightforward. I've been to my fair share of these before. It was pretty much what I expected."

"Very good," she said, smiling again, and then bounced off to oversee the stacking of the chairs.

"Hey. It's Milo, right?"

The girl had approached me so quietly that I had no idea she was there, and took an involuntary step back from her.

"Yeah. Hannah?"

She smiled at me too, a small and slightly rueful expression. "I just wanted to apologize for earlier. I didn't mean to be in your room when you got there. It was just a misunderstanding."

"Yeah, whatever. No harm, no foul," I said.

"Have they found you another one yet?"

"Another what?"

She blinked. "Another room."

I laughed. "Why would they find me another room?" Was it my imagination, or did she actually turn even paler as I watched her?

"I told you to ask the nurses for another room," she said, and there was definitely a slightly panicked edge to her voice.

I laughed again, though it was only my nerves doing the

laughing. "I don't even know who you are. And I doubt the nurses would give me another room just because you told me I needed one. Besides, what's wrong with the one I have? You know, besides the fact that it's here in this godforsaken hellhole?"

I'd meant the last bit as a joke, but she didn't even crack a smile. She opened her mouth and closed it again, picking at a stray thread dangling from the tattered cuff of her oversized sweater. She dropped her eyes to the floor.

"I just... I really think you might be... more comfortable in another room, that's all," Hannah said quietly.

"*Is* that all?" I asked.

She looked me in the eyes just long enough to take my breath away with something nebulous and desperate in her expression, but then she turned and left without another word.

"You've got the Ballard girl onto you, huh?" A scrawny pimpled kid with Coke-bottle glasses right out of a cartoon sidled up to me as I watched her walk away.

"Onto me? What is that supposed to mean?" I asked.

"That chick is scary. Messed up." the kid shook his head. "I know you just got here, but I'd keep my distance if I were you."

"Great, I'll keep that in mind," I said. "Just out of curiosity, is there any particular reason I should take your advice, seeing as you could just as easily be the messed up one around here?"

The kid shrugged. "Guess not. Just thought I'd warn you, since she's taken an interest. I wouldn't want her interested in me."

He walked away. His words didn't make me any more nervous than I already was. He hadn't told me anything I hadn't guessed about Hannah the second I'd laid eyes on her. Besides, from what little I caught of his brief, almost bragging little monologue during the group session, I had him pegged as a Look-At-Me, and so I pretty much dismissed anything that came out of his mouth as attention-seeking bullshit.

Back in the doorway of my room, I looked around. It was small, nondescript, and slightly depressing. There was a bed, a desk, and a closet, all empty. The sight of the bars through the dusty window panes was disturbing, but I'd known they'd be there. Even though the sunlight streamed in between them, they pulled a trigger in my head, a sort of mild claustrophobia, but I shook it off. My own stuff was still packed away in two bags where I'd tossed them into the middle of the floor. I tried to find something—anything—that might explain why I would want a different room, and then laughed out loud at myself. After all this time, I couldn't believe I was actually taking a Fox seriously.

§

Okay, so even the best of us have to eat our words at some point or another, and mine became a not-so-tasty midnight snack that evening—well, at 12:27, to be exact. There I was, in the middle of some deep and glorious beauty sleep, and then suddenly, without understanding why, I was sitting straight up in my bed, heart pounding, palms sweating, and with a panic of unknown origin coursing through my body.

I stared wildly around the room. Nothing. There was nothing out of place. For good measure, even though I knew it was childish, I looked under the bed, in the closet, and through the bars of the window, down onto the pitch-black yard below. No proverbial monsters. Everything was quiet and still. I slumped back onto my pillow, which smelled slightly mildewy, and took a deep, shaky breath. I must have been having a dream I couldn't remember, or else some noise had woken me. This place was one big mystery, full of unfamiliar sounds and smells and sights that were bound to be unsettling until I got used to them. And usually, I was out the door again before that could even happen. I reasoned that it had nothing to do with the fact that a strange girl with strange eyes thought there was something wrong with my room. Yeah, that wasn't it.

A small sound echoed in the hallway outside. I slid back off of my bed and pressed my face to the tiny window in my door. Hannah was there, sitting with her knees pulled up to her chin, nodding off with her back pressed to the wall directly opposite my door. The sight of her made my pulse race again. What the hell was she doing here, sitting outside my room like some sort of stalker?

I reached down and checked my door, but it was locked, so I didn't think there was any way she could have gotten inside. At the little clicking sound of the jiggling handle, her head jerked up and her eyes flew open. Before I could pull away from the window, she caught sight of my face. We stared at each other for a long, tense moment. Then she just raised a hand and flicked it in a casual wave, before cupping it back over her knee and resuming her silent vigil. Her expression betrayed not a bit of embarrassment or any other emotion that should have accompanied being caught on such a creepy little stakeout; she appeared totally at ease.

I knew there was a button near my bed that I could activate to alert a staff member, but for some reason, I felt no desire to push it. Instead, returning her wave awkwardly, I shuffled over to my bed and lay back down. I never heard anything else from the hallway, and I never got back up to check if she was still there; somehow, I knew she was. It was a long time before I fell asleep again.

The next morning when I woke up, I ran to the window like a kid at Christmas to see if Hannah was still there, but she was gone. I felt weirdly sad about it, though I couldn't begin to explain to myself why that might be. It didn't actually make any sense. Shouldn't I be relieved that she was gone?

I spent way too much time picking out what to wear, but something about the process made me feel like myself; after all, if I didn't care, then what the hell was the point of it all anyway? No one else would appreciate that I looked fabulous, but at least I would, and that was something I could hold onto in a place where they just keep ripping shit away from you.

It took two tries to find the cafeteria, a hideous blend of '70's linoleum floors, fluorescent lighting, and burnt orange plastic furniture that made me wish I'd stayed lost. I checked in with the unsmiling woman by the door, signing in and putting on a nametag, the final touch of indignity to my carefully chosen ensemble. I searched the sign-in sheet for Hannah's name, but it wasn't on the page I could see. By the time I emerged from the buffet line with my tray of tasteless cafeteria food, there were no empty tables. I started scanning the room for the emptiest one I could find, but stopped when I saw I was being flagged down.

The kid with the coke-bottle glasses was waving energetically at me from a table he was sharing with three other kids. I considered ignoring him, but quite honestly, I was intrigued. I mean, it's always nice not to be the kid in the corner eating by yourself, even if it meant sharing your table with a bunch of freaks in a mental facility. As the new kid, I could easily be considered the freak among freaks, so rather than encourage that image, I headed for the table and sat down.

"Milo, right?"

"Yeah. Sorry, I don't actually remember…"

"Trevor," the kid with the glasses said. Then he pointed everyone out in turn. "Jacob, Colleen, and Meghan."

"Hey," I said in a general vague greeting. They all nodded back, saying nothing.

"So, we wanted to know what happened last night," Trevor said, leaning towards me conspiratorially.

"Sorry, Trevor, you're going to have to be a little more specific," I said, mutilating the top of a little cardboard carton of milk so that I could pour it onto my corn flakes. "It was a pretty wild and crazy night. Can you narrow it down?"

Trevor shared an excited look with the others. "Really?"

I snorted. "No, not really. Are you kidding me? What the hell is there to do in here? I read some magazines and fell asleep."

I watched all four eager faces deflate around me. "Oh," Trevor said. "We'd heard you were the reason Hannah was back in solitary."

My spoon paused en route to my mouth. "What do you mean?"

"Hannah Ballard was moved out of the girls' hall in the middle of the night," the girl named Meghan said. She had bleached blonde hair grown out at the dark roots and had drawn an elaborate design of hearts, stars, and flowers all over her own left hand with a black pen. "We heard her yelling and screaming down the hallway when the nurses dragged her out at like, three in the morning."

"Her roommate Carley said she was caught sneaking back in, and that she'd been down on the boys' floor to see you, and she got caught in your room," said the other girl, named Colleen. She had a very round, freckled face that was lit with the manic sort of glow only a really juicy rumor could ignite in some people.

The boy named Jacob laughed quietly. "You are such an idiot."

Colleen turned an affronted look on Jacob. "What? It could be true! Why would Carley say it if it wasn't true?"

Jacob just shook his head and smirked at me with an appraising glance. He'd clearly taken one look at me and decided there was no way I was the type who would sneak girls into my room. I took one look at him and decided he was a hideous bitch.

Colleen was still eyeing me suspiciously, with a half-smile. "Are you saying that she wasn't down in your room last night?"

I shook my head. "No, she wasn't in my room," I said, which was technically true. "So where is Hannah now?"

"Well, we call it solitary, you know, like in prison movies," Trevor said. "The staff calls it re-entry therapy. Basically she's had all of her privileges and social activities revoked until they decide she's learned her lesson. And they took her out of her regular room and put her in one of the rooms on the behavioral floor."

"That sounds like it sucks," I said, trying to sound off-hand.

"It does," Colleen said. "That's kind of the point. It's how they stop people from breaking the rules."

"Have any of you ever had to do it?" I asked.

"I did once, when I first got here," Jacob said. "They said I was 'resistant in my therapy settings.' You throw one chair at a doctor and they get all defensive."

Meghan giggled, staring soppily at Jacob like he was the most badass, and therefore most attractive, thing she'd ever seen. I could actually see her future clichéd relationship struggles playing out across the cafeteria table, and it was all I could do not to laugh out loud with my mouth full of cornflakes. Hitch your wagon to a star, sweetie.

"So, how long until they let her back into her regular routine?" I asked, trying to sound casual about it. The truth was that I was much more interested in what was happening with Hannah than I had any logical reason to be.

Trevor shrugged unconcernedly. "A few days, probably, as long as she cooperates with the restrictions they put on her. She's been in there a lot, but it's never been for very long."

"Yeah, I'd say she's pretty good at it by now," Colleen said.

"So what's the deal with her, anyway?" I asked.

"You mean what is she in for?" Trevor asked, again with the prison terminology.

"If you want to put it like that, yes."

All four of them looked at each other in a darkly significant sort of way, and I immediately regretted asking them, sure I was now going to get the hallway gossip version of the truth, which, most of the time, barely resembled the truth at all.

"She hallucinates," Meghan said at last. "Like, all the time. Voices and people that aren't there. She's been in institutions all over the state her entire life."

"They bring in special doctors just to see her. Carley says she's been on every med they can throw at her, and nothing works," Colleen added.

"Yeah, well, Carley is a chemistry experiment herself," Jacob said. "But she's right, Hannah's running out of options here. They're going to move her soon, I bet. Someplace higher security. Someplace permanent."

Trevor nodded. "She freaks everyone out, including the staff."

"Right," I said, losing what little appetite I had for my now soggy cereal. "Well, I guess I should be happy she wasn't in my room, then."

§

I didn't see Hannah at all that day; so that part of the gossip was true, at least. I couldn't stop looking for her, though: in the hallways, before group therapy, in the rec room during free time. I couldn't shake the feeling that it was my fault she was being punished, no matter how much I told myself that was stupid. I hadn't done anything wrong. She was the one outside of my room in the middle of the night—the room that she warned me away from, for whatever insane reason. I'd ignored her; of course I had! Whatever issues she had with my room, they were obviously a side effect of her well-documented hallucinations. By all accounts, she did this sort of thing all the time. I had nothing to feel guilty about, and certainly nothing to be scared of.

Until that night.

It began the moment I walked into my room for quiet hours at eight o'clock. I pulled the door shut behind me to find my suitcase and duffel bag stacked neatly by the door. I stared down at them, trying to remember why I'd moved them there, instead of leaving them under the bed, where they were out of the way. Then I noticed the shape of the duffel bag: not flaccid and crumpled, but plump and rounded. I nudged it with my foot.

It barely budged. It was packed.

Even more confused, I crossed over to my bureau and pulled the drawers open one by one. All empty. I drew back the closet door: nothing but a cluster of empty hangers.

What the hell?

I walked right back out of my room and down the hallway to the staff desk, where a nurse was on duty.

"Excuse me, but am I being moved?" I asked.

She frowned at me. "Moved? Moved where?"

"That's what I'm asking. Am I being put in a different room? A different hall? Sent home early for good behavior?"

She picked up a red three-ring binder. "What's your name, again?"

"Milo Chang."

"What room are you in?"

"12A."

She flipped through the binder, frowning deeply and muttering to herself. "No, there is no room change scheduled. What made you think you were being moved?"

"Because someone was in my room and whoever it was packed up all my stuff!"

"Why would anyone do that?" the nurse asked me, her tone skeptical.

"I have no idea! Why do you think I'm out here, asking you?" I shouted back.

The nurse's expression became instantly stern, and I could recognize impending disaster in the slant of her eyebrows. I did not want to get on the wrong side of any of these people in my first week here. I'd seen nurses and other staff members hold serious grudges against the kids with attitude problems, and that was one road I did not feel like skipping on down, at least not right now. I took a deep breath and forced a smile back on my face.

"Sorry. I didn't mean to yell. I'm just a little freaked out that someone touched all my stuff, that's all. Is it possible someone did a room search, or cleaned in there, or something like that?"

The nurse continued to scowl at me. "Room searches are with cause only. Cleaners don't come until Wednesday."

"Okay, then," I said, smiling even more broadly in my mounting panic. "I must have, uh... moved that stuff myself and forgotten about it. Thanks for your help."

I went back to my room and stood in the open doorway, staring at the bags like I was waiting for them to do something interesting. When they didn't start singing show tunes or yodeling, I mentally slapped myself and pulled them into the middle of the room, where I set to unpacking them again. I couldn't explain what had happened, so I did the logical thing and decided to ignore it completely. Then I sat on my bed and started writing a comic book letter to my sister.

This was a thing of ours. I didn't want her imagining the worst about the places I kept being sent away to, so I drew my experiences into little comic strips called *The Astounding Adventures of Milo*. They all started with something that really happened, something lame, like getting lost on the way to the cafeteria or playing solitaire during free time, but usually ended with ninjas or a spaceship, or me riding off on a winged unicorn. She was way into unicorns, and I was way into sending home the gayest illustrations possible to further indirectly piss off my father, so it all worked out nicely.

I was at it maybe twenty minutes or so when the light on my bedside table flickered and went out. I reached over and tapped it a few times, and the bulb sort of blinked and flashed temperamentally before flaring back on again. I went back to my drawing.

A few moments later, it happened again. I reached into the lamp and twisted the bulb to tighten it, and picked up my pen. As I laid it to the paper, the bulb exploded.

Tiny shards of glass and filament flew everywhere, and I threw my notebook up in front of my face to protect myself from the shrapnel. Then I sat frozen in the semi-darkness, my heart racing and my breath coming in quick, rattled gasps.

Okay, I told myself, as calmly as I could. *Okay. That was just a lightbulb. It's an old building, and the lightbulb blew out. Just a little power surge. Nothing to freak out about.*

I stood up, a little unsteadily, if I'm being honest, and crossed over to the other side of the room, where another lamp stood in the corner by the window. Carefully, because my hands were shaking, I pulled off the shade, unscrewed the lightbulb, and carried it back to the bedside lamp. I yanked my sleeves down over my fingers to avoid cutting myself as I removed the jagged remaining base of the shattered bulb still lodged in the lamp, and then slowly screwed in the new one. It flared to a gentle glow.

See? Problem solved. Nothing to worry about.

The words were still on the tip of my inner voice's tongue when the lamp flew across the room, crashed against the opposite wall, and broke into about a million pieces.

I can't be sure how long it took for the nurses to come running, but I know that I hadn't moved a single muscle from where I stood, frozen in horror, staring at the remains of the lamp like a gawker at a celebrity sighting.

I don't think I even heard their questions until the third or fourth time they asked me. By the time I was able to tear my eyes away from the lamp, they were already shaking me by the shoulders and using words like "shock" and "medication".

"Milo. MILO. Answer me. What happened?"

I found her face, which was offensively close to mine at this point. Her breath smelled like coffee. "I... the lamp broke."

"Yes, I can see that. What happened? Why did you throw it?"

All I could smell was coffee. "I didn't throw it. It... it just broke."

The two nurses looked at each other, then at the pile of lighting carnage in the corner. "It just broke?" asked Coffee-breath.

"Yeah."

There was another strange smell that had caught my attention. It was weirdly metallic and stung my nose, like it was charged with electricity.

"Milo, now is not the moment to be dishonest. That lamp has obviously been thrown. Now tell me why you did that, please."

I rubbed furiously at my nose, which was starting to tingle. The smell, whatever it was, was starting to give me a headache. "I'm telling you the truth. It just broke. It must have fallen, or..." I looked around the room in vain for something that might have caused the lamp to do what it had just done, but I couldn't concentrate.

"Milo," Coffee-breath said again, wrapping her mouth around my name like an adult wraps her hand around a bratty kid's arm when she's telling him off. "I'm going to give you one last chance to explain to me why you destroyed New Beginnings property."

Some sort of energy in the room was pulsating around me. It was dark and negative; I could actually feel it enveloping me. The metallic smell was getting stronger, starting to burn. Eyes watering, nose stinging, and my fear finally breaking over me like a cresting wave, I rounded on the woman in sudden anger. "I already told you I didn't do it. But here's something I haven't told you yet: I would strongly recommend you chase that next pot of coffee with a healthy dose of mouthwash, sweetness, because your breath could strip paint!"

And that, kids, is how you land yourself in solitary on your second night in a mental institution. I hope you were taking notes. There will be a quiz at the end of the story.

Coffee-breath's eyes went wide in shock, and the other nurse let out a quick bark of a laugh, before quickly composing her face again into a stern expression. Then they both took me by an arm and marched me out of my room and into the hallway.

"Stop! Stop her! Margaret, grab her!" a voice echoed from our left. We turned just in time to see Hannah barreling down the corridor and skidding to a stop beside us, where Coffee-breath, who was apparently called Margaret, abandoned her hold on me and grabbed onto Hannah instead.

"Are... you... okay?" Hannah gasped at me between heaving breaths, as she bent over and clutched at her side.

I stared down at her, and it dawned on me that she knew. She had come running down here because, somehow, she knew what had just happened in my room. How the hell did she know?

"Milo? Are you okay?" she repeated, her eyes raking me from top to bottom as though assessing me for visible damage.

"I... yeah, I'm okay," I said.

"Okay isn't the word I'd choose," Margaret said, adjusting her hold on Hannah so that she had one arm pinned behind her back. "He's destroying property and disrespecting staff. In fact, he's on his way to a stint in the behavioral hall, so you'll have some company." She turned to two more nurses, both male, who had just arrived breathless beside us. "What's the matter," said Margaret, "can't keep a handle on one tiny patient? What is this, the third time she's gotten out of a locked ward on your watch?"

"Give it a rest, Margaret," the burlier of the two said, taking Hannah from her.

Hannah didn't struggle or respond. In fact, she wasn't paying the slightest attention to anything the nurses were saying. Once she had satisfied herself that I was alright, she had begun staring, with unsettling intensity, through my open bedroom door.

As she did so, the strange, metallic smell began to dissipate, and all my bizarre symptoms—the stinging in my eyes and nose, the pounding headache— vanished without a trace. That energy, that terrible energy was gone, and I felt light and free again. I took a deep, unfettered breath and then looked over at Hannah in wonder.

"How the hell did you do that?" I asked her.

"I wish I knew," she muttered, and before either of us could say another word, the male nurses marched her, none too gently, back down the hallway and through the double doors.

§

Every attempt at an apology was completely ignored; I might as well have been begging and pleading with the wall. I tried every excuse in my little bag of tricks, and turned on what I consider to be an intoxicating amount of charm, but Margaret was not interested in forgiving me. Nope, her only interest was revenge, and that revenge came in the form of tossing me, even as I spewed a constant stream of remorse, into my very own room on the behavioral ward.

"Remember when you asked earlier if you were being moved?" Margaret asked, with a perverse smile that showed every one of her coffee-stained teeth. "It turns out you are getting your wish after all."

"It wasn't a request!" I shouted as the door closed on me.

I was so mad at myself that I would have yelled, if that wouldn't have made me look even more unhinged than she already thought I was. I knew better than to pull shit like that when I was in one of these places. It just wasn't worth the fallout, which I would now be dealing with for the remainder of my stay, not to mention the crap I'd get from my parents when the inevitable phone call was made to inform them of my outburst.

My new status as a troublemaker earned me a new schedule, which was even more abysmally awful than the old one. I was removed from all social activities, was banned from the common areas, and now had double sessions one-on-one with the good Doctor Mulligan, who talked to me with the kind of condescension usually reserved for dogs who shit in the house. And worst of all, my recreational time was now replaced with menial tasks meant as punishment. I cleaned graffiti off of the walls, folded piles and piles of sheets, and stuffed envelopes full of pamphlets and literature on patient services. It was reporting for this last task, on the third day of my sentence, that I found myself in the same room as Hannah. She was sitting at the table, already folding bright pink flyers emblazoned with the names of various eating disorders. I dropped into the seat next to her, the nurse hovering over me to make sure I started my work without complaint. I waited a few minutes after the nurse retreated before I spoke.

"Hey."

"Hi."

"So, here we are. Doing time together."

She allowed herself a small smile. "Yup, I guess you could put it that way."

"I'm pretty new to the cell block. You'll have to show me the ropes. Rumor around the place has it that you are a frequent flyer over here."

The smile was gone as quickly as it appeared, and I regretted the joke. "Sorry. Sometimes I don't know when to keep my mouth shut. Actually, I never know when to keep my mouth shut." I stuffed a few envelopes in silence.

"It's fine," she said at last. "I shouldn't be surprised that the other kids told you that. I mean, it is true. I'm here all the time. I'm sort of famous for it."

I tried to leave it at that, but I'm too damn nosy for my own good, so I took a deep breath and asked the question I was dying to know the answer to. "So... why are you here? Or I guess I should say, why are we both here? Because you and I both know I didn't throw that lamp, and I'm willing to bet that it didn't throw itself."

She put down the envelope she was holding and began tracing her fingers absently over a thin white scar on her wrist. "I owe you an explanation. I know that. I'm really sorry I didn't just give you one before, but... well, let's just say that explanations rarely go well for me."

"How do you mean?" I asked.

"I mean that when I actually decide to give the real explanation, I usually wind up scaring someone off or landing myself on a new med," she said with an utterly humorless laugh. It was the saddest, most hollow laugh I'd ever heard, and it dug out a little hole inside me.

That was the first place I made room for her in my life.

"Whatever you have to tell me can't be as strange as what already happened to me," I said, with a stab at encouragement. "I'm already scared, and I promise I won't go telling tales to those hags no matter how weird your explanation is," I said, cocking a thumb over my shoulder at the forms of the two nurses stationed by the door.

Hannah raised her eyes from her battered wrists and locked onto my gaze. She seemed to be deciding something, and I felt myself go completely still, like I was posing for a painting. I held my breath, waiting to see what her verdict would be, if she would judge me worthy of her secret. I felt the little hole in my chest open wider, as though aching to receive whatever it was she might have to tell.

Finally, she reached into her pocket and pulled out a little folded square of paper. Carefully, she opened it up and smoothed it gently on her knee, where we could safely peruse it without the nurses noticing. It was a patient profile, like the one they undoubtedly had of me and every other kid in the place stashed away in some filing cabinet somewhere. This one was obviously old, though. The paper it was printed on was yellowed and curling at the edges, and the information looked as though it had been entered manually on a typewriter. A small black and white photograph was stapled to the upper left-hand corner.

"Who's this?" I asked, leaning closer to her so that I could scan the paper.

"His name is Jeffrey Stone. He was the first patient assigned to that room when New Beginnings first opened in the '70s. Of course, it wasn't called New Beginnings back then. It was a private psychiatric hospital called The Fielding Youth Rehabilitation Center. It was a place that rich people could send their kids to secretly. They paid absurd amounts of money for the 'experimental' treatments and 'innovative' therapies they offered, not to mention the privacy and discretion of the staff. At least," she said, rolling her eyes, "that's what the pamphlets advertised. There was a stack of them filed in the same box where I found this."

"Sounds horrifying," I said, looking at the face frowning up at me from the photograph. He had close-set dark eyes and a pair of eyebrows that were dangerously close to meeting in the middle. "So what does this kid have to do with... anything? I mean, he's gotta be, like, a senior citizen now."

"He would be, if he was still alive. Which he's not. Say hello to the kid who threw your lamp."

A long silence stretched between us. My mouth went dry. I swallowed hard and cleared my throat before I dared to break it. "I don't get it."

Hannah looked me in the eye, and again I could not move or look away. "Your room used to be Jeffrey Stone's room. That's where he stayed when he came here. That's where one of his "innovative therapies" went wrong and he died in 1976. See?"

She pointed to a date at the bottom of the sheet, next to the typed word, "DECEASED."

I stared at the place she was referencing, but couldn't force the word to make sense; it just looked like a random grouping of letters. "I still don't..."

"Wow, you're really gonna make me come right out and say it, aren't you?" Hannah said, with a slightly exasperated laugh. "Okay, then. He's a ghost. There's a ghost haunting your room, and he wants you out of there."

I blinked. She held my gaze unflinchingly. I swallowed again, maybe just a bit convulsively, but I definitely kept my voice calm as I said, "And you know this because..."

"I can see him. Well, not just him. I can see ghosts in general. I see them almost everywhere I go. I have ever since I can remember, and I can't do anything to stop it."

Two things smacked me in the face at the same time. The first one was pretty obvious. This girl was telling me she saw ghosts, which in generally accepted reality, did not actually even exist. It was ridiculous. It was the very Fox-iest confession that could have come out of her mouth. In just about any other circumstance, I would have smiled politely, backed away slowly, and booked it the hell out of the room. There may have even been some screaming and hand-flapping involved. But the second smack stunned me where I sat, and I felt no desire to flee. This smack came from the realization that I actually believed her. I didn't doubt a single word of what she was telling me.

I opened my mouth, not sure of what was going to come out of it, and heard myself say, "So, what am I supposed to do about a hostile, dead roommate who won't leave?"

For a second, she looked as stunned as I felt. Then, her face split into a huge smile, and she let out a peal of laughter that made the nurses look up from their magazines for the first time.

"What's so funny?" I asked, starting to wonder if I should have done the whole running and hand-flapping thing.

"It's just... that's it?"

"What's it?"

"No staring? No questions? No running away screaming?" She shook her head, still smiling. "I'm not used to people believing me at all, let alone without a moment's hesitation."

"Well, I'm not used to crazy bitches telling me they see dead people, but we all have to adapt, I guess."

She laughed again, and this time I joined in. We laughed more and more until the nurses were staring and we had to compose ourselves, dropping our heads and snorting silently over our work. We didn't want to look like we were actually having fun, or they might decide to separate us and give us some other mind-numbing drudgery instead.

Finally, the laughter played out and we were both left staring down at the dour face of Jeffrey Stone. His expression leeched the rest of the humor from the situation.

"Seriously, though," I said, pointing to him. "You see them all the time? Like, right now in this room?"

Hannah shook her head. "Not all the time. I mean, it's not constant, but it's pretty close. They have a tendency to find me when I move to a new place. I've gotten good at ignoring them, but sometimes I get one like Jeffrey that makes it difficult."

"How many are there at New Beginnings?"

"Seven in the building. A few more on the grounds."

"So, the doctors call them hallucinations and you just have to go along with it?"

"What's the alternative?"

"I don't know. Proving it? Showing them evidence, or whatever?"

Hannah laughed again, but it was a bitter little sound. "It's a lot harder than you think, even with people who've seen something strange, like you have. Sometimes I would get fed up with pretending and try it. It only ever ended one way: a severe psych eval and stronger meds. Trust me, if you saw some of the places they wanted to put me, you'd stop trying, too."

"Yeah, I guess I can see that," I said. "Sometimes it's just easier to pretend, isn't it? Just go along with it."

"I'm guessing you've got some experience with that, too," she said quietly. I could feel that penetrating, analyzing gaze on me again, but I didn't mind, somehow. After all, she'd just trusted me with her biggest secret in the world, and I was practically a complete stranger.

"Well, not like you," I said. "I mean, I can't imagine hiding what you have to hide. But, yeah, I've done my fair share of capitulation, just to survive."

"Like what?"

"Well, there's all kinds of euphemisms for why I'm here, but it all boils down to the same problem. I'm gay and my dad can't handle it."

She just looked at me expectantly, waiting for me to go on.

I put up my hands in a gesture of surrender. "I know, I know. It comes as a real shock. After all, I'm so masculine. I mean, can't you just feel the testosterone rolling off me in waves?"

She giggled. "Oh, is that what that is? I thought I felt something."

"Yeah, it's pretty hard to ignore. Anyway, I realized early on that he thought there was something wrong with me, even before I could have put into words what it was. It was the way he looked at me, with this little wrinkle between his eyes, like I was doing something distasteful just by being there. I hated it when he looked at me like that, so I started doing the things he seemed to want me to do. I tried really hard, but generally failed miserably at whatever it was, usually one sport or another. Actually, I discovered I was a pretty good long-distance runner, and I got really excited that at last I'd found the thing that was going to satisfy him. But after watching me run one race, he told me I needed to quit track. He never told me why exactly, but it must have been the way I looked when I ran; instead of making me look like the other guys, I think it just made me stand out even more by contrast."

"That's awful," Hannah said.

"It's no legion of ghost stalkers, but it sucks, no lie," I said, trying to keep it light. "That's not the worst of it, though. I was so desperate to get out of the last place he sent me that I wrote home and told him I had found a girlfriend, and that I couldn't wait to introduce her to them when I got home."

"You... invented a girlfriend?" Hannah asked, making an obvious effort to keep the judgment out of her voice.

"Worse than that," I said. "I actually asked some poor girl out. Her name was Haley, and she was so desperate for male attention that she would have thrown herself at a serial killer on death row if he'd so much as winked at her. I knew how vulnerable she was, knew I would damage her somehow, but I asked her out anyway. It's probably the shittiest thing I've ever done in my whole life."

"But he gave you no choice," Hannah said, and placed her tiny hand on my arm. It was cold and stiff, like it was made of porcelain. It only added to the aura of fragility.

"I don't know if that's true, but it felt true," I allowed. I didn't shy away from her hand. There was something comforting about it. I focused on its cool pressure while I finished my story. "Haley must have known on some level that I was using her, but she ignored it, just like I did. Haley was released a couple of weeks after me, and we put on this hideous performance of a relationship for like, six months. I brought her over for dinner, held her hand, kissed her good night, used couple-y nicknames that make you want to vomit, all of it. But everyone kept demanding more of me; she wanted more, my dad wanted more, and soon I couldn't pretend any longer. It all cracked and fell to pieces under the pressure and the scrutiny. Haley wound up on suicide watch, and I, after a series of unfortunate life choices I won't get into, wound up here."

Hannah pressed her little hand into mine, and I took it as easily as if it had been Phoebe's. We sat for a few minutes in the silence, not looking at each other.

"Wow, you're a real downer, huh?" she said at last, her face utterly serious.

I burst out laughing. "Yeah, sorry, that was a real ray of fucking sunshine. I should save that kind of thing for group sessions. I bet I'd get a therapy gold star."

"Thank you for telling me. I think it's good for me to remember that other people have to pretend, too."

"See?" I clapped her on the back. "Doesn't it make you feel better to know that you're just one of the freaks?"

"I fit right in," she said, smiling. "What a relief!"

"Just another one of the unloveables. Congratulations."

"You know," she said, her expression brightening, "that would be a great name for a band."

I considered this. "You're right, sweetness, it certainly would. A really hipster one that only did covers of underground girl grunge bands from the '90s. We could write some incredibly deep lyrics, what with all our teen angst. Do you play any instruments?"

"Nope, not even a little. You?"

"Not since my mandatory piano lessons during elementary school. I've completely blocked all memory of the wretched thing. I guess we're shit out of luck."

"I guess so."

"So, in the meantime, what do we do about this stud?" I asked, tapping a finger on the scowling face of Jeffrey Stone.

Hannah sighed. "I don't know. He's been in that room since he died, and he's really adamant about staying. I'm not sure I'll be able to convince him to leave, even if I do get the chance to go back in there."

"Maybe I can just request another room?"

"I don't think the staff members are going to be very accommodating of your requests, now that you've been identified as 'behavioral.' Unless…" her voice trailed away and her eyes glazed over in thought.

I let the silence spiral as long as I could tolerate before I finally burst out, "What? What is it?"

"I was just thinking," she mumbled vaguely.

I rolled my eyes. "I can see that. Care to let me in on it?"

"Right, sorry," she said, shaking her head. "Well, like I said, Jeffrey will be really angry if you go back in there, now that he thinks he's got his room back. I don't think he'll be quiet about it, especially if we provoke him."

"And why in the name of Vogue would we want to provoke him?" I asked warily.

"We wouldn't if it was just us, but if the nurses were all there, it might just be the perfect solution to both of our problems."

"Okay, I'm intrigued. Elaborate," I said.

"If we get him really angry, angry enough to cause some more stuff to fly around the room—then what choice will the staff have but to believe us?"

I thought about it for a moment, and then my face split into a grin that may or may not have qualified as evil—I'm not at liberty to say at this time.

"Do you think we could provoke him into throwing something blunt directly at Coffee-breath's head?"

§

It took two more days of pointless manual labor and sucking-up on my part before it was decided that I could rejoin the general population. Amidst other usual indignities, I'd been made to write an excessively long and flowery apology letter to Coffee-breath, which I then had to read out loud to her while she mugged and scowled at me. It was laced with sarcasm that went right over her head, which was the only way I could secretly salvage my pride. I'd been sure I couldn't take another minute of it, but now, as I stood facing the open door of that room again, I seriously considered walking in there and breaking something just so they would send me back to solitary.

"Well, here you are again. Home sweet home," Coffee-breath said.

"Yup. Feels just like old times," I said quietly, staring around the room. Nothing looked out of place. Not a single clue as to what was probably lurking invisibly in the corners, tucked in the shadows. I took a deep breath.

I stepped over the threshold, still holding that deep breath in.

I wished suddenly for Hannah's little porcelain hand in mine, the cold, fragile, reassuring pressure of it. She'd told me what to do, and what to say. I just didn't want to do it without her. After all, ghosts were her specialty, not mine. Damn her repeat offender status, or she might have been able to come with me.

Okay, I told myself. Here goes nothing. And possibly everything.

"Margaret, could I just ask you a question?"

Coffee-breath turned back to me, clearly aggravated. "You could. Doesn't mean that I'll answer it."

"Lovely, thanks. I was just wondering what kinds of alternative therapies you all have here for... you know, difficult cases."

She frowned at me. "What do you mean, difficult?"

"Don't you ever have cases that need even more than a trip to the behavioral ward? Don't worry, I'm not suggesting I'm about to get difficult," I said, as she gave me the stink-eye. "But there must be some kids who just don't cooperate with that. So, what do you do with them?"

The light closest to the window began to flicker ever so slightly. I felt my pulse quicken.

"We have alternative treatment plans to fit many different scenarios," Coffee-breath replied, her tone still suspicious of why our conversation was headed down this road. "We assess the patient and the situation and create an individualized plan to fit that patient's needs."

"But you must have, like, extreme measures, right? Like for emergencies or really crazy outbursts," I pressed, as the light flickered just a bit faster. "Come on, you can tell me. You must have seen some really intense stuff since you've been here, right? I'm sure they save all the really difficult stuff for the most experienced staff."

She drew herself up a bit with pride. "I've dealt with some very challenging patients, yes."

"Of course you have," I said, shamelessly stroking her ego. "So, what's the really juicy stuff? Electroshock therapy? Hydrotherapy? Lobotomy?"

She looked shocked. "We don't do those kinds of things here. That would be illegal!"

The light was really flickering now. It caught her eye for the first time, and she watched it curiously.

"Oh, come on," I said, waving her off with my hand. "The suits don't know the reality of what you all deal with here. Come on, spill. Do you use surgical measures? Sensory deprivation? There must be a back room, a secret ward down in the basement."

"No, of course not!" Coffee-breath said, trying to give me an indignant look, but the light, flashing madly now, had completely captured her attention. She walked over to it and tapped on the shade, peeking into the top and adjusting the bulb as she said, "I don't know what gave you that idea, but we've never condoned practices like that here."

"Oh sure, not on the record," I said, raising my voice to make sure Jeffrey was paying attention. "I'm talking off the record."

"Milo, that's quite enough!" she said sternly, reaching down and unplugging the light from the wall. It continued to flash and blink like a strobe light. "What is going on with this light?" she muttered.

An energy was building in the room, a sort of static electricity. I could feel it raising the hairs on my arms and tingling across my skin. Jeffrey was going to make himself known at any moment, I just knew it.

Just a little bit more…

"Just between us girls, Margaret, come on! What do you do to the really screwed up ones?" I cried.

She opened her mouth to answer me but screamed instead. Every light, inside the room and out of it, exploded at once. The lamp in her hand flew from her grip and smashed into the ceiling before falling to the ground. I heard the shouts of the nurse out at the desk as all of the recessed bulbs in the hallway popped and went out at the same moment.

In the darkness, silhouetted by the only light left, the glow of the streetlamp outside the window, her crouched and shaking form rose to a standing position.

"What… the hell… was that?" she whispered between terrified gasps.

"That was what happened to that lamp a few days ago," I said. "I told you I didn't throw it. It's also the reason I'd like another room, please."

She looked at me. Her expression was hard to decipher in the newly minted darkness, but then she said, in a tremulous voice, "I'll go make the arrangements now. Make sure you don't leave any of your things."

"Don't worry," I said. "I won't."

§

Three days later, after settling into a new room and acclimating back into the general population of Foxes, Look-At-Mes, Periodics, and Fixer-Uppers, I walked into the cafeteria for breakfast to find Hannah sitting at a table in the corner. No one was sitting within two tables of her; it was as though someone had drawn an invisible line that they all knew not to cross, lest her special flavor of crazy be somehow contagious. I got my tray of food and walked over to her table.

"Hey."

"Hey, yourself."

"Well? Aren't you going to ask me how it went?" I asked.

"I don't need to. I saw Jeffrey already, and he's very happy to have his room back."

"Oh. Well, don't you want to hear the details? It's a pretty thrilling story. And the best part is, Coffee-breath is totally terrified of me now."

"It's nice to have them scared of someone else for a change," Hannah said, smiling. "Okay, tell me all about it."

She pulled out the chair beside her and I sat down in it. And it felt right, sitting beside her.

Beside her, I decided, was my new place to be.

6

FINN'S STORY

THE WARM FLORAL SCENT of her still lingered on my clothes—hints of it brushed my face like impromptu kisses when I turned my head just the right way. It was like carrying a secret around in plain sight—a joke I told to no one and yet laughed about to myself all day.

It was mine. She was mine. Sometimes I still couldn't believe it.

Perhaps that edge of incredulity would allow me to bear what would happen next. Because if it seemed too good to be true, perhaps I could convince myself it never had been true at all.

"Carey. Get up."

I rolled over and squinted into the darkness. Seamus was standing over my bunk, arms crossed over his chest. I glanced at the clock on the wall. It was three o'clock in the morning.

"Seamus? What's happening?"

"Get up and get dressed."

My heart began to race. "What's happening? Has something happened? Are we under attack, or—"

"No one's in any danger. Just get dressed and come to my office."

Baffled but relieved, at least, that I wasn't preparing for some kind of immediate battle, I scrambled into my uniform, laced up my boots, and shuffled into Seamus' office, slapping at my cheeks and rubbing vigorously at my eyes to rouse myself to full consciousness. Bloody hell, I was sore. Lack of sleep in that blasted Traveler caravan had done a job on my muscles.

I found Seamus sitting behind his desk signing a stack of papers. He barely glanced at me as I cleared my throat to announce myself, and pointed to the empty chair opposite him with his pen. Without further ado, I dropped into it and waited. He was clearly in no hurry to explain what this was all about, and I wasn't going to rush him.

At last, he put his pen down, leaned back in his chair, and rubbed his forehead as though he had a devil of a headache. Then he looked at me, shaking his head.

"I warned you. All those years ago, I warned you, and you just couldn't listen to me, could you?"

This pulled me up short. "Pardon?"

"Do you take me for an idiot, Carey?"

"I... never have before, sir," I said slowly, trying to catch up, to figure out what in blazes he was on about.

"I told you that girl was trouble. I told you to keep well away from her, to distance yourself."

Where my insides had been writhing with confusion a moment before, I suddenly seemed to have no insides at all—just the hollow, echoing space that dread carves out in you when it takes hold. I licked my lips, which had gone horribly dry.

"I wondered, once the two of you were back here again. I admit there were moments I wondered. I thought you'd come to your senses. I thought you had discipline. I can see now that I gave you entirely too much credit," Seamus said, giving me a look of pure disgust.

In that moment, I felt absolutely no impulse to lie—that much I remember clearly. Whatever else might happen, the time for lying—if there ever had been a time for such a thing—was past. Whatever Seamus knew and however he knew it, no falsehoods on my part, however well-spun or convincingly delivered, would change that. I was also a shit liar.

I said nothing, choosing instead to meet Seamus' gaze steadily and let him prove his case, as it were.

When it became clear that I had no intention of either confirming, or denying his accusations, Seamus reached into his pocket and flung something across the table at me. I caught it by sheer reflex and looked down at it, bewildered. It was one of my poetry books—the one, I realized with a sinking feeling, that Jess had illustrated for me. But how had Seamus gotten his hands on it?

"We've just had a visit, from the High Priestess of the Traveler Durupinen, no less," Seamus said. "You ought to take better care not to leave your love tokens lying around, Carey. One of the Traveler Guardians found this in the caravan after you left."

I swore internally. What a bloody fool I was. What a bloody, careless fool. Though I knew the poetry in the book did not mention Jess by name, there were verses of an intimate nature, and of course, her artwork filled the pages in between. Seamus could add two and two.

"There was also a sketch," Seamus added, when I still didn't speak. "It seems Miss Ballard left it behind."

I didn't need Seamus to elaborate. I knew which sketch he meant, and I remembered vividly what it portrayed.

"What happens now?" I asked quietly.

"You ought to be raked over the coals in a public hearing before the Council," Seamus spat. "Both of you should."

"Should. Are you saying that's not what's going to happen?" I asked, meeting his eye.

"Much to my chagrin, no," Seamus admitted rather grudgingly. "The High Priestess does not want anything to overshadow the Coronation, nor does she want to spend the first days of her Priesteshood entrenched in an embarrassing spectacle over the Code of Conduct. It is, of course, her choice how to handle it."

"But you would have preferred the public spectacle," I replied.

"I would have preferred not to waste the opportunity to demonstrate to our ranks just how unacceptable your conduct has been," Seamus returned. "Making an example of you would serve as a warning to others, a warning I think it would do them good to hear." He sighed. "Nonetheless, the High Priestess has decided to sweep it all under the rug to spare everyone the humiliation. Your clan holds tremendous power and you have shown great service to Fairhaven and the Northern Clans in the past. The High Priestess believes these to be sufficient reasons to deal with this situation surreptitiously. Therefore, you are to be transferred."

As though from miles away, I heard my own voice ask, "Transferred where?"

"Skye Príosún," came the answer.

It took several seconds for the words to penetrate my brain, and when they did, I found I could barely breathe. Skye Príosún was our most remote outpost, the very furthest reaches of Northern Clan power. It was also a barren, isolated place, and a post there was as much a sentence for the Guardian as it was for the prisoner. No Caomhnóir chose a post at Skye—it was understood that a position there was a metaphorical slap in the face, a judgment on your worth and abilities as a Caomhnóir. It would not be missed by anyone who learned of my assignment there that I had been demoted and disowned by the Fairhaven leadership in the very starkest of terms.

Seamus was watching my face carefully as I absorbed this news. "There's no point in asking your clan to intercede on your behalf," he said, misreading my expression.

I snorted with disgust at the notion. "Oh, come off it, Seamus. I would never ask them to, nor would they agree to do so, as you know full well." The thought was absurd. Clan Gonachd had only ever concerned itself with consolidating its power and influence. The salvation of a wayward son of the clan would not be worth sustaining damage to the clan's reputation. They would be more than grateful to bury me deep in the bowels of Skye Príosún rather than take ownership of my misdeeds. The same, of course, would not be true if I was my sister Olivia or my cousin, Peyton. But I was not.

"When?" was all I could think to ask.

"Effective immediately. You are to pack your things at once. We leave in thirty minutes for the helipad."

"And I'm to have no opportunity to fight this? No course of appeal whatsoever?"

"Oh, you can make a fuss, certainly," Seamus said, with something remarkably like a sneer. "You can shout from the rooftops if you like—demand a hearing, call witnesses, do your worst. But you know the outcome will be the same, so why not save both yourself and Miss Ballard the public flogging you'll receive if you reject the High Priestess's frankly merciful offer to deal with all this privately?"

I wanted to argue, but even in my shock I knew he was right. Absolutely no good would come of fighting this transfer. All I would do was humiliate Jess and possibly endanger the Council seat that Hannah had fought so hard to win. Clan Sassanaigh had already faced years of ridicule and rejection. How could I heap more on their heads, selfishly, just to delay the inevitable?

I couldn't. That was the hard truth of it.

"Then I suppose there's nothing left to say," I replied. "I'll gather my things, then." I stood to go.

"Nothing to say, is there?" Seamus asked, shaking his head at me. "Not a word of apology to your brethren for your weakness?" He made a sound of disgust through his nose. "I had you pegged as better, Carey."

My hand was on the doorknob when I turned back to him.

"Love is not weakness, Seamus. If I'm better in any way, it's because that woman helped me find the best that was in me, and it will be a frostbitten day in the hottest reaches of hell before you'll ever hear me apologize for loving her, to you or to anyone."

Back in the bunk room, I pulled my duffel bag out from under my bed and began to fill it as quietly as I could. Everything felt numb—my fingertips, my brain, my heart. There was not a blessed part of me that was able or willing to absorb what was happening—that I was leaving her. That I would not even have the chance to say goodbye. It was unthinkable—unbearable.

My thoughts turned to Ileana. Surely, she had not broken the boundaries of Durupinen jurisdiction simply because she suspected Jess and I had a relationship? What business was it of hers if a couple of Northerners broke the Code of Conduct? No, she had to have discovered—or at the very least, suspected—how Irina had escaped the boundaries of the Traveler camp and, by extension, its intended punishment for her. This was revenge—revenge against Jess for interfering in Traveler law. Ileana knew that Traveler justice could never be exacted on Jess, so she made sure that Northern Clan law would be brought to bear instead.

"Finn? What are you doing?"

Startled, I turned to see Bertie sitting up in his bunk, squinting through the darkness as he tried repeatedly to mash his glasses onto his face.

"Bertie. No worries, mate. Go back to sleep," I said, attempting a casual smile, hoping he would simply roll over. No such luck.

"Why are you packing? Are you going somewhere?"

I hesitated, but what was the point in lying to the poor bloke? He'd hear the truth soon enough, and I'd rather he heard it from me. After all, he might be the only person who had the chance.

"I am, as a matter of fact. The truth is, I'm being transferred. Tonight," I said, sitting back on my heels and sighing.

Bertie's round face crumpled with confusion. He sat up and swung his legs over the side of his bed. "Transferred? But I don't understand. Are Jess and Hannah going somewhere? They've only just won the Council seat, where could they—"

I shook my head. "I'm no longer assigned to Clan Sassanaigh. I've been reassigned to Skye Príosún."

Bertie's eyes widened and I watched the realization play across his face. It was so awful to watch, I found myself half glad that he was likely the only person I'd have to tell face-to-face.

"But, I don't understand. Why would they transfer you? You're... you're one of the best Caomhnóir they've got! Jess and Hannah need you!"

"I appreciate that assessment, mate, but it seems Seamus disagrees with you. Jess and Hannah will be fine. There are plenty of competent Guardians here who can take over for me." Even as I said it, a golf ball sized lump lodged itself in my throat, and I could barely choke out the words.

"No, they can't transfer you!" Bertie said, standing up now and looking half-panicked, half-indignant. "I'll vouch for you! They're making a mistake! Who should I...?"

I jumped to my feet and placed a restraining hand on his shoulder, shushing him at the same time. "I appreciate that, mate, but there's nothing you can do. It's been decided. There's no point arguing with Seamus. You may as well bang your head against a brick wall."

"But why? Why is he doing this to you? I... I need you here."

He uttered this last bit so quietly that it took me a moment to decipher what he had said, and in those few seconds his face turned beet red with embarrassment. I struggled for the right thing to say.

"You don't need me here," I said, as dismissively as I could, as if the idea was absurd. "You've worked hard and you've become a brilliant Caomhnóir for Savvy."

"I'm not brilliant. I—I'm barely competent," Bertie muttered.

"You're devoted," I corrected him. "And loyal. And hard-working, which is more than I can say for some of the lazy, selfish sods around here. They resent their charges, but you don't. And that makes you a better protector than they can ever hope to be."

Some of it was true, and the rest was only half a lie, which I forgave myself for telling as I watched the words fill Bertie up, buoying him in what I knew would be a rough sea ahead for him. Half the lads only left him alone because they knew I'd pummel them if they gave him a hard time.

"I'll be in touch," I promised, knowing full well I may have to break it. "I want you to do something special for me, though."

Bertie threw out his chest and set his jaw. "Name it, Finn. Name it and it's done."

"I need you to keep an eye on Jess and Hannah for me, and their new Caomhnóir as well. Make sure he's up to scratch, yeah? And write to me—keep me up to date on what's happening here. I'll...

this is only temporary. I'll be working on getting myself back to Fairhaven as quickly as I can."

Bertie nodded once, sharply. "I won't let you down, Finn," he said.

"I know you won't. And I asked you, mind, none of the rest of these tossers, so let that be a reminder of what kind of Caomhnóir I think you are."

He grinned, which was all I needed to be able to leave the poor bloke behind. I zipped up my bag, clapped him on the back, and strode from the room before I could change my mind.

§

I remember very little of the journey to Skye. Whether my mind was attempting to protect itself from the reality of what was happening, I'm not sure; but when I look back on the trip—first the car, then the helicopter—I can tease out only a few blurry images, all of them silent. The only truly clear memory I have is stepping out of the chopper and onto the lawn, staring up at the place where—for lack of a better analogy—I would be serving out my sentence for my perceived crime. It loomed before me, looking every bit the impenetrable fortress it was touted to be. I had seen it before only once, when I was assisting with a prisoner transfer, and then had not even entered the place.

I doubted that the prisoners currently locked away in its bowels felt more dread upon their first glimpse of the place than I did in that very moment. Fairhaven had never felt further away.

Seamus had insisted on accompanying me—though whether to gloat or because he thought me a possible flight risk, I couldn't be sure, and it was his purposeful strides I followed through the imposing front entrance and into the outer courtyard.

The space seemed to be in use as a training area for the Caomhnóir. Scattered all around within the perimeter of the high stone walls, there were groups of men sparring, marching, and mending weaponry. Every one of them looked up upon my arrival, and there was not a friendly nod or a wave amongst them. Charming.

Seamus motioned me forward to stand beside him as he was approached by an older Caomhnóir who limped forward, eyeing me like a hawk with the one eye that did not wear a grubby leather patch. This man, I knew, had to be Eamon Laird, the Commander over all Caomhnóir at Fairhaven and a man with a reputation for almost thuggish cruelty. The heavy scarring that badly disfigured one side of his face pulled one corner of his mouth into a permanent sneer.

"This is him, then?" Eamon barked without greeting or preamble. The look he gave me was nothing short of repulsed. I felt my fists clenching at my sides and quickly shook them out. I wouldn't do myself any favors losing my temper with the leadership before I'd even put my bag down.

"Yes. Finn Carey of the Clan Gonachd. Here's his file," Seamus said, handing it over to Eamon, who opened it at once and began perusing the contents. I wondered what was in the file—test scores and write-ups, surely, but what else? What sorts of records did the leadership keep on the rest of us? I realized I had absolutely no idea.

"What a waste," Eamon replied, clicking his tongue against the roof of his mouth. "Such promise. Another bright prospect derailed by temptation."

Here, again the insinuation that my relationship with Jess had been nothing more than a pathetic loss of will power in the face of lust. Did these men truly not grasp the idea that a relationship between a Durupinen and a Caomhnóir could be anything other than a product of female machination, the siren song and its hapless victim? I expected no less in the newly indoctrinated Novitiates, but surely experience had taught these men that real life was rarely so simple, so easily dismissed? How sad to realize their thinking had never evolved past such infantile notions about human interaction.

"Little chance of falling victim to that here, unless you fancy filthy inmates in chains, Carey," Eamon said with a dry chuckle, which Seamus echoed.

"No, sir," I replied stiffly, keeping my eyes on the file in his hand. If I locked eyes with the man, I might just kill him.

"Right, then," Eamon replied, snapping the file folder shut and tucking it under his arm. "Well, we'll see what we can find for you here to keep your mind on your sworn duty, won't we? I expect you'll be cursing the woman's name in no time. Best thing for you. I imagine she's just carrying on her cozy existence, isn't she, and letting you take the fall?"

I managed, with difficulty, to not tackle the man where he stood, but it was a near thing. It became clear in that moment that I was somehow going to have to bury an awful lot of what was raging inside me if I hoped to survive here without being court-martialed.

Seamus and Eamon began discussing a litany of details related to my transfer, but I was only half listening. It was daytime now at Fairhaven. When would Jess realize I was gone? Would anyone explain to her what had really happened or—the thought occurred with a stab of horror—would they lie to her about what had happened to me? Would they perhaps tell her that I had left of my own accord? That something had happened to me? Would they say something to make her think—God forbid—that leaving her was my choice? I should have given a message to Bertie, to make him promise to deliver it. Why hadn't I thought of it? What the hell was wrong with me?

A roiling panic had begun in the pit of my stomach, the walls around me suddenly feeling as though they were closing in. I focused on taking deep, steady breaths. The last thing I could afford to do was to lose consciousness in front of my new Commander.

"West!" Eamon shouted over his shoulder. A short and stocky Caomhnóir with a thick neck and the stubbly red beginnings of a beard jogged over at once, looking expectant. "Show Caomhnóir Carey to the sleeping quarters and then to the kitchens for something to eat."

West looked me up and down once, appraisingly, and then jerked his head over his shoulder toward the second set of doors. "This way, then," he said, and strode off, leaving me to jog behind him to catch up.

I looked back over my shoulder to see Seamus watching me. I'm not sure what I expected; a wave? Some sort of acknowledgment that he was leaving me on this godforsaken rock to rot? If so, I was a fool. He turned without a word, without a gesture, and walked off in the direction of the front doors and the helicopter. Within minutes he'd be in the air again, on his way back to Fairhaven, where even now Jess must be realizing that something was terribly wrong.

Damn it all to hell.

"This way," West called, and I turned back to him. He paused long enough to be sure I was following again, and then resumed his walk into the *príosún*. His legs were extremely muscular, but short, and he moved them almost comically fast to maintain his pace.

"Carey, is it?" he asked, tossing the words over his shoulder as we walked straight through the cavernous central chamber of the *príosún*, stairs winding up around us dizzyingly high to doors and galleries and, impossibly, still more stairs.

"Yeah, that's right. Finn," I answered distractedly as I tried to get my bearings.

"Peter Westingbrook," he replied. "We tend to go by last names around here, but Westingbrook is a mouthful, so everyone just calls me West. You can, too, I suppose, if you like."

"Right. Cheers."

"We don't get many Council clan blokes around here," West said, shooting me an almost amused expression. "You must have cocked things up good and proper to wind up with this here lot."

I didn't reply, and when I didn't, West seemed to realize he wasn't going to get any details out of me and dropped it. He pointed a stubby finger over his left shoulder. "Mess hall just there, but it's closed now until lunch. That's where we all eat, normally. Meals at six, noon, and six sharp. Don't miss the bell, because they won't feed you in between, and shifts are long without a proper tuck in. Food isn't bad and there's plenty of it, unless you're a prisoner, of course." West seemed to think this was a jolly good joke, and chuckled to himself, but I left the laughing to him.

"Sleeping quarters right through here," West went on, pushing open a heavy oak door with a black latch on it and stepping aside to let me through. The room was cavernous and very long, with rows of bunks running the length of the space on both sides, interspersed with tall, narrow, leaded glass windows. The floor was bare stone, with a threadbare, faded purple rug running down the middle like a mockery of a Hollywood red carpet. There was no air of tidiness or military order to the place, like back at Fairhaven—personal belongings were jumbled under the beds and wrinkled bits of uniform and crumpled towels littered the backs of chairs and bedside tables.

West walked straight down the middle, pausing only to kick a boot back under the foot of a bed I was quite sure wasn't his. I followed him about three-quarters of the way down the carpet until he halted and pointed.

"Anywhere you see a pile of blankets folded on the end of the bed, that bunk is free for the taking. There's no rhyme or reason to it, but a bit of advice, and you can take it or leave it. Makes no difference to me, as it goes. Knox snores like a bloody freight train, so you'll want to steer clear of him, he's third from the end, this side. And Wells is a right knob, he'll steal your cigarettes soon as look at you, and he smells like a bull in summer no matter how often he showers, which is never often enough. He's that one there with the newspaper on it, though I'm buggered if I know why, the thick bastard can hardly string a sentence together, let alone read one. Other than that, it's luck of the draw, really."

Deciding to accept the free advice, I gave both of the indicated beds a wide berth and chose a bunk on the end right in front of a window through which, if the sky was clear, I might just catch a sliver of sunset above the outer wall. West nodded his approval of my choice, though I did not ask for it, and stood by casually picking at a scab on his elbow while I unpacked a few things and shoved my duffel bag under my bed.

"Right. Nosh?"

"Yeah."

He turned and walked back the way we had come in, leading me back through the circular central chamber and onward into the kitchens. Generally, kitchens are kept somewhat hidden from diners, in the hopes of keeping the public from contaminating an otherwise clean and orderly workspace. In Skye Príosún, it appeared that the opposite was true. The place was truly chaotic. Pots and pans loudly clattering, as workers cursed and shouted to be heard. Cleanliness did not seem to be a priority, and it was with an internal mantra of "stiff upper lip" that I accepted the bowl full of beef stew and the hunk of bread West managed to scrounge for me. Luckily, it tasted much better than it looked, and I tucked in without further hesitation, not because I was truly hungry, but because I was smart enough to know that I should eat when food was offered to me.

"What happens now?" I asked when I had eaten my fill.

"You'll follow me and a few of the lads on shift. Shadow them, like, so that you can learn the ropes of how we patrol all the parts of the *príosún*. There's different protocols, see, for different wards and different times of day. You'll have to learn 'em all quick, because Eamon will have you on your own before the end of the week, and he'll expect you not to fuck up."

"What's the shift schedule?" I asked.

"Six hours on, six off, five days a week, with one day reserved for training and one for rest," West said. "And believe me, you're going to need that day of rest."

"What about the boundaries? Where can we go?" I asked.

"Within the castle, we've got the bunks, the mess hall, the gym, the library, the weapons hall, the rec room, and the courtyard. In the rec room, they've got computers, which you can use to send emails and the like, but be warned—they monitor everything that comes in and out. There's no privacy, like, and the same goes for phone calls, so best not try to ring anyone you're not supposed to be talking to."

He mentioned it casually enough, but I knew that meant the reason for my posting at Skye had already spread like wildfire through the ranks. Still, it was decent of him to warn me off trying anything that might get me into further trouble. Even so, I felt my heart sink. No chance of getting a message to Jess somehow.

West went on, "Outside the castle, we've got the grounds, which extend all the way to the beach, though it's a bugger of a climb down there, and the 'round about forty acres to the inland side. And twice a month you can get leave to drive into Portree for a pint and a glimpse of civilization. Although, whether you actually get that leave will depend on the reasons you've been assigned to this outpost."

"What do you mean?" I asked, a bit more sharply than I intended.

"Come on, mate, we all know why we're here," West said, with a surprisingly cavalier shrug. "This is the last stop for Caomhnóir, and there's no use pretending it's not. We've all wound up here because we've made a right mess of things in one way or another, and now we've got to make the best of it. Leave to Portree is considered a privilege, not a right, and like any privilege, you've got to earn it from the higher-ups."

"I see," I said, absorbing this information. It seemed likely that Seamus' main concern would be that I would somehow try to communicate with Jess, and I knew that he would do whatever he could to prevent that. It was possible, therefore, that my file, currently being perused by Eamon, would contain instructions to limit my privileges in such a way as to make that a virtual impossibility. I could feel my anger toward Seamus—toward the entire system—curdling into a diamond-hard lump in my chest.

"Anyway," West went on, rather cheerfully, "regardless of why you're here, keep your head down and work your arse off, and you'll likely have leave privileges in no time. Eamon cares much more how you handle yourself here than how you fared before you walked in the doors. They post the weekly list on the notice boards outside the Commander's offices. Matter of fact, I'll take you there next, and we can get your marching orders for the afternoon."

West talked my ear off all the way down to the Commander's offices, explaining the locations of the different wards and the protocols for handing off shifts. West was an affable enough sort of bloke, but I was in no mood to make chums. To admit I should form alliances and maybe even friendships meant admitting that I would be on this godforsaken rock indefinitely, and I was in no way ready to face that possibility.

Over the next few days, I found myself reverting to survival mode. At night, when I could not distract my brain from the grief of losing Jess, I was plagued with terrible nightmares, most of them involving me wandering through misty woods or winding castle passages, trying to answer her desperate cries for help but unable to find her no matter how long I looked. When the fear of drifting back into the dreams left me sleepless, I tried to write. I pulled one of my black books out from beneath my mattress and opened it to a blank page, staring down at it, willing my pain into words so that I could exorcise it from me, siphon it off onto paper and cast it away from me. But for the first time in my life, I found that the words would not come—that I had reached a mental space where the words could not reach me, could not help me make sense of what I was feeling. Again and again, I was forced to give up, put my pen away, and pore instead over the delicate strokes of Jess' artwork in the margins until sleep swept me off into wandering nightmares once again.

During the waking hours, I slogged through shift after shift, committing the regulations for each ward to memory, which was a welcome distraction for my overwrought brain. I endured the whisperings and mutterings of the other Caomhnóir, who were no doubt sizing me up, trading the rumors and stories they'd heard about me, and determining whether they ought to make overtures of camaraderie or join forces against me. I expected nothing less. There was a pecking order in any Caomhnóir setting, and these men wanted to know where I was going to fit into it. I had no desire to assert myself in any way, and yet I knew I had to protect myself if I wanted any peace within the walls.

At the end of my first week, I had my first training day, which I must admit I had been dreading. Physical combat was the bluntest way, the most animal way, to establish one's place in the pack, so to speak, and I was not keen to put myself on such obvious display. If I performed too well, I would be deemed a threat. If I performed too poorly, I would be relegated to target status. There was a fine line to walk if I wanted to maintain the privilege of being left alone, and I did not relish the idea of having to fight people to do it.

Sparring training took place in rotating groups. After a ten-kilometer run out on the cliffs and a battery of physical exercises, we were split into two groups, one for sparring with weapons and one for hand-to-hand combat. I buried myself safely in the middle of the pack during the running and the rest of the training exercises, but there would be no more blending in once we were paired off and began to fight. I was sorted into the hand-to-hand group first and paired off, by chance, with West. I breathed easily for a moment. West was as close to a friend as I had in the place, and he had continued to be helpful and cordial to me since I'd arrived. We locked up and began to fight. I let him land a few blows and I made sure to get in a few of my own. When the instructor called us off a few minutes later, we shook hands and looked each other in the eye, and I thought I saw respect gleaming out at me. Whether he knew I had held back, I didn't know, but there was no resentment in his gaze, so I chalked it up to a win.

The next round, when my name was called, a bloke I knew as Knox loped into the circle. He fancied himself something of an alpha, I had gathered. He was tall and muscular, with dark hair and rather close-set blue eyes. His nose had the permanently bulbous appearance of having been broken on more than one occasion. He was rarely seen around the place without a few hangers-on, and he was one of those who liked to draw attention to himself at meals or in rec, besting people at games of cards and boasting crudely about conquests. He had also not troubled to keep his voice down when speculating at meal times what a Council clan darling was doing knocking around with the lot of outcasts on Skye. I would have to play this a little differently, I knew. West's pride wasn't so easily wounded, but Knox, for all his bluster, had the kind of manhood that bruised like an overripe peach.

The bell clanged, signaling the start of our fight. Knox wasted no time going on the offensive, and I had no choice but to call on my reflexes to avoid being pummeled. I dodged blow after blow, watching Knox's ire rise like the mercury in a thermometer. The more frustrated he got at his inability to land a blow, the sloppier his technique became, and I was able to turn the tables on him, stunning him first with a hook to the jaw, then a knee to the ribs, and finally, executing a leg sweep that left him panting on the ground on his back. The bell clanged again, signaling my victory.

I held out a hand to help him up, not sure he would take it, but after a moment of consideration, he did. He looked me over, his eyes still blazing.

"So, you got by on more than your Council connections, did you, Carey?" he muttered.

"Can't have mummy fighting all my battles for me, can I?" I replied smoothly.

Knox's expression was hard to read, but there might have been a nugget of respect in it. I didn't think we'd be chums by any stretch of the imagination, but he knew now I wasn't to be trifled with, I was confident of that, at least.

By the end of training that day, I had managed, with some strategic effort, to earn myself a bit of leverage. My Commanders knew I was capable, and my fellow Caomhnóir knew better than to tangle with me. For the first time since I'd arrived, I felt just a bit of solid ground beneath my feet, which was good, because I needed something to anchor myself to, or my grief over Jess threatened to carry me clean away. I dug in as the days, and then the weeks, and then the months slipped by.

Keep your head down, I told myself. Keep your head down and your mouth shut and show them you can be trusted. I would have to earn any respect or privilege there was to be had within the walls of Skye Príosún, and there was no hope of seeing Jess again without both. My reputation was the only leverage I had, and I had to start rebuilding it here.

§

Just as I began to wonder if anything could possibly break the monotony or the isolation, I found myself eligible for leave to Portree for the first time since I had arrived. I had no expectation, given the manner in which I had been reassigned, that I would ever be considered for such a privilege, but there I was, having my back slapped by West, who began rattling off the many pubs, restaurants, and shops I would have the pleasure of visiting when I was there.

"Are... are you sure my name's on that list?" I asked, for I hadn't even bothered to check.

"Dead sure, mate, I just read it myself!" West replied jovially. "Well done. That may be some sort of record, earning leave that quickly."

I forced a smile. The last six months had been the longest of my life. The idea that this development had happened "quickly" was a concept my mind could not properly wrap itself around. "Brilliant," I managed, and left him to prattle on about Portree, for which I gave not a care in the world because it did not contain Jessica Ballard. Instead, my mind began to reel, wondering if there was any possible way I might use my time in Portree to communicate with Jess. Might I simply find a local public telephone box? Would there be an internet café I could perhaps sneak into? Did internet cafés even exist way the hell out here, and would the leadership have some way of preventing me from using them if they did? Would I be allowed to go anywhere alone, or would we all be expected to keep tabs on each other, like a pack of children tasked with babysitting one another? It seemed I was about to find out, and yet, I'd barely had the chance to imagine the possibilities when a second opportunity fell, seemingly from the cold, star-strewn Scottish sky, right into my lap.

It was Monday, my day of rest that week, which meant I could luxuriate in unconsciousness for as long as I liked. The dreams still popped up, but that day they left me mercifully to my own devices, and so I slept like the dead until nearly ten o'clock in the morning. I'd missed breakfast by hours, but I wasn't bothered. It had been so restorative just to achieve the kind of sleep where both body and mind rested simultaneously, I felt I could have gone all day without food and been quite cheerful about it. I took a long shower—I'd long ago grown used to the tepid water temperatures which were all the *príosún* had to offer—and dressed at leisure. I'd just decided that a stroll along the cliffs was what I needed, and had begun to make my way out to the grounds when I noticed the clump of Caomhnóir hovering around the notice board. I was used to seeing this sort of thing on the day the leave list was posted, but that had gone up two days earlier. I made my way to the back of the group and found West trying to elbow his way to the front.

"What's up?" I asked him, craning my neck to see over the heads of the crowd in front of us.

"Off-site security detail," West replied, eyes shining.

"What does that mean?"

"It happens when there's a big Durupinen gathering somewhere. They want extra security, so they assign some of us to the job and ship us over to the mainland to help out. It doesn't happen often. I wonder what's going on that needs the extra manpower."

I pondered this as we waited for the crowd in front of us to read the notice and disperse. Of course, I'd been involved with such events before. The Airechtas alone had required dozens of extra Caomhnóir shipped in from all over the Northern Clan territories. I had never stopped to consider that some of them must have come from the various *príosúns*, but now that I thought about it, it made perfect sense. I could also understand why so many of the men would be excited about it; chances to leave the island were few and far between.

"There's no way my name will be on that list," I muttered to West as we shuffled forward. "I haven't been here long enough to earn a privilege like that, surely?"

West shook his head. "It's got nothing to do with seniority, not this time. The Council won't care who's been here longest. All they care about is who can provide the best protection. The most skilled, the most adept, the very best protectors—that's who they'll demand be sent their way."

My heart sped up. Was it even possible?

At last, the men ahead of us cleared out and we could see the notice in full:

Off-Site Security Detail
Event: Wedding for Clan Dílseacht
Positions: Border Details and Vehicle Inspections
Dates: 19-21 June

And there, on a list of approximately a dozen names: Carey, Finn.

I stared at it in shock, reading it several times to convince myself that it was, indeed, my name. That I was, for the first time in months, going to have a chance to leave this island. My addled brain didn't seem capable of absorbing it. A hearty clap on the back jolted me out of my shock.

"Well done, mate!" West was saying. "See, I told you! Three days off the rock! Blimey, that's the first one I've made in almost a year."

"Cheers," I said dazedly. "And... well done, yourself."

I turned in the direction of the library, West still prattling on at my side about off-site details and what they were like, but I was barely listening. Excitement was expanding inside me like an explosion, and it was all I could do to stop myself from whooping.

I knew whose wedding this must be. Róisín Lightfoot was the only member of Clan Dílseacht who had been engaged recently, as far as I knew. Clan Dílseacht and Clan Gonachd were thicker than thieves, everyone knew that. That meant my family was sure not only to be invited, but perhaps even to be included in the wedding party. But this was not the realization that had my heart in my throat. Clan Dílseacht was on the Council, and there was no way in hell they would hold a wedding for a member of their Gateway without inviting all of the Council clans. It would be an unforgivable breach of tradition and etiquette. It would also mean an opportunity to show off just how wealthy and well-connected they were to the rest of the Northern Clans, and Patricia Lightfoot would never squander such a chance. So, surely wedding invitations had already made their way into the hands of every Council clan, and were even now being accepted.

And that included Clan Sassanaigh.

Was it possible... was I kidding myself into hoping... that Jess and I might find ourselves within sight of each other for the first time since I'd been transferred? I felt like a child wishing for the moon—it was so inconceivable, so ludicrous, and yet, there it was, so close that I almost fancied I could touch it.

I shook off West outside the library with some completely invented excuse about needing to visit the armory to have the smithy take a look at my dagger, and instead took off across the grounds and toward the cliffs, hoping the salt air would clear my head enough so that I could think.

It was impossible that I could be in the same place as Jess and not find a way to see her. My heart could not conceive of it. And yet, I couldn't believe I was being permitted to take a post in a place where she might be. Had Seamus overlooked this possibility? Had he perhaps not made provisions against off-site details in my file? After all, it had taken months for me just to earn the right to drive an hour up the road to a pub. Perhaps there had been a time stipulation? Perhaps I had passed some sort of test by following the rules for this long? Or, perhaps Seamus or someone else in leadership already knew that Jess wouldn't be in attendance for some reason? I had to find out, but how could I get the information without drawing attention to the fact that I hadn't reformed in the slightest?

The answer came to me so suddenly, it seemed to smack me right in the face. Of course. There was one person I could call, one person who, if I begged and groveled sufficiently, might be willing to help me. I loathed the idea, but there was not an ounce of my pride I would not swallow in order to see Jess again, and so my mind was made up. Turning on my heel, I made my way back toward the castle and into the rec room, where I sent the one email I could think to send that would make any chance of a reunion possible. Then all I could do was wait and pray for an answer.

That night, I began having nightmares—nightmares from which I would awaken suddenly, drenched in a cold sweat and shaking from head to foot. They started out just like the nightmares I had when I first arrived—I was wandering through foggy landscapes, hearing Jess calling out for help, but unable to find her. I wouldn't have thought the dream could get worse, but my mind found a new way to torture me. In this new iteration of the dream, Jess' cries led me right to her. I could see her ahead, calling out, wringing her hands, my name still shivering in the air between us. But as I reached her, I found I could not touch her—my hands passed right through her as though she was one of the spirits it was our duty to protect. She could not see me—her desperate eyes stared right through me as she continued to call for me, to demand why I had deserted her. What had she done, she begged, to deserve this? How could I have left her alone? And all I could do was shout pointlessly in a voice she could not hear.

I rolled over and sobbed into my pillow, the dream emotions still freshly tangled with the waking ones, so that I could hardly make sense of them. And then, all of a sudden, as it began to sort itself out, I found myself laughing—actually laughing—into my pillow. At first, the impulse made no sense, but then the thought that had sparked the laughter floated its way to the surface of my mind. If Jess knew that I was imagining her wandering helpless in the woods like some damsel in distress, she would slug me right in the face.

I laughed until my throat felt raw and my sides hurt. It was the first time I'd really laughed since I'd arrived at Skye Príosún, and I was bloody thankful for it.

§

I'd begun to lose hope that I'd receive a response to my email as the day of my leave in Portree approached, so when I opened my email the evening before to see the message waiting for me, I sighed with relief. All I had to do now was shake off the lads for a bit once we got there, and I'd be free to make my case.

All of the Caomhnóir on leave that day were divided into groups and assigned to vehicles. I piled into the van with West, Knox, Wells, and Jensen, and we set off on the winding road to Portree, Jensen driving like a right lunatic, as I had been warned he would.

"Bloody hell, Jensen, if this is how you drive before we head to the pub, the cows in the fields better run for cover on the way home," Knox grumbled.

"Ah, sod off, Knox, you wanker," Jensen replied, "or you can bloody well walk to Portree."

The back and forth continued in this manner, culminating with Jensen stopping the car and trying to pull a hysterically laughing Knox out of the passenger seat and into the ditch on the side of the road, knocking him about the head repeatedly until Knox agreed to lay off his driving skills. In spite of the tomfoolery, we managed to pull into the main street of Portree before midday. While the others argued about whether to walk the shops or see what was playing at the cinema, I pulled West aside.

"Oi, I've got to meet someone down at one of the cafés, all right? I'll catch up with you in a bit."

West's eyebrows rose so high, they disappeared into his shaggy red hair. "Is that so? What are you up to, Carey?"

"Nothing you need concern yourself about," I assured him with a genial punch on the arm. "I'll catch up with you lot at the pub, all right?"

West looked like he still wanted to interrogate me, but I didn't give him the chance, turning my back on him and striding off down the street. I glanced down at my watch. If I hurried, I would get there on time.

Portree had at one point been a fishing village, and it retained much of the nautical charm. The buildings clustered shoulder to shoulder overlooking the bay, like so many wives gathered anxiously with their eyes on the horizon, waiting for fishing boats to find their way home at the end of the day. If I hadn't been so blasted nervous, I might have stopped a moment to enjoy the freedom and the views, but not today.

I cut away from the water's edge and down a narrow street which took me to another road full of shops. I'd asked her to meet me outside a café West had told me about, and she'd agreed. If she hadn't backed down—if she hadn't changed her mind—she should be sitting waiting for me right around the next corner…

As I rounded the curve of the road, I spotted her, sitting outside of the little café, arms crossed truculently across her chest, picking fretfully at the edge of a scone she had no intention of eating. Her eyes were hidden behind a pair of enormous sunglasses that she hardly could have thought necessary in the overcast Scottish afternoon, but I could clearly see the rest of her face, which was twisted into a perfect knot of stony aggravation.

I'd never been so happy to see my sister, Olivia.

So intent was she on destroying the innocent scone on the plate in front of her that she didn't see me approaching until I had nearly reached the table. Wiping her hand hastily on a napkin, she jumped to her feet just as I stepped around the table to greet her.

"Olivia. Thank you so much for—"

SMACK!

Rather than embracing me, Olivia had reared like an angry cobra and slapped me across the face as hard as she could. The blow rang through my cheekbone and rattled inside my head, making me stagger.

"Liv! What the bloody hell did you do that for?" I gasped.

Olivia let forth a mad cackle of incredulous laughter. "What did I do that for? You're lucky I don't kill you where you stand, after everything you've put us through over the last few months!"

"Liv, I'm sorry, I—"

"You're sorry? You're sorry?! Is that all you can say, after dragging our clan name through the absolute gutters, all because you couldn't keep your bloody hands to yourself? How could you, Finn? And with her of all people! She and that mad sister of hers stole our family's Council seat! They've destroyed our reputation and now you've gone and taken what's left of it and stomped all over it, and then you had the utter gall to summon me here like some kind of—"

"Liv, get a grip on yourself," I snapped. "People are staring."

It was true. Tourists had frozen on the pavement on either side of the street, mouths hanging open, gaping at us openly. The presence of gawking strangers was just enough to bring Olivia to her senses, and she sank slowly back into her chair.

Still tensed in case she struck again, I lowered myself into the chair across from her. When she did not speak first, I took the chance to get a word in. "I didn't summon you here. If I recall from our email exchange, I begged fairly shamelessly. That said, I know I had no right to expect you to come, so thank you."

"Don't you dare thank me," Olivia grumbled. "I'm not here for you. No one in our family has had the chance to speak with you since this all happened, and I didn't want to miss the opportunity to make sure you knew just how angry we all are."

"Message received," I said, rubbing ruefully at my still throbbing cheek.

Olivia's face crumpled, and I knew that tears had sprung up behind those oversized sunglasses. "Oh, Finn, how could you?" she whispered. "Is it… is it even true?"

"Yes. It's true," I replied.

She dropped her head into her hands with a groan.

"Liv, listen to me. This wasn't some stupid fling. I would never risk everything for a dalliance. I'm in love with her, Liv." The words did not come easily—my sister was not a person in whom I'd ever confided much, and perhaps it was this that pulled her up short.

"In love? In love with Jess Ballard? You can't be serious, Finn."

"I am. I am serious. As serious as I've ever been in my life. Come on, Liv, you know me. We haven't always gotten along, but you're my sister and you know who I am. You know how seriously I take my calling—how badly I wanted to prove myself, to rise in the ranks of the Caomhnóir. It's all I've ever wanted. It's what I've worked toward my whole life. Do you honestly think I'd throw all of that away for nothing?"

"Haven't you?" she snapped.

"No. She's everything to me, Liv. I'm nothing without her."

Olivia pulled her sunglasses down over the bridge of her nose, staring into my eyes as though searching for something there. When she found it, her eyes went wide, and her lip started to tremble.

"Oh my God. You really are in love with her, aren't you?" she whispered.

"Yes."

"You idiot," she whispered, the tears escaping down her cheeks now. She flung off her sunglasses at last so that she could brush and bat the moisture from her face. "You fool, Finn Carey! How could you have fallen in love with her?"

"I didn't do it on purpose, I assure you," I said. "If love was the kind of thing you could overpower with reason, I'd have shaken it long ago, believe me. But there's nothing I can do, Liv. My fate was sealed from the moment I saw her."

Olivia was looking at me with a strange combination of dawning horror and pity, as though she'd only just this moment realized that her brother was capable of such a thing as falling in love.

"And I know our clans have clashed, Liv, but be reasonable. Jess is as much a victim of circumstances as we are. You don't have to like her, but you haven't got anything against her, not really. Marion is the reason everything's gone to hell for Clan Gonachd and you know it. She's always been too ambitious, too ruthless, and the only thing she's ever managed to earn for our family is a long list of enemies and a damn good case for treason."

Olivia folded her arms and glared at me but did not argue. Bless her, she was stubborn, but she wasn't stupid. Our mother and Marion had had more than one row in recent years over Marion's continued attempts to claw her way into higher positions of power. I had tried to steer well clear of it all, but word still got back to me. Peyton may have been undyingly loyal to her mother, but the rest of us knew that Marion was more of a liability than an asset these days. The truth was that we'd all be better off if Marion simply faded into obscurity and let Clan Gonachd lick its wounds and try to recover what dignity it could. But of course, we all knew her better than that.

"And I am sorry," I added, sensing her weakening just a bit. "I never meant to hurt you or anyone else in our clan. But surely you can see how ludicrous it is for all of us to have to keep living like this? The Prophecy is over. There's no more reason to fear Caomhnóir and Durupinen relationships! Why should Jess and I be punished for—"

"Because we have rules, Finn! Because we have laws, and they're supposed to apply to everyone! If you think I'm going to agree that we should throw out every tradition we have just so you can carry on with Jess Ballard—" Olivia began, firing up again.

"Okay, okay," I said, raising my hands in surrender. "Look, I didn't ask you here to argue. I just… I wanted to apologize. And I also wanted to ask you a favor."

Olivia's eyes narrowed to slits. "What kind of favor?"

"Are you going to Róisín Lightfoot's wedding?" I asked.

Olivia blinked, clearly confused at the sudden turn the conversation had taken.

"Of course I am. She's one of my best friends, you know that. She's asked both Peyton and me to be bridesmaids," she replied.

"And do you know if Jess or her sister Hannah will be there, too?" I pressed.

Olivia rolled her eyes. "Unfortunately, yes, they both will. I was helping Róisín with the seating chart only last week. She had no choice but to invite them, I suppose, though she certainly seems much keener on them than I am. But all the Council clans will be represented." She narrowed her eyes again. "Why do you ask?"

"I'm going to be there, too, Liv. At the wedding. The Lightfoots have enlisted additional security from the ranks at Skye and I've been selected for the detail."

Olivia stood up, looking angry again. "Finn Carey, if you are asking me to help you desert your post and run off with—"

"Of course not, now sit down, Olivia!" I hissed through clenched teeth. "I would never ask you to do something like that. Deserting my post would be a crime, and I would never involve you in something like that. I only want to see her, Liv. Five minutes, that's all I ask. I never... I never got to say goodbye."

The emotion nearly choked the words off, and I could feel the tears fighting their way to my eyes, despite my fierce efforts to resist them. It was this, perhaps, that made Olivia sink quietly back into her chair. I was quite sure she'd never seen her big brother cry once in her entire life.

"They'll never let you," Olivia said at last. "Seamus would flay you alive if he caught the two of you together. You'd lose every privilege you have. You'd probably never see the outside of Skye Príosún again."

"I know, but I've got to risk it, Liv. Please."

"How? How would you possibly pull it off?" Olivia asked, her voice cracking now.

"I don't know, that's why I need your help. I've never been to this estate where they're holding the wedding reception. Do you know anything about it? Have you ever seen it?"

Olivia nodded. "Yes, I've been there twice now, once for a tour with the other bridesmaids and once for a tasting."

"Well, can you think of anywhere you might have seen on the property, some outbuilding or something that we could use to meet?"

Olivia thought for a moment, then shook her head. "There's nothing close enough to the main house. They aren't using the grounds for the reception, and Jess would have to cross half an acre of open gardens before she got to any groundskeeper's sheds. She'd be spotted."

"What about the garages?" I asked.

Again, Olivia shook her head. "They're closer, but they'll be crawling with valets. The kitchen entrance is right there as well, so staff will be coming in and out."

I ran my hands through my hair, trying both to think and to stave off the feeling that this was all going to be impossible.

"Wait," Olivia said. "There might be another way, inside the main house."

"Inside? Liv, surely every inch of the place will be crawling with..."

"Not the top floor," she replied. "There's a whole floor that's off-limits to the public during events, but they showed us on the tour—just as a point of interest. There's a hidden staircase in the ladies' powder room off the main entrance hall and it leads up to a whole hallway of old servants' quarters."

"And there's no one up there? No staff or anything?" I asked, feeling the tiniest of sparks of excitement igniting in the pit of my stomach.

"None, as far as I could tell. They don't use it for anything now. It's like an attic," Olivia insisted, folding her arms across her chest, smiling smugly as though she'd just bested me in a round of chess.

"Do you think you could find a way to get Jess to meet me there during the reception?" I asked.

"Will you be able to get away? You'll be on duty, won't you?" Olivia asked, looking skeptical.

"We have a rotating break schedule. It's standard protocol. All the men will need to eat at some point, so they'll stagger our dinner breaks. I can slip away during mine, beg off to the loo or something," I said.

"How will I know what your schedule will be?" Olivia asked.

"I'll find a way to let you know, don't worry," I said. "Does that mean you'll do it?"

Olivia bit her lip. "I'm still furious with you!" she hissed.

"I understand that. You can be furious with me for the rest of your life, if it suits you. I won't complain. But please, Liv. Please do this for me."

She jiggled her knee rapidly, arms still crossed, face still knotted up as her anger and her love warred with each other. Finally, she let out a sound that was half-sigh and half-groan. "All right! All right, I'll do it. But Finn, know this, I will not take any unnecessary risks for you. If it looks like I might be caught, or if anything goes wrong, I'm going to walk away, and I'll deny this ever happened, do you understand me? Clan Gonachd will not sustain any more damage on your account, not if I can help it."

"I can't ask for more than that," I said. "Thank you, Liv. From the bottom of my heart, thank you."

"You can keep your thanks, I don't want them," she snapped, replacing her sunglasses and rising abruptly from her chair. She snatched her purse from the table and pointed to the undrunk cup of tea and the scone. "You'll handle that, of course," she said.

I smirked. "Of course."

"What's this then, Carey?" a voice called from behind me.

I turned to see Jensen and Knox loping up the pavement toward us, their faces alight with knowing smiles. I swore under my breath.

"All right, lads?" I asked, trying to smile back.

"So, who's this then, Carey? Surely, you couldn't have charmed a complete stranger into a date in less than half an hour?" Knox jeered.

"Oh, I don't know, she don't look that charmed to me, to be honest," Jensen said, grinning. "All right, darlin'?"

"You must be a right prat, Carey, meeting her here," Knox added. "We all know how you landed on Skye. What's to stop us from alerting the superiors that you're still breaking the Code of Conduct right under their noses?"

I stood up, but it was Olivia who surged forward, Olivia who pulled off her sunglasses and gave them a vicious glare which, by all rights, ought to have melted them where they stood. "I'm his sister, you knuckle-dragging cretins," she spat at them. "And unless you'd like me to lodge a formal complaint with your Commander about your behavior on leave, you'll sod off and find another female to harass with your pathetic slavering."

"This isn't Fairhaven, love," Knox replied, his face clouding over.

TALES FROM THE GATEWAY

"You won't find the kind of bowing and scraping you're accustomed to in your cozy little castle, not out here on this rock."

Olivia gave him a look of pure disdain. "Well, then, that explains why you've been left here to rot on your precious 'rock,' now, doesn't it?"

She turned to me. "Take care of yourself, Finn." And with a curt nod at me and one last, withering look at Knox and Jensen, she stormed off, leaving, as she often did, a loaded silence in her wake.

§

Oddly enough, it was Olivia's presence on Skye that first clued me in that something was amiss amongst the ranks at the *príosún*. It started that afternoon on leave, as we sat in the pub, trading rounds of pints and trying to forget where we were. Knox, Jensen, and Wells were griping back and forth, lamenting their lot in being stuck where they were. This I was used to; resentment was thick in the air at Skye, which was no surprise. But as I listened, the conversation took an odd turn.

"...where they get off talking to us like that. Like we don't put our bloody lives on the line every day keeping them safe." Knox was saying.

"They don't know the half of it. What if we just stopped doing our jobs, eh? Just opened up the cells and let all those Necromancers out? They'd stop their sneering right quick, wouldn't they?" Wells roared.

"Christ, keep it down, Wells," West said, slapping Wells on the arm. "The Code of Secrecy, mate…"

"Hang the Code of Secrecy!" Wells replied, wiping his mouth and signaling the barkeep for another round. "Hang the Code of Conduct. Hang the whole bloody system."

"Hang it all," Jensen agreed in slurred tones.

"I reckon Carey knows what I'm talking about don't you, mate?" Wells shouted, raising his glass to me from across the bar. "He's been screwed good and proper by the Code of Conduct, haven't you? I reckon you'd like to tell a few Durupinen where they can shove their bollocking rules and codes, wouldn't ya?"

"Nah, not Carey," Jensen said with a dismissive laugh. "He's still half in love with one, isn't he? I bet he'd lay right down and beg if she asked him to."

I kept my head down and refused to engage, though I'd have loved nothing more than to properly introduce both of their faces to my right hook. I'd seen them in sparring practice and knew beyond a shadow of a doubt that I'd have them both out cold on the pub floor before they could remember how to make a fist, and that was when they were sober. To do it when they were pissed like this wouldn't have been sportsmanlike, even if it would have been enjoyable.

"I reckon Booker's got the right idea, after all," Knox went on, bored with my lack of reply. "I reckon we ought to see what he's on about, don't you think?"

"What about Booker?" West asked. "What's this load of tosh, then?"

"Booker don't think we should take it lying down. He says we could band together... fight back," Knox replied in a ridiculous stage whisper.

"Fight back against who?" West asked, chuckling.

"The system," Knox replied, nodding his head seriously, but spoiling the effect by belching.

"Yeah, okay," West said, rolling his eyes. "Good luck with that, mate."

"Don't get all high and mighty with me, Westingbrook," Knox said, firing up and sneering his way through West's full surname. "You think Booker's full of shite? You ought to listen to what he's got to say. He's got ears to the ground, mate. He's heard some things that would make you stop and think why you tolerate your lot the way you do."

"Booker's a prat and so are you," West said dismissively. "Keep your head down and that big mouth shut, Knox, before you find yourself in a cell instead of guarding them."

"I might take me chances," Knox muttered, taking a swig from his fresh pint. "You ought to listen the next time you make your rounds, West. Seems the best ideas are coming from inside the cells these days."

"Ah, piss off," West said, and slid off his stool, laughing and shaking his head.

"What's Knox on about?" I asked as West came to sit down beside me.

"Ah, don't listen to him, he's pissed."

"But what was he saying about Booker?" I pressed. "He's one of the deputy Commanders, isn't he?"

"That's right," West said. "You haven't had to interact with him much, have you? He handles disciplinary action, mostly, and you've been a proper angel since you got here." West chuckled good-naturedly. "Yeah, Booker's a real bitter type. Rumor is he got sent here for abandoning his post with his pledged clan. Not sure what happened, or if it's true. Anyway, he's got a real sore spot when it comes to the Durupinen, especially the Council. I reckon he bad-mouths them a fair bit."

"Bad-mouths the Council?" I asked, eyebrows raised. "And he's in leadership? How does that work?"

"Out here, it don't matter much," West said, shrugging. "We don't have much occasion to interact with the Council, or Durupinen at all, for that matter. Booker is good at what he does, which is whipping troops into shape, so if he's a bit... well, hostile, what does it matter?"

"Whipping them into shape for what, though?" I asked. "If it's not to reform themselves and better serve the clans, what's it all for?"

West shrugged again, clearly undisturbed by the turn the conversation had taken. "Dunno. You want another?" he asked, nodding at my nearly empty pint.

"No, I'm all right. Cheers, mate," I said, and he slumped off to the bar, leaving me with my own thoughts.

§

Knox had planted the seed in my mind, and I now began to view my environment through an entirely different lens. Certain patterns began to emerge, and I filed them away with increasing concern. The way the men talked about Durupinen, for example, began to leap out to me. More and more, I would pick up on comments and jokes, and the tone was far more troublesome than anything I'd ever heard in the barracks back at Fairhaven. I also noticed that, over the weeks, the most vocal of these men seemed to be assigned, more and more, to the highest security Necromancer wards. This struck me as odd. When I had first arrived, the rotation through the wards had been fairly regular, but increasingly, we seemed to have settled into smaller spheres of duty. Knox, Wells, and Jensen, I noticed, were regularly assigned together and to the same few wards. When I mentioned it to West, he shrugged it off as he did most things.

"What does it matter?" he said, barely taking his eyes off of his steak and kidney pie. "The less I have to deal with the Necromancer scum in those wards, the better, I say. Let them lot deal with it."

But all I could think about was what Knox had said at the pub: "The best ideas are coming from inside the cells these days." If any Caomhnóir could find common ground with a Necromancer, he wasn't one I trusted to be in charge of them.

The next thing I noticed—and it raised my hackles at once—was an increase in transfers of Necromancer prisoners. All of a sudden, more and more, I was seeing them being led from their cell blocks to the interrogation rooms or the Commander's wing. I'd have thought nothing of it six months ago—perhaps a recent breakthrough in Tracker investigations meant they were needed for more questioning. And yet, I saw no Trackers on the premises during these transfers. I wondered if my isolation at Skye was making me paranoid, and yet, I could not shake my increasing concerns. It felt like nearly every day, I saw or heard something that sent alarm bells jangling away inside my head.

One night in early May, I was finishing up my shift in one of the high-security spirit wards. Truth be told, I hated working the spirit wards. The prisoners didn't need to sleep, and so their moans, pleas, and rants were nearly incessant. It was a brutal place to be assigned a double, and I had a pounding headache that night as I descended the staircase on my way back to the bunks, thinking only of taking two paracetamol and falling face-first into my pillow. The pain in my head was so bad that I almost didn't notice the open door. I would have walked right past it, if Booker hadn't appeared.

The door led, I knew, to a lecture hall used for occasional trainings. As I rounded the corner to the landing, Booker marched up from the lower half of the staircase and slipped into the room, giving me a curt nod and closing the door behind him. Before he had closed it, though, I caught a glimpse of what was happening inside: a darkened room, a group of perhaps a half dozen Caomhnóir, candles, a Circle upon the floor. As the door shut, one of the men looked up, and I locked eyes with Knox. Then the door had closed, the handle had latched, and I was left alone on the landing with nothing but the lingering smell of burning sage in my nostrils and a litany of questions running through my mind. Not wanting to draw attention to myself, I continued down the staircase, my formerly exhausted brain now wide awake and reeling.

TALES FROM THE GATEWAY

Caomhnóir were regularly drilled in the practicing of Castings, but not at two o'clock in the morning, and not by Booker, who was not in charge of training, and anyway, there were no trainings on the official schedule until Thursday next. I also knew that Knox was supposed to be in bed at the moment, having worked the previous shift, according to the schedule. What the bugger was going on?

All hope of sleep now gone, I proceeded not to my bed, but to the assignment board outside of the Commanders' offices. Carefully, I read through the full schedule of shift assignments and activities for the day, noting the changes that had been made in red pen since I'd last looked at it, which indicated swaps or sick leave. As I had suspected, no trainings were being held anywhere in the *príosún* that night, and Knox was not currently on shift.

Next, I hurried back to the bunks, where an official sign-in was posted. Every time we finished a work shift and were signing in for a sleep shift, we had to sign the log, which was then verified by the shift Commanders at the time of shift change. There on the log, was Knox's name, meaning he was supposed to be in bed. I scanned the list and slipped into the dormitory, making note of the empty beds. I reconfirmed them against the posted list and found seven beds were empty that were supposed to be occupied, Wells and Jensen among them. And the initials of the Commander who had accounted for them all? Booker.

I stood there for a moment, unsure of what to do. Every instinct I had was screaming at me that something wasn't right, but how ought I to proceed? Surely the top of the command chain—people like Eamon Laird—would want to be alerted if shifts were being improperly regulated? Perhaps he even knew about it, and could offer a rational explanation as to what I had seen? I decided to retreat to my bunk, see what time the missing Caomhnóir returned, and go see Eamon in the morning, when he was sure to be in his office.

I took the pain-killers for my headache, but sleep did not follow. I lay in my bed, my entire body tensed, my eyes staring up at the ceiling, waiting for the sounds of boots. About an hour later, the door opened and all seven of the missing Caomhnóir returned to their bunks together, whispering to each other. I could not make out a word of their conversation, but found it telling that they returned as a group. When I got up in the morning and checked the log, not a single trace appeared that any of them had been absent from the dormitory for any length of time. On paper, they'd all been in bed for the duration of the night. My mind made up, I stopped in the mess hall to force down my portion of breakfast, and then made straight for the Commanders' offices.

I found Eamon at his desk, head bent over a pile of papers, a pencil clamped tightly between his teeth. When I knocked on his open door, he looked up and let the pencil fall into his hand.

"Carey?"

"Yes, sir. I wonder if I might have a word?"

"If you must. Come in, then."

I entered the office, but my nerves would not allow me to sit. "Sir, I noticed something a bit odd last night, and I felt it my duty to bring it up to you, in the interest of security."

Eamon put down his pencil, scowling at me. "Is that right?"

"Yes, sir."

"Well, go on then, Carey. Let's have it."

And I explained, in as much detail as I could, what I had seen on my way down from the spirit ward, and also the inconsistencies in the logs and shift reports. Eamon listened to me with a completely impassive face, betraying so little reaction that I might have been giving my report to a statue rather than a living, breathing Commander.

"Is that all?" he asked when I was done.

"I... yes, sir. I think that's everything."

"Let me ask you a question, Carey. Do you think you are personally aware of every gathering, meeting, schedule change and event that occurs within the walls of this fortress?"

"I... no, sir. I don't presume to possess that kind of knowledge."

"That's right. You're at the bottom of the heap here, Carey. This place is full of activity, most of which does not concern you in the slightest."

I shifted uncomfortably from one foot to the other. Did this mean he knew about the gathering I had witnessed? Was I relaying information he already had?

"I understand that, sir. I was just concerned that the information on the log didn't match up with—"

"Was that log signed?" Eamon asked, cutting me off.

"Yes, sir."

"By a Commander?"

"Yes, sir. Commander Booker."

"I see. So, have you come down here to call Commander Booker's integrity into question?"

"No, sir. I simply wanted to..."

"Let me explain something to you, Carey," Eamon said, and his tone sharpened considerably. "Your Council clan status seems to have given you the false impression that anyone in this fortress gives a good goddamn about your opinions. We don't. I don't care one whit about your bloodline, your pedigree, or how many goddamn laws your mummy has passed. Here, you're only as good as your word and your work ethic. You understand me?"

"Yes, sir."

"Whatever you've cooked up in your mind, whatever conspiracy theory you've convinced yourself of that puts you on some kind of moral high ground over your peers, you can forget about it. You've been assigned here to keep your head down and do as you're bloody well ordered, do you hear me?"

"Yes, sir."

"Now get out of my office and don't presume to waste my time again, unless you'd like to find yourself on another double tonight."

"Understood, sir," I replied, nodding my head and backing out of the office, closing the door behind me.

Out in the hallway, my heart and mind were racing. Eamon's words, far from convincing me to forget about what I'd seen, had only convinced me more thoroughly that something was wrong. More alarming still, the leadership was in on it, and that meant that there was no one left to tell, no one to whom to report.

I was so distracted that I turned the corner and nearly walked right into Booker, who was on his way back into the offices. His face, when he saw me, turned instantly to stony disapproval.

"Carey," he said with a curt nod. He was carrying the clipboard with the shift log on it. He did not miss my eyes flicking involuntarily to it and then away again.

"Good morning, sir," I replied, returning the nod and then walking on. I could feel his eyes on my retreating back all the way down the corridor until I turned the corner.

It was as though the walls of the *príosún* were closing in around me. I couldn't be sure who I could trust, or what I could tell them. Even West, whom I considered something akin to a friend, wouldn't be safe to confide in anymore. He was too easy-going, too trusting of everyone. There wasn't a thing he couldn't find a way to shrug off, and while this was sometimes admirable, now it felt downright dangerous. I had never felt so isolated in all my time at Skye.

Even as I felt that isolation begin to close in around me, a ray of hope burst through my chest, and I clung to it like a drowning man to a life preserver. In a few short weeks, fate willing, I would see Jess. Even if only for a few minutes, we would be able to speak to each other. There was no one in the world I trusted like I trusted her. If I could relay this information to her, make her understand the significance of what I had witnessed amongst the ranks of the Caomhnóir here, I knew she would find a way to raise the alarm. It was not the way I had envisioned spending our few stolen moments together, but now it was clear that she was my only chance.

My immediate panic seemed to calm itself. There was a path forward. Get to Jess. Tell her everything. Trust that she would pass the information along to the right person. If I could just keep my head down that long, avoid any more suspicion, and keep my eyes peeled, I might just be okay.

More than ever before, I found myself counting the seconds until we would see each other again. Only now, it was more than just my heart that depended upon our reunion: it might just be the safety of the entire Northern Clans.

7

HANNAH'S STORY

"HANNAH, TALK TO ME."

"No."

"Please, sweetness."

"NO!"

I was pressing my pillow over my head with every ounce of strength I had, but it still wasn't enough to keep Milo's voice out.

"Come on. I can't keep apologizing indefinitely. At some point, you're going to have to forgive me."

"No, I don't. I can do this forever. I'll walk around with this pillow on my head for the rest of my life. I'll start a new fashion trend," I sniffed.

"Hmmm... edgy, but I'm not sure it would catch on," he replied in a mock-thoughtful voice that made me want to throttle him.

"Very funny. Now go away."

He didn't answer, but I knew he was still there. I could feel him, his energy pushing and prodding against the pillowcase, willing it aside. I waited, holding my breath. Finally, I heard him sigh dejectedly, and the sound was like a punch in the gut. "Fine. Take a little time. I'll come and check on you in a bit."

Don't, I thought to myself. Please don't.

It had been one week. One week since he'd... made his decision. I still couldn't bear to think about it, even though I knew that my best friend was right there in the room with me—that he wasn't really gone for me the way that he was gone for other people. This knowledge didn't soften the blow at all—if anything, it made me feel worse. I remained, despite his best efforts, utterly inconsolable.

Of course, I hadn't known he was still earthbound at first, because he'd had no idea what the hell he was doing. It took him a full two days to realize where he was, and another two days to figure out how to manifest himself, how to move around, and how to focus his energy in such a way that he could reach out to me. Meanwhile, I'd spent four days crying constantly, refusing to eat, and reaching out into the mental space around me, tugging on energies and bright spots, searching for any sign of him, hoping I would find him but also hating myself for hoping it. And when I finally found him, and he finally grasped enough about his state to show himself, I wanted nothing more than to never have found him at all.

I know. That sounds really messed up. But hear me out before you write me off as the worst best friend in the history of ever.

The guilt had always been the worst part of what I could do. Unless you've experienced it, you just can't imagine it. Most people would assume that being scared frequently is the worst part, but they'd be wrong. It's unpleasant, of course, being confronted with ghosts just popping up out of nowhere—like living in a low-budget horror movie that relies on cheap jump scares to keep you on the edge of your seat. And there is an element of that—of living life permanently on the edge of your seat. But the truth is that human beings can get used to almost anything. We're surprisingly adaptable like that. And so, by the time Milo... left... and then came back, I was quite accustomed to living life on the edge of my seat. I made the edge as comfortable as I could and settled in for the long haul, because if one thing was clear, it was that the spirits, however they had found me, were not going away.

No, the worst part was not the sudden entrances or the sometimes gruesome appearances. It has always been the guilt, pure and simple. I understood guilt at an age when most children have scarcely understood that other people possess feelings at once as strong and tender as their own, and it all stemmed from the fact that spirits didn't simply appear to me: they needed me for reasons none of them could properly explain.

Imagine being four years old and having grown adults appearing to you in the night like monsters from under your bed, begging for your help. Imagine sitting in school trying to take a third-grade spelling test with a ghost standing behind you, demanding you look them in the eye when they're talking to you, you insolent brat. Imagine trying to navigate the horror of a seventh-grade girls' locker room, dying of shame as a ghost follows you into the shower in its quest for your undivided attention. And through it all, what I felt more than anything was guilt—guilt because they all seemed to think that I alone could help them... and I had absolutely no idea what they were talking about. I'd lived with the guilt of that—of my inability to give them what they needed—since I could remember.

But this guilt I felt now, about Milo, was an entirely new animal—a beast I didn't know how to wrestle with. Because never before had someone I'd known chosen to become a ghost because of what I could do. Just thinking the thought made my skin crawl and my stomach heave and my head want to explode. It was unbearable.

"But I knew there was a chance I could still be here for you!" he had told me when he appeared for the first time, his voice tinged with an incomprehensible note of pride.

For me. For me. He wanted to leave everything except me. And so, he did.

I rolled to my side and vomited right over the end of my bed and then spent the next hour scrubbing the carpet with violently shaking hands until my fingertips were red and raw.

The next day I dragged myself to group, not because I wanted to be there, but because dragging myself was preferable to someone else dragging me, which is what would have happened if I hadn't shown up. Dr. Mulligan had already hinted at a meeting with my team to "reassess my services," which was group-home-speak for "you'd better get your shit together and show us you're coping or we're going to medicate/transfer you." I'd had this threat made to me so many times over the years in so many different settings that I could see it coming just by the way someone cleared their throat or looked over the top of their glasses at me. I had also become very adept at convincing people I was coping—at least, until the next public spirit encounter that I was unable to convincingly ignore.

As usual, everyone at group treated me like I had a particularly virulent strain of leprosy. In fact, it seemed to be worse today. They weren't even bothering to keep their whispers to a level I could reasonably pretend to ignore.

"Jesus, she looks like hell..."

"Surprised she hasn't offed herself..."

"Should she even be here..."

Dr. Mulligan shot them all reproving looks before turning and smiling at me, patting the chair beside her, inviting me silently to sit down while also singling me out as someone she might need to "handle" during our session. I dropped resignedly into the chair, folding my legs up onto the seat and resting my chin on my knees, hoping that a closed-off physicality might send the signal for people to just leave me alone. The chair next to me on the other side remained empty as the rest of the kids settled into their seats, and Dr. Mulligan, looking over at it in vague confusion, gave a quiet gasp. I knew right away what had happened.

She had miscounted. That was supposed to be Milo's seat, but Milo was no longer there to sit in it.

She stood up, face flushed pink, and reached out to pull the chair out of the circle, but I placed a hand on it.

"No," I said quietly.

"What's that, Hannah?" Dr. Mulligan asked, attempting to keep her smile pasted on her face, but failing.

I looked up at her and felt a possessive kind of anger blaze up behind my eyes. "Leave it," I said.

She looked as though she wanted to argue with me, as though this might be some sort of learning moment for the group that she could seize on. I could almost hear the line of inquiry forming in her head."Let's all talk about Hannah's feelings. Why don't you want me to take the chair, Hannah? Talk to me about the empty chair, Hannah. What does it represent to you?" But just as she opened her mouth to say it, she looked into my eyes and her face went quite pale.

"No," I whispered again. Inside my head, I was screaming at her. "If you take his chair... if you dare take his chair and erase him like that, I swear to God, woman..."

Dr. Mulligan withdrew her hand and swallowed hard before sitting back down. "Well, shall we get started, everyone?" she asked, a little too loudly.

I kept my hand on the chair, just in case.

Meghan started, as I knew she would, because Meghan wasn't happy unless group turned into a breathless, captive audience bent on analyzing her every private thought. Milo couldn't stand her. He called her a "Look-At-Me," one of his made-up categories for the kids who populated places like New Beginnings. The description had never been more apt than it was that day, as Meghan, who had barely had a passing acquaintance with Milo, launched into a ten-minute monologue detailing her devastation over his death. By the time she was finished, punctuated by lots of nodding and sympathetic noises from Dr. Mulligan and a few of the other kids,

I wanted to leap across the circle like some kind of jungle cat and slap the phony tears right off her cheeks.

"Hey, thanks for saving my seat," came Milo's voice. I managed not to look, but rather felt him settle into the chair beside me, and I quickly pulled my hand away. I wanted to shout for him to leave, that he was only making this worse, but of course, I couldn't do that in a room full of people. Instead, I pressed my lips together and pulled my hood up over my head in a gesture I hoped he would interpret as, "Leave me the hell alone." If he noticed, he ignored it.

From the corner of my eye, I could see him shaking his head at Meghan. "Someone slap this girl. Can you believe her? 'A hole in her life' without me? Oh, please. Histrionic personality disorder, table for one."

I covered an involuntary snigger with a cough, then cursed myself. It would only encourage him if he thought I was listening. Thankfully, no one else in the circle seemed to have noticed my slip-up. Meghan was still rambling on, twisting a strand of over-processed blonde hair around one of her fingers and sniffling theatrically into a wad of tissue.

"Remember when she started flirting with me over the summer, to make Jacob jealous?" Milo went on snorting with quiet laughter. "And when I told her I wasn't into girls, she insisted that gay boys were just boys who hadn't met the right girl yet, and that she could convince me if I'd just go back to her room and make out with her? And then when I refused, she wrote 'Faggots will burn in hell' on the door of my room in permanent marker? Ah, good times, good times."

I maintained a straight face this time, but it was a close call. I'd just managed to completely compose myself when Milo let out a sound like an angry cat.

"Did she... did she write my name on her hand in Sharpie?" His voice rose to an absolute shriek of incredulity. I looked over and, sure enough, amongst her usual array of self-inflicted skin graffiti, Meghan had scribbled Milo's name onto the back of her hand, enclosed in a heart.

It happened in the blink of an eye. Once second, Milo was sitting beside me, fuming, and the next second, he was across the circle in front of Meghan. I could feel his energy building like the pressure in the atmosphere, making my ears pop.

"Milo, don't!" I blurted out.

Suddenly, the soda can in Meghan's hand exploded. Lemon-lime soda sprayed into the air like a geyser, soaking her face and splattering everyone around her. Colleen squealed and fell sideways out of her seat. Jacob swore and jumped up, throwing his arms over his head. Milo, however, shot back into his seat, a terrified look on his face.

"Holy shit, did... did I do that?" he whispered.

Everyone else, however, was now looking at me.

"What... how did you... what the fuck, freak?" Meghan shouted, pointing at me.

Dr. Mulligan held up a hand. "Meghan, that's enough, that language is completely—"

But Meghan was hysterical. "Didn't you hear her?" she shrieked, pushing dripping wet hair out of her eyes and pointing dramatically at me. "She... she said something about Milo and then my soda exploded!"

"Your soda exploded because of carbonation, Meghan," Jacob snorted. "Jesus Christ, get a grip."

"But didn't you hear her?!"

"What, so people can't talk now?"

"I'm telling you, she did it! She doesn't belong in here with normal people! Why isn't she locked up?" Meghan shrieked.

Jacob laughed. "Are you actually calling yourself normal now?"

"Shut the FUCK up, Jake!" Meghan shouted, rounding on him now.

"You probably shook the can before you opened it," Jacob said.

"It was already open when I sat down!" Meghan shouted back.

"That's enough, both of you!" Dr. Mulligan was also shouting now. Meghan jumped out of her seat and strode over to Jacob, tossing the can to the floor and spilling the rest of the contents on Colleen's purse, causing her to start swearing and shouting, too.

Under cover of the chaos, I slipped out of my chair and fled the room, closing my door behind me. The door, of course, was no deterrent for Milo.

"Look, Hannah, I'm sorry, I didn't mean to—"

"You can't do stuff like that, Milo!" I hissed at him. "You're going to get me in trouble!"

"I don't even know what I did!" Milo cried. "Or how the hell I did it! What happened in there?"

"Just because you don't have a body anymore doesn't mean you can't touch things!" I snapped, still fighting to keep my voice low, desperate not to draw any more attention to myself. "Ghosts have a lot of power. It's your... your energy. You can concentrate it, you can focus it on things and manipulate them."

"I can?" Milo asked, a smile dawning on his face.

"Yes. Especially when you're experiencing really strong emotions. But you'll be tired and drained after you do it."

Milo's smile slipped just a little. "Yeah. Yeah, now that you mention it, I do feel a little... hey, what should I try next?" He floated over to my desk and bent low over a pencil, trying to move it across the surface.

"Nothing! Don't try anything! Just stop!"

"Why?"

"Because the last thing I need is even more weird shit happening around me!" I cried. "Do you want to get me sent to solitary, or worse, kicked out and sent to the state hospital?"

"No, of course I..."

"Then stop with the poltergeist tricks!" I begged.

"Okay!" Milo said, zipping away from my desk and raising his hands up in surrender. "Okay, I'm sorry, I'll stop!" He lowered them and smiled. "But at least you're looking at me!"

I crossed my arms and scowled at him. "Only because you tricked me."

"I didn't trick you!" Milo insisted. "But hey, isn't this preferable to the pillow thing?"

My eyes filled with tears. "You don't get it, Milo."

"What don't I get? Explain it to me!"

"I don't want to see you like this!"

"But—"

Both of us froze as we heard the handle on my door jiggle. Milo vanished on the spot just as the door swung open. A beautiful, blonde, statuesque girl stood on the threshold clutching a suitcase in one hand.

"Carley!" I gasped. "What are you doing here? I thought..."

"You thought I was done with this place? Yeah. Me, too."

She brushed past me to the bed that used to be hers and heaved her suitcase up onto it. Carley had been my roommate at New Beginnings until about three months earlier when she had been cleared and released to go home. Her half of the room had been empty ever since. Every day I'd expected to walk in and find myself with a new roommate, but it had never happened. Colleen told anyone who would listen that she'd overheard two of the nurses talking and saying that Carley's parents had continued to pay for the space, because beds in programs like New Beginnings were in high demand and they wanted to make sure she had a guaranteed place to go.

"You know, because, like, all they do is travel. They can't be bothered to take care of her if she, like, relapses or whatever," she had insisted.

"Rich people are such trash," Jake had added.

"Shut the fuck up, Jake, your parents are loaded and everyone knows it," Meghan added with a well-practiced roll of her eyes.

"Hey, my dad owns a couple of auto body places," Jake replied, firing up at once. "He does alright, sure, but not like Carley's parents. They've got more money than they can spend."

Everyone knew that Carley's family was really rich. Her parents were famous socialites and Carley had exploited her family's position into an enormous social media following that hung breathlessly on her every update. Her stints in and out of places like New Beginnings were nothing more than dramatic episodes in the weird internet reality show that was her life. The staff even allowed her phone access—which was supposed to be prohibited—just so she could manage her views and comments. She even made money off them, getting paid stupid amounts to endorse stuff as an "influencer." Everyone around her was rabid to bask in just a single reflected ray of her fame, which was weird, when you saw how much she actually hated all of it.

"It's not that I'm not happy to see you, but... what happened?" I asked Carley as she opened the suitcase and started putting clothes away in her drawers.

"Life," Carley sighed. "Turns out there was more of it out there than I remembered. You probably read all about it, didn't you?"

Carley always assumed that everyone followed her exploits religiously, which I suppose must just be a mindset that famous people get. The truth was that I'd never spent more than a few sad moments scrolling through her posts on a rec room computer before deciding I didn't want to contribute to the system that, as far as I could tell, was slowly crushing her twenty-four-seven under pressure so powerful it was a miracle she hadn't already been reduced to Carley-dust. But the other kids at New Beginnings had made no such decisions, and so all the details trickled down to me eventually. Partying. A much older playboy as her on-again, off-again paramour. Feuds with other social media darlings. A viral paparazzi photograph in which her left breast was prominently featured. About five million comments that somehow seemed to suggest, at the same time, that she was way too skinny and also had gained a ton of weight.

I nodded and left it at that. I really didn't want her to have to go into the details. Instead, I just asked, "Are you okay?"

She shrugged again. "You know," she said. "The usual."

She started hanging gorgeous designer pieces in the closet next to my sweatshirts. Everything still had a tag on it, as though she'd stopped on her way over and walked into Bloomingdale's with an empty suitcase. "Anyway, what are you asking about me for? I feel like I should be asking about you."

I frowned. "About me? Why?"

She stared at me. "What do you mean, why? Hello? I heard about Milo."

I swallowed hard. "Oh. Yeah."

"That must have sucked," she said. The words sounded trite and dismissive, but she didn't mean them that way. That was just how she talked. Her eyes, as she looked at me, were full of sympathy.

"Yeah, it did. It still does," I admitted.

"I hope he at least had a chance to tell that dick of a father of his off before he went," Carley muttered.

I just shrugged. Milo had left a letter for his family. He didn't tell me what was in it, and I would never ask him. None of that belonged, in any way, to me.

"I see you're keeping things neat again," Carley pointed out, gesturing over to my side of the room, where evidence of my 'keeping things neat' or, as my doctors liked to call it, obsessive-compulsive disorder, was abundantly apparent. Every book, organized by color, size, and alphabetical order. Every pen and pencil lined up in perfect parallel lines. Every speck of dust scrubbed away, every fold of my sheets and blankets tucked and crisp and perfect. I'd had it under... well, not total control, but more control recently. I'd loosened my crushing grip on the defenseless inanimate objects in my life by degrees. I'd stopped focusing on creating right angles, allowed my pens to huddle together in a coffee mug, even left my bed unmade for a whole afternoon. But then, of course, Milo...

"Yeah," I said. "It's... um... yeah, I'm..."

Carley smiled knowingly. "Just a bit of spring cleaning, right?"

I smiled back. "Yeah. Just a bit."

Carley nodded, giving me a wink. "Looks good. So anyway, hopefully this is just temporary. Who knows, maybe we'll walk out together this time," she said, squeezing my shoulder.

She always said this to me, and she'd been in and out six times already since I'd met her. She knew I was never getting out, but it never stopped her from saying it. And honestly, in a weird way, I could sense palpable relief in her every time she walked back in and saw me standing there. There wasn't much Carley could count on, but she could count on her strange little roommate contained within these walls, waiting for her when she slipped up again.

"Come on, let's take a selfie! Reunited at last!" Carley said brightly, pulling out her phone and throwing her arm around me. As always, I looked at her before I looked at the camera.

"No posting?"

"No posting. Just for us," she said, crossing her heart, like I knew she would.

She flung her arm around me and we turned to the camera and smiled. Well, I smiled a bit. She made a sort of enigmatic expression that involved pursing her lips and sucking in her cheeks. She pressed the button and the image froze in time, a gorgeous blinding sun and its insignificant shadow, occupying little more than negative space beyond the reach of her glow.

Carley was one of the only kids in New Beginnings—or anywhere, really—who wasn't scared shitless to be around me. I'm not really sure why that was, but it was true. Nothing about my condition seemed to faze her. She barely batted an eyelash when I was less than successful at hiding a visitation, and she never demanded that I explain myself. In fact, for someone who had lived with me on and off for the better part of two years, she had asked me remarkably few personal questions. She knew I didn't follow her on social media, though, where every tiny detail of her life was packaged for public consumption, so maybe she was just returning the favor. I never pried, so neither did she.

I sometimes thought about how very easy it would have been for her to exploit our relationship for social media popularity. I mean, how many sympathy likes and shares could she have gotten on photos and updates of her chronically psycho little friend? But she never did it—never even mentioned me, and while that might make other people feel invisible, it made me feel safe.

Up close, unfiltered, unedited, I thought Carley looked as unhappy as I'd ever seen her. Even her army of makeup brushes couldn't hide the deep owlish rings under her eyes, nor the telltale puffy redness that only came from excessive crying. And once she had unpacked her things, she didn't, as was sometimes her habit, descend at once upon the rec room to bask in the attentions of the rest of the kids. Instead, she slid herself carefully into a pair of black leggings, cozy slipper socks, and a gray sweatshirt that had been intentionally cut and sewn back together so that it hung alluringly off one shoulder. Then she climbed into her bed, her movements strangely fragile, and commenced a long, silent scroll of her phone. Her face grew sadder and sadder the longer she looked at the screen.

I walked over, plucked the phone out of her hand, and handed her a book. She looked up at me, almost disoriented. "Why don't you unplug for just a teensy bit," I suggested to her. "All of that will still be there in a couple of hours."

"But I have to respond to—"

"No, you don't," I told her gently. "Don't respond. Don't even look at it for a bit. In fact, it will make you even more interesting than usual. Where's Carley? She's always here! She hasn't posted in hours! You'll be the talk of the internet just by doing nothing."

She smiled a little, nodded dazedly, took the book, and rolled over onto her side. I listened for a few minutes to her quiet breathing and the occasional turn of a page, and then I put the phone away in her top dresser drawer and snuck out of the room.

My gentle knock on Dr. Mulligan's door was met at once with a friendly, "Come in!"

I pushed the door open and peered around it. "Dr. Mulligan? Do you have a minute?"

"Hannah!" she replied, tossing her pen down and carefully closing the file she had been writing in. "I've always got a minute. Come on in. I was very nearly on my way down to see you."

"Oh. Well, I'm glad I saved you a trip, then," I said, closing the door carefully behind me. "I just wanted to talk to you for a second, about Carley."

"Oh yes," Dr. Mulligan said, shaking her head and draining the last of the coffee in her tumbler. "I'm so sorry about that. I meant to give you a heads up about Carley's return this morning in group, but things sort of... well..."

"Exploded?" I suggested.

"An apt word choice, yes," Dr. Mulligan replied, smiling appreciatively. "Anyway, you ought to have been informed that you were getting a roommate again. I apologize for the oversight."

"Oh, I'm not upset about that," I said, stepping around the armchair in front of the desk and dropping into it. There was no need to be asked to sit down in Dr. Mulligan's office. "I'm not complaining. I'm glad she's back... well, no, not really, but... you know what I mean."

"Yes, I know what you mean," Dr. Mulligan said with a small smile. "These aren't the circumstances in which we would have wanted to see her again."

"Right," I said, nodding. "And the thing is... well, it's about her phone privileges."

Dr. Mulligan frowned. "The decision to allow Carley her phone was not made lightly. If that's something you feel is unfair, you are free to bring it up with—"

"No, I'm not complaining!" I said, cutting her off. "I'm not asking for special treatment, and I don't care if Carley gets it. I know she's... well... famous."

I managed to stop myself from saying "rich," which I imagined would not have gone down so well. No one wants to be accused of treating people differently because of money. Dr. Mulligan was sharp, though, and I think she knew what I had very nearly said. She raised one eyebrow, and her tone warned me to tread carefully.

"What about the phone privileges, then?" she asked.

"I don't think the access to all the social media stuff is good for her," I blurted. "She gets kind of... obsessed with it. Phone calls and texting are a different story, but... have you ever even seen her accounts?"

Dr. Mulligan bristled. "I'm not one for that type of mindless entertainment."

"It's not mindless, and for someone like Carley, it's anything but entertaining. Every single picture or video she posts gets thousands and thousands of replies, and while lots of them are nice, nearly as many are really hateful and negative," I said, shuddering.

"Hateful how?" Dr. Mulligan asked.

"Like, just judgmental and awful. Telling her she's too fat, too thin, that she's ugly, that she needs plastic surgery, that she wears too little clothing, or that she should show more skin, it just goes on and on," I explained. "And some people might be able to ignore things like that, just choose not to read them, but... I don't think Carley can."

Dr. Mulligan considered this for a moment. "When Carley entered treatment here, it was made clear that she needed access to her phone for a variety of reasons. Those photos and videos you're talking about are a source of income for her. She's built a kind of internet brand for herself, and while I'm not entirely clear on how all of that works, it seems she has to continue interacting on those sites regularly in order to maintain her contracts."

"I understand all of that, but..."

"Her parents made it quite clear that unfettered access to social media was a stipulation of her admittance here."

"Why do they care?" I asked, feeling anger start to froth in the pit of my stomach. "They've got more money than they know what to do with! Whatever money she's making from her brand, it can't be more important than her getting better!"

"I will bring up your concerns at the next staff meeting," Dr. Mulligan said, her tone a bit clipped and dismissive. "But I don't expect they'll budge on that matter. Carley's parents were very clear..."

"Carley's parents aren't doctors!" I cried. "Why should what they want carry more weight than what Carley needs to get better?"

Dr. Mulligan did not reply, and in her silence was all the answer I needed.

"Money, huh? So, how much are they donating to the place?" I asked, folding my arms across my chest.

"Hannah, that is inappropriate. I shouldn't even be discussing this with you," Dr. Mulligan said, her face quite red now.

"But someone has to be advocating for her!" I cried, rising out of my chair. "Someone has to care more about whether she's okay than whether they can put an aquatherapy lounge in the east wing!"

"Enough!" Dr. Mulligan snapped, and I quickly sat again. She looked angrier than I'd ever seen her, and when she spoke again, I could barely hear her clipped and quiet words. "Thank you for bringing your concern to me. I will assess the situation, and perhaps suggest to Carley that she... allow herself some time each day to take a break from her various internet obligations."

I shook my head. "She won't do it. It's like an addiction, Dr. Mulligan, she's obsessed with..."

But the look on Dr. Mulligan's face effectively ended the conversation. It was no good. I'd done what I could do. "Anyway," I said, standing up, "thanks for listening."

I turned, but she stopped me. "Hannah, your concern for your friend is admirable, but you're not a medical professional. And in any case, I think your focus right now should be on yourself, how you are coping with Milo's death, and how you are going to move forward in your treatment."

"You're probably right," I said, automatically, because there was no point in contradicting her. "I'll, uh... start focusing on that."

She wasn't going to let me off this easily, and I knew it. Sure enough, she pressed onward.

"How are you doing? With everything?"

"Fine," I said.

"Hannah, you know that word isn't allowed in my office," Dr. Mulligan said sternly. "It either means nothing, or the exact opposite of what it should. Descriptors, please. Feeling words."

If I could have rolled my eyes without her seeing, I would gleefully have done so. Instead, I sighed resignedly and told her the part I could tell her. "I'm sad. Really, really sad. And lonely."

Dr. Mulligan gave me an encouraging smile. "We're all sad. But you'd be less lonely if you could bring yourself to participate a little more fully in the communal times. Play a card game. Watch a movie. Share a little more in group."

"No, that makes it worse."

"How?"

"Because Milo was the one I did all that stuff with. So, doing it alone just feels ten times worse than not doing it at all."

"But you aren't alone. All of the other residents are—"

"You heard Meghan today," I cut in. "She thinks I'm a freak. They all do. Why would I torture myself by trying to engage with them, just so they can watch me like a science experiment the whole time?"

"But if you don't even try, Hannah, if you don't make an effort to show them that you aren't what they—"

"I shouldn't have to! It's exhausting! Why is it on me to earn basic decency and respect? That should be a given. They should be the ones making an effort!"

"Why did you call out Milo's name today in group?" Dr. Mulligan asked suddenly, pulling me up short. I panicked, stalling for time for my brain to work.

"What?"

"You shouted out Milo's name right before the soda can exploded," Dr. Mulligan repeated. "What happened there?"

"That was... that was just a coincidence," I said, perhaps a bit too casually in my effort to repair the damage. "I was about to tell her off for using Milo like that, and she spilled her stupid soda."

"Using Milo like what?" Dr. Mulligan asked.

"Like he's a prop in her melodrama," I replied snappishly. "I'm sure you've realized this, but Meghan has an unprecedented talent for making everything about herself. She didn't care about him, and the only thing she'll miss about him is having one more body to drag into her self-penned romantic crises."

"Other people are allowed to grieve Milo in their own ways," Dr. Mulligan said reprovingly.

"She's not grieving, she's performing!" I shouted. "And that's exactly why Milo was..." I stopped myself, backtracking. "That's exactly what Milo would have said if he'd been there."

"You'll get through all of this easier if you let yourself realize that we all share in Milo's loss," Dr. Mulligan said softly. "It doesn't just belong to you. You don't have to bear it alone."

I laughed. It sounded hollow and empty and dead in my own ears. "Yes, I do."

"Have you thought any more about what we talked about? About the new treatment we discussed?"

I swallowed hard. A powerful antipsychotic med, just approved by the FDA for use in minors, and I was a prime candidate for the clinical trials. I'd been on drugs like it before, and they'd turned me into a zombie, though they had dulled the impact of spirit visitations as well, mostly by keeping me practically oblivious to the outside world. No, thank you. If I had to choose between being a head case and being a vegetable, I knew my choice.

"No," I said. "But I will."

And though she called after me, she allowed me to leave her office. When I returned to our room, I found Carley sound asleep, her phone back in her hand, and fresh tear tracks running through her makeup.

§

One of the good things about having Carley back was that Milo made fewer attempts to visit me in our room. He knew how hard it was to maintain a façade of sanity in front of Carley, and he didn't complicate matters by trying to talk to me while she was in the room. And she was in the room a lot—much more than on any other occasion when she'd checked in for a stint at New Beginnings. But even when Carley wasn't around, he didn't accost me. He just sort of hung out in the background, inviting conversation but never initiating it himself. Maybe it was because of the fiasco in group, but he stayed way back when the other students were nearby. He was probably afraid that he would accidentally blow something else up. He took to hanging around the back corner, occasionally trying to manipulate a pack of playing cards.

As for me, my feelings of guilt only multiplied. My best friend had remained earthbound as a ghost to stay with me, and I was ignoring him, punishing him for wanting to look out for me. What the fuck was wrong with me? What kind of heartless person does that? I was the only person he could possibly talk to, and I'd abandoned him. But seeing him like that... every glance, every conversation was like the jab of a knife between the ribs.

It's your fault, Hannah. Jab.

He stayed because of you, Hannah. Jab.

He never would have done it if he hadn't known what you could do. Jab. Jab. Jab.

It was unbearable. My anxiety began to spiral. I started looking desperately for a release, and before long, found myself looking down at my own arms, at the criss-crossing of little scars, wondering how it would feel to replace one pain with another, just for the relief. It had been several years since I'd coped in that way, and the fact that I had allowed the thought to pop back into my unguarded head made me feel sick and angry.

Meanwhile, everyone around me was watching me spiral, but no one could understand the real reason, because I couldn't tell anyone without convincing them I'd gone officially over the mental cliff they'd watched me teeter on for years. The doctors and staff eyed me with wariness and concern, while the other kids had all but broken out the tubs of popcorn waiting for me to snap. Every time

I tried to shift my attention outward, to distract myself from my own misery, all I could see was the staring and the concern. And as fragile as I felt, it was nothing to the way Carley was deteriorating.

I doubted Dr. Mulligan had said a single word to the board about the phone access for Carley, but if she had, it had made no difference. I did what I could to distract her, to engage her in any other activity, from board games to movies to any one of the dozens of classes and workshops offered to residents. Sometimes she drifted along to one with me, but more often than not, she stayed in bed, glued to her phone. The frustrating part was that she was doing everything required of her, as far as the doctors were concerned. She never missed a group or individual session. She participated and said all the right things. She ate the food they put on her plate, which they monitored closely, as disordered eating was one of Carley's many issues. As far as they were concerned, she was going right down their checklist, a complete success. But they didn't see the way she lay awake at night, the way she tumbled down a rabbit hole of self-loathing every time she picked up her phone or sat down in front of a computer. Carley had gone through these motions too many times, knew what she needed to do to keep the staff happy, and made sure she did it. Sure enough, a few short weeks later, she was packing up her bag again to return home, where her public socialite life was waiting, ready to swallow her whole once again.

Later, I wondered if she knew. As she packed her suitcase, as she chatted about where she was going to get dinner that night, about the party she was invited to on Saturday, about how her boyfriend was hinting about taking her away to Cabo for the weekend. I wondered if she knew, as she pulled me into a hug that felt like a cry for help.

I think she must have known.

Less than a month later, I was coming back in from the cafeteria when Milo popped up out of nowhere in the hallway, scaring the hell out of me and making me drop my cup of tea all over the floor.

"Damn it, Milo!" I shouted, before catching myself and dropping my voice. "You can't do that! You know you can't do that!" Down the hallway, through the open door to the rec room, I could see necks craning, curious faces looking to see what the commotion was.

"It's just me again!" I called loudly into the room, making them jump and look away. "Just crazy Hannah Ballard making a scene with another one of her invisible friends! Nothing to see here!"

"I'm sorry," Milo replied, crouching down so that he could talk to me as I sopped up the spilled tea with a wad of tissues from my cardigan pocket. "I didn't mean to freak you out. I just... I need to talk to you..."

"Milo, we already talked about this," I muttered. "I really just need you to—"

"I know we did, and I respect that. And I... I wouldn't even be here right now if it wasn't really important," Milo hissed.

"What could be so important that you couldn't just wait for me to get back to my room where I wouldn't cause a scene?" I muttered. The tissues were falling to pieces in the puddle of tea, making an even bigger mess. I sighed.

"I... well, that's the thing, really. I need you to... just don't go back to your room, okay?"

I chanced a glance up at Milo. "What do you mean, don't go back to my room?"

"Just... just don't, okay? Go do something else for a little while. Go to the rec room, or... or the reading room or something."

I frowned at him. "But why?"

"I just... can you just do this one little thing for me? I just need a little time to... just, please, Hannah, okay?"

I stared at him now, all pretense gone. He looked almost frantic.

"Tell me why."

"No."

"Milo, tell me!"

"No. Please, Hannah. Please, just listen to me."

We looked into each other's eyes for a long moment, trying to communicate without words. He was screaming at me, screaming at me to listen.

I should have listened.

Before I could even ask myself why I was doing it, why I was ignoring him when he was clearly trying to look out for me, I had jumped to my feet, abandoned my tea disaster in the middle of the floor and took off toward my room, Milo floating along behind me the whole way, shouting for me to stop, to listen...

I felt her there the moment I put my hand on the doorknob. Her energy shot through me like a bullet, and I turned to Milo. His face was so, so very sad.

"Don't, Hannah. Please."

I opened the door.

Carley was crouched in the corner of her bed, her back pressed to the wall. Her face was a tear-stained mess of makeup tracks, and her hair was a tangled nest. She was wearing a satin dress and one stiletto heel. When she looked up and saw me there, her eyes were wild, her voice echoing to me from a place I couldn't reach.

"Don't make me go back out there, Hannah! I can't go back out there!"

She flickered out of focus, then back into focus, like an image on a screen.

I didn't speak to her. I stepped out and shut the door again, muffling her cries.

"I'm so sorry," Milo whispered. "I'm so sorry, sweetness. I tried to warn you."

"When?" I managed to croak out, even as my throat seemed to swell shut against the howl of grief fighting to escape my mouth.

"I don't know," Milo replied, and I could hear the tears in his voice. I squeezed my eyes shut so that I wouldn't have to see them. "I honestly don't. I just felt the energy in the building shift, and I knew there was another... someone else like me here. I followed the traces and I found her there, in your room. I didn't know what to do, but I thought, maybe if I could get her out of there before you saw her... Oh, sweetness, I am so sorry."

The ground beneath my feet felt like quicksand. The entire hallway seemed to be spinning. Not only could I not cry, not scream, but I also couldn't breathe. Blackness was gathering around the edges of my vision. Vaguely, I heard a voice, footsteps coming toward me.

"Hannah?! Hannah, are you alright?!"

"Carley... Carley..."

"What about Carley? Hannah, take a deep breath, honey."

It was Dr. Mulligan. She caught me just as the ground started rushing up to meet my face.

"She's... I can't... help me, please. I can't keep... I don't want to... help me."

And then everything went mercifully black and silent.

§

I could probably remember more of the next few weeks, but I don't want to. The hospitalization lasted forty-eight hours, during which they tried to protect me from the details of what had happened to Carley. Even later on, when I was able to bring myself to read about it, there was too much speculation and rumor to dig through to uncover the truth at the heart of it all. What I did know was that it didn't matter if it had been intentional or accidental. I knew what had killed Carley. She was drowning and the world reached out a hand only to use it to shove her head further beneath the surface.

As soon as I could speak, I asked for the new antipsychotic, and it was granted immediately. The world around me faded into gray and shadows and ambiguity. Milo and Carley and the other spirits were still there, but I could push them away now. And with them, all the living people blurred into the background, too. Conversations were senseless background noise. Faces dissolved into nothingness. I didn't know how I looked to the other residents of New Beginnings, and I didn't care. For the first time, I had found an off switch for the world. All I cared about was not feeling. Not feeling. Not seeing. Not hearing. Not being. I retreated into the vacuum of me, and I might have stayed there forever if she hadn't shown up, come crashing through the void like an asteroid, shattering my cocoon into a million needling shards and jolting me back into reality.

My sister.

I had drifted throughout my day, drifted back to my room, and there she was, standing in the middle of the room, reading one of my notebooks. What startled me most about her was how clearly she appeared to me—a single resolved figure in a blurred sea of undefined nothingness. Her very gaze, as her eyes met mine, seemed to reach across the room and shake me by the shoulders.

"What are you doing in my room?" Her appearance had startled me so thoroughly out of my walking stupor that I could think of no other question to ask.

She seemed startled as well. She did not answer me, but only stared with an alarming mixture of emotions chasing each other across her face.

A face I could have sworn I knew, and yet, I couldn't place it. I shook my head. No. No, I didn't want to be dragged back into reality this way, not when I'd become so adept at avoiding it. I would force her into the background, like all of the others.

"You shouldn't be here," I told her. "I took my meds. I haven't missed any in over a month. Why are you here?"

"I... came to see you," she said.

That voice. Hadn't I heard it before?

No. No, I didn't care. I refused to feel, to acknowledge. I closed my eyes. I willed the fog to descend. "But you shouldn't be here. I shouldn't be able to see you." I opened my eyes again and found her still clear, still staring at me with eyes that felt familiar. "No! You aren't supposed to be here! They promised!" Desperate now, I lunged for the intercom.

"Wait! Stop! Please don't press that button! Just hear me out! Hannah, I'm real, okay? I'm a real person."

"What do you mean, real?"

"I mean I'm not a ghost. I'm not like the others you've been seeing."

"Not ghosts. Hallucinations. Dr. Ferber promised that—"

"—Fine! I'm not a hallucination either."

What was going on? What did this girl know of ghosts? Where had she come from? Why did she know my name?

"Are you my new roommate? They didn't tell me I was getting a roommate." And even as I asked it, the specter of Carley's death reared up in my chest, threatening to overwhelm me, and I had to fight to push it back down beneath the fog. I kept asking questions just to stave off the onslaught of reality.

"No, I'm not your roommate. I'm not a patient here."

"What are you doing in my room? Why are you touching my things?"

"My name is Jessica. I came to get you out of here. Don't you want to get out of here?"

"I don't want to stay here, but I have nowhere else to go," I snapped at her. Why wouldn't she just blur away, like everyone else! Why was she burning through so clearly, so loudly?

"What if there was somewhere else you could go? What if there was a home waiting for you, a real one, not another place like this? Would you want to leave then?"

The question was almost enough to make me laugh. I sat on the end of my bed, trying to distract myself by straightening the blankets, which I hadn't realized until this moment I had allowed to become wrinkled. How long had they been that way? "Yes, I want to leave. But they would never let me. And even if they did, why would I go with you? Who are you, anyway?"

"I'm someone who understands what's been happening to you. Those people you've seen since you were little? I can see them too."

I was angry that I had no choice but to look at her, to acknowledge her again. Why couldn't she just leave me alone? "I don't believe you."

The girl came and sat down on the very end of my bed, as far from me as she could while still daring to share the space. I fought against the desire to move as far from her as possible, to put as much distance between us as I could. I barely heard what she said next.

"It's true. I know everyone told you that they were hallucinations, but they aren't. They're ghosts, people whose spirits are trapped here. I can see them too, I promise you."

I didn't know who this girl was, or what the hell she thought she was doing here, but she wasn't going to get me to admit to anything. "No, ghosts aren't real. In therapy, they told me that my illness—"

"—You aren't sick, Hannah. They just don't understand what you can do. Listen, I can prove it. I just met your old roommate, Carley."

My fingers froze on the edge of the blanket. I could hardly breathe. "You couldn't have. She's—"

"—Dead. I know. But I just saw her."

I was shaking now. "I don't believe you."

"What about Milo?"

How could she know? There's no way she could... "I... I don't know anyone named Milo."

"Yes, you do! He told me you were friends."

Two could play at this game. Milo would never give me away to some stranger, that much I was sure of. "What does he look like?"

"Really thin with shaggy dark hair and blue eyes, likes to play solitaire in that common room downstairs."

She could have gotten that description from anyone, I told myself. She would have to do better than that. "What did he say to you? Did he tell you anything?"

The girl nodded eagerly. "He seemed pretty interested in sharing his personal information, actually. He told me he was committed here for depression, anxiety, attempted suicide, and an addiction to prescription pain killers. He's the one who told me how to find your room. He also told me I needed a new hairstyle and that he could tell I was crazy just by talking to me."

TALES FROM THE GATEWAY

I fought back a hysterical urge to laugh. "That sounds like something he would say," I admitted.

I stared at the girl, right into her eyes. She stared back, not defiantly, but openly, eagerly, as though she was hoping I could read the truth in her eyes. And for one, strangely clear moment, I could.

"You really did see him, didn't you?"

I saw the relief break over the girl's face. "Yes. I'm telling you the truth, I promise."

"That doesn't explain how you knew I was here or why I should go anywhere with you," I said, unable to quiet the almost hysterical suspicion that the girl was somehow trying to trick me.

The girl appeared to be steeling herself. And then she spoke, "About ten months ago I started having these Visitations—the same kind that you've been having for your entire life. Ever since it started, I've been in search of the reason why. And just last night, I got the answers I was looking for."

"Why? Why can we see them when no one else can?" The question escaped my mouth without conscious thought, the question I had asked myself a million times in my life, and never with the hope of an answer. My eyes blurred with sudden tears.

"It has to do with our heritage, our bloodline. You and I were both born into a line of women who have this... ability. We're related, Hannah."

"Related?" I whispered.

"Yes. We're sisters."

I couldn't think. I couldn't breathe. She couldn't have said the word I thought I heard. She couldn't have meant it about me.

"But I don't have anyone. I've never had anyone," I managed at last.

"I know. I didn't know about you, Hannah. I didn't know you were here, or I would have been here sooner. I'm so sorry."

"I don't have anyone," I repeated, because it was the only truth that I knew, and my drugged brain would not let go of it because to let go of it was to let go of myself. "Only the dead people. I only have the dead people."

"But you do now, Hannah, that's what I'm trying to tell—"

The girl stopped speaking suddenly and fished a phone out of her pocket. During her hushed and hurried conversation, I felt like I was pushing the boulder of information she had just dropped upon me up a mental hill, trying to reach the top, to reach the moment it would tumble over the other side and I would be able to understand it. But I felt so weak, and the boulder was so heavy, and I was so, so tired.

The girl—Jessica, her name was Jessica—hung up. "Hannah, I'm really sorry, but we don't have a lot of time for explanations right now. I promise you that I will answer every question that you have, every one that I have an answer to. But right now we need to get out of here. Will you come with me?"

I couldn't even bring myself to speak. My brain was trying to protect me from what must surely be some kind of trick or a trap or a lie. But a tiny voice had woken up in the back of my head, and it was shouting at me as though from miles away, its message almost lost in the vastness it had to cross to reach me:

Trust her. Trust this girl.

Without deciding to, I agreed. I tried to stand, but stumbled, and the girl—Jessica—offered me her hand. After a split-second hesitation, I took it.

We both gasped.

A powerful current, almost like electricity, pulsed between us. Yet rather than wanting to break apart, the current only bound us more closely together. A gust of wind blew our hair around our faces, and the quiet of the room was suddenly alive with voices, bleeding through the walls, echoing from the floors, emanating from everywhere.

Jessica pulled her hand away just as I jumped backward, knocking into my desk in my haste to get away from her. "What was that?" I demanded, but she looked as shocked as I felt.

"I don't know, but I don't think we should let it happen again," she said. "Are you okay?"

I considered this. I could feel nothing now but a faint tingling in my fingertips and the pounding of my palpitating heart. "I think so," I said.

And then all hell broke loose. Everything happened so fast, I could barely process it. The place went into a code pink lockdown, and before we could decide what to do or where to go, we'd been locked into the room together. It was crumbling. This tiny sliver of hope in the form of a stranger who claimed to be my sister was about to be crushed before I'd even completely convinced myself it was true. I couldn't let it happen. I had to know what would happen if I followed this girl outside of these walls—if I took that hand just one more time.

Well, spirits had gotten me into this mess, and spirits were going to get me out of it.

I'm still not sure how I managed it, as drugged up as I was, but the feeling of Jessica's hand in mine had burned a small peephole of clarity through the haze, and I acted instinctively.

I shoved Jessica safely away in the closet and, just as the nurses arrived with their threats of more drugs, I closed my eyes and reached out.

This is it, I called out to the spirit energy around me. For years you've asked for my help, and I've never known how. But I felt something a moment ago, when I held that girl's hand, that's going to change all of that. But none of it will matter if we can't get out of here, and so I need you all. Come to me, please. Help me so I can finally help you.

And they came, all of them, as though they had been waiting in the wings for this very moment. And after years of feeling like I had no control at all, how easy it suddenly was to control them. It was as though each of them was tied to an invisible, mental string; and all I had to do was tug on them with a single thought, and that thought was obeyed instantly. And in that moment, I really only had one thought: Get me out of here. A single point of my finger, and the room was a tornado of whirling spirits, shattering glass, and flying furniture. The nurses who had kept me locked up and sedated for years were sprawled unconscious on the ground, and the door we needed to escape through stood open. In my shock at what I had just done—or rather, what the spirits had done for me—I released my hold on all the strings, and spirits were free again.

"Hannah? Are you alright?" Jessica put a hand on my shoulder, making me jump.

"Yes. I'm alright," I said automatically, because I had no other words to describe the heady, powerful feeling still flooding through me, ebbing away now, leaving me drained and foggy once more. I met Jessica's eye and tried to smile, but I couldn't. She was looking at me with something like fear, but a moment later it was gone as she took charge. "We've got to get out of here, now!" She grabbed my arm and we ran.

But something was happening to me as we dashed through the halls toward freedom—with every step, I was growing weaker. It was as though my limbs were slowly filling up with sand, and my mind as well. We took the stairs down to the kitchens, destroying a door sensor along the way, and with each step, I grew less and less aware of our surroundings, less and less in control of my body. I felt myself slipping away.

Just a little further, I urged myself. You're almost there.

My vision had dimmed to shades of gray as Jessica dragged me across the lawns toward a waiting car. She pulled me into it, slid me across the seat, and slammed the door. I had one whiff of leather interior, one fleeting glimpse of a beautiful, frantic-eyed face in the rearview mirror, and then my body and mind gave out and I slipped gratefully into unconsciousness.

§

I felt the last of the bleariness and fog swirl away down the drain with the hot soapy water, felt my muscles relax into real awareness for the first time in weeks. I turned the temperature up higher and higher by degrees, searing away the shell into which I had retreated for so long. Something vital inside me had shifted, a reversing of poles, or else a re-centering of gravity.

I felt better. I felt like me.

I'd woken to the careful ministrations of the beautiful face from the car—my aunt, Karen. After assuring me that I was safe, that no one would be coming after me, she urged me gently to sip some water, then to eat a little toast. The effects of the escape, as well as my medications, were fading, and after a while, she had suggested I take a shower and change into some clean pajamas, which she had folded meticulously on the end of the bed. Maybe it was the crisp and perfect lines of the clothing, or the way she so tenderly continued to smooth and arrange them even as she picked them up to hand them to me, but I had agreed. Now I thought I might just stay in this shower for the rest of my life, burning through layer after layer of memory and watching it all drift away from me on clouds of steam.

"Sweetness? Can I come in?"

For the first time since he'd left and then come back, the sound of Milo's voice was a welcome one. I smiled a little to myself.

"You're here."

"Of course, I'm here! What, did you think I was going to wallow away my afterlife in that hellhole without you?"

"I don't know. No, I guess not. I'm just... I'm just really glad to hear your voice."

"So, does that mean I can come in?"

"Sure."

"I'm just... checking on you, because, well... I mean, shit." Milo let out a long, slow breath.

I almost laughed. "I know, right?"

"Sorry, but that's all I've got," Milo chuckled. "I'm low on eloquent sound bites at the present time. That was one wild exit out of that place. But seriously, how are you feeling?"

I considered this, before deciding on the right word. "Awake."

I felt rather than saw Milo's smile. "Well, that's something. Welcome back."

"Thanks." I paused. "I really wasn't sure if you'd still be here."

"What do you mean?"

"After the way I treated you."

Milo gave a sad laugh. "After the way you treated me? Are you kidding? Sweetness, you've got nothing to apologize for."

I let the water keep running because it was easier to face my shame with the sound of it muffling his voice, with the steam cloaking his expression.

"Yes, I do. Even if you don't need to hear it, I need to say it, Milo. You stayed behind for me. I thought it was all my fault, but all that does is remove your agency. It erases you, and your choices. I never should have taken that from you. I have to let you own that. I'm really sorry."

Milo's voice was thick with tears. "Apology totally unnecessary but gratefully accepted, sweetness."

"Thanks. And I'm... I'm really glad you're here, and I'm going to let myself think it and say it out loud. You chose me, so I'm choosing you. If... if that's still okay?"

Milo snorted in an exaggerated way, which I knew meant the emotion had gotten too real for him. "As if you had a choice. I'm basically, like, your permanent stalker now, so get over it."

I laughed. It felt weird and rusty, but also good. I shut the water off, pulled a fluffy white towel from the rack, and wrapped myself in it. It smelled faintly of lavender and fell all the way to my ankles. When I stepped out of the tub, I saw Milo sitting cross-legged on the double vanity, smiling at me. I boosted myself up and sat beside him.

"They're going to be waiting for me down there, huh?" I asked.

"Yup."

"I'm kind of scared."

"I don't blame you," Milo said. "But scared can be good. At least it means you're here, you know?"

"Yeah."

"They seem... genuine, Hannah. They seem really worried about you."

"Yeah. I just... I guess I never really let myself wonder what it would be like to have a family. Not since I was a kid. It was a self-preservation thing."

"I know. Especially because families don't always work out the way they're supposed to," Milo said.

"Exactly."

"But... they risked a lot to get you out of there. I don't think they're done risking stuff for you. They obviously care. And... well, you might finally get some answers, you know? About why you can do... this." He gestured between the two of us and smiled again.

"I know. It's just..." A small, slightly hysterical laugh bubbled up and escaped me. "Well, it's actually kind of terrifying when you might finally get the things you've been praying for your whole life."

"Ironic, isn't it?" Milo said gently.

I slid down off the sink and turned to face the mirror, looking into my own face. Only now, I could also see her face, too. My sister, Jessica. My nose was actually our nose. My dark eyes were actually our dark eyes.

"A sister," I whispered to our shared features. "A twin."

And for the first time ever, our smile smiled back at me.

TALES FROM THE GATEWAY

The complete works of E.E. Holmes
THE WORLD OF THE GATEWAY
The Gateway Trilogy (Series 1)
Spirit Legacy
Spirit Prophecy
Spirit Ascendancy
The Gateway Trackers (Series 2)
Whispers of the Walker
Plague of the Shattered
Awakening of the Seer
Portraits of the Forsaken
Heart of the Rebellion
Soul of the Sentinel
Gift of the Darkness
Tales from the Gateway

THE RIFTMAGIC SAGA
What the Lady's Maid Knew
The Rebel Beneath the Stairs

E.E. Holmes is a writer, teacher, and actor living in central Massachusetts with her husband, two children, and a small, but surprisingly loud dog. When not writing, she enjoys performing, watching unhealthy amounts of British television, and reading with her children. Please visit www.eeholmes.com to learn more about E.E. Holmes and *The World of The Gateway*.

Made in the USA
Middletown, DE
16 May 2024